DRAWN THAT WAY

ALSO BY ELISSA SUSSMAN

Stray

Burn

DRAWN THAT WAY

ELISSA SUSSMAN

Interior illustrations by Arielle Jovellanos

SIMON & SCHUSTER BFYR

NEW YORK LONDON TORONTO SYDNEY NEW DELHI

An imprint of Simon & Schuster Children's Publishing Division
1230 Avenue of the Americas, New York, New York 10020

For information about special discounts for bulk purchases, please contact
Simon & Schuster Special Sales at 1-866-506-1949 or business@simonandschuster.com.
The Simon & Schuster Speakers Bureau can bring authors to your live event. For more information or to book an event, contact the Simon & Schuster Speakers Bureau at 1-866-248-3049 or visit our website at www.simonspeakers.com.
Interior design by Hilary Zarycky
The text for this book was set in Adobe Garamond Pro.
The illustrations for this book were rendered digitally in Procreate.
Manufactured in the United States of America
First Edition
2 4 6 8 10 9 7 5 3 1
Library of Congress Cataloging-in-Publication Data
Names: Sussman, Elissa, author. | Jovellanos, Arielle, illustrator.
Title: Drawn that way / Elissa Sussman ; illustrations by Arielle Jovellanos.
Description: First edition. | New York : Simon & Schuster Books for Young Readers, [2021] | Audience: Ages 12 up. | Audience: Grades 10-12. | Summary: Seventeen-year-old Hayley Saffitz, a confident, ambitious, aspiring animation director, participates in her idol's summer program but must risk her blossoming relationship with his son if she is to prove she is as talented as the boys.
Identifiers: LCCN 2020057258 | ISBN 9781534492974 (hardcover)
ISBN 9781534492981 (paperback) | ISBN 9781534492998 (ebook)
Subjects: CYAC: Internship programs—Fiction. | Animation (Cinematography)—Fiction. Sexism—Fiction. | Dating (Social customs)—Fiction.
Classification: LCC PZ7.S965663 Dr 2021 | DDC [Fic]—dc23
LC record available at https://lccn.loc.gov/2020057258

For Dad
Who gave me big dreams and equally big feet

"Even with primitive materials, one can work small wonders."
—LOTTE REINIGER

BB GUN FILMS ANNOUNCES FIRST-EVER SUMMER INTERNSHIP

Bryan Beckett, the creative force behind BB Gun Films, announced on Monday that they would be opening their doors to a select group of high school interns.

Beckett made waves in the animation community ten years ago with the release of the critically lauded film *A Boy Named Bear*. Inspired by and named after his own son, Beckett directed and wrote the film about a boy whose imagination is so powerful that he's considered a risk to himself, his government, and the world. It won Beckett his first Oscar.

After news of his custody battle over Bear was leaked to the press, Beckett became known for his extreme privacy, rarely granting interviews. That secrecy extended to his studio, and all films in production.

Beckett made an exception a year ago when he recorded a CalTED Talk for the California Animation Institute (CalAn). The ninety-minute video offered a rare glimpse into the mind of the director/producer who has been dubbed "the keeper of

America's imagination." In it he discusses his process, why he wears the same outfit every day, and why he thinks that "a curious, creative mind is the most formidable weapon in the universe."

The announcement of the internship sent shock waves through the animation community, and it seems fair to assume that this could be a once-in-a-lifetime opportunity for a few lucky students.

One can only imagine the wisdom a visionary like Bryan Beckett will dole out to his freshman class of interns.

From the official release:
"In order to be eligible for the internship, students must be entering their senior year of high school. Accepted applicants will work at the studio during the day and be housed at the nearby CalAn campus. They will be assigned mentors and work in teams with their fellow interns to develop and produce four short films to be screened at the end of the summer."

Applicants must fill out a questionnaire—now available on BBGunFilms.com/SummerInternship—and submit a portfolio of their work. Details regarding format can be found on the website.

CHAPTER ONE

I had arrived.

Leaning over my steering wheel, I got my first real, up-close look at my future. It was big and bright with round, swooping architecture and a giant wrought-iron gate that was currently wide open. I'd seen the building from the freeway almost daily on my way to school, and I'd even driven past the main entrance once or twice or two dozen times before, but I'd never had a reason to pull up to the studio entrance. Until today.

This was the place where a pencil and a piece of paper could be the start of something extraordinary. I'd been imagining this moment—this day—for weeks.

A Boy Named Bear had been made for my generation—for *me*—and we'd all grown up with Bryan Beckett teaching us the proper way to tell a story. Now I was going to be one of the lucky few to learn it directly from him.

No. Not luck. I wasn't an intern at BB Gun Films because I was lucky—I was an intern at BB Gun Films because I was good at what I did. Because *I* knew how to tell a story. With *my* pencil and paper, I'd beaten out almost five thousand students for a coveted slot in what was possibly the only internship program BB Gun Films would ever do.

It was the first step toward my future. An apprentice at eighteen, a storyboard artist at twenty, head of story by twenty-four, and directing my first feature way before I was thirty. That was the plan.

Next to me, Dad let out a low whistle. I knew exactly what he was seeing. "So this is the house that cartoons built," he said.

"They're not *cartoons*, they're animated films," I said for the thousandth time. "And this multibillion-dollar *studio* was designed by Andrew Howard."

Dad's eyebrows rose. "The guy who did the children's museum in Argentina?" He looked over at me. "*Now* you show an interest in architecture?"

I shrugged. We were both aware that my architectural knowledge was limited to all things BB Gun. I knew Dad would notice the design, but I was also hoping it would impress him. That the studio would impress him.

"For seventeen years, I've tried to encourage a love of art," Dad said. "And *this* is how you repay me. By becoming obsessed with cartoo—" He cleared his throat as he caught my glare. "Animated films." He was joking. Mostly.

"Behave," I said. I wanted him there and not there. After all, it had taken a lot to convince my parents to let me do this internship. It was clear that they hadn't even thought I'd get in, but when I did, I'd had to sit through several discussions where my parents weighed the pros and cons of agreeing to let me spend the whole summer doing what they saw as nothing more than an unpaid internship in a field they knew nothing about.

In the end, they'd agreed because I'd assured them it would look good on a college application. They didn't see what it really was: an opportunity. A chance to prove myself. To them. To my peers. To Bryan Beckett himself.

I rolled down the window to talk to the security guard. "I'm checking in for the evaluation," I said. "I mean, registration. For the internship." My face was hot, but the security guard didn't even blink—no doubt I wasn't the first awkward teenager he'd spoken to that day.

"Driver's license," he said. "Is he on your guest list?"

"Yes, sir," Dad said, and saluted, trying to be cheeky. He was ignored.

"I'll need your ID as well," the security guard said.

We passed them over and waited while we were checked off on the list the guard was holding. I drummed my fingers along the curve of my steering wheel. I could only imagine what it would be like once we passed through those gates. Would I feel different? Special?

I wanted to feel special.

The security guard cleared his throat and I looked up to see that he was holding out our licenses, his gaze focused on my tapping fingers.

"Sorry." I reached out with one hand, stilling the other.

"You can park on the first floor," he said with a hint of a smile. "And welcome to BB Gun Films, Hayley."

I grinned, goose bumps spreading all over my arms. This was it. *This* was the moment.

Even the parking structure was cool to look at. The whole thing had the feel of an oversize jungle gym, with the metal painted bright colors and each floor named after a different, famous BB Gun Films character.

Floor number one, unsurprisingly, was Bear, the title character from their first film. The wild child was portrayed with his

5

characteristically messy, leaf-strewn hair and muddy face, his hands on his hips and his preadolescent chest puffed out.

We all wanted to be Bear when we were little—a child whose imagination was so impressive that it threatened the status quo. It took me years to fully appreciate the nuances of the film, but when I was a kid, I was simply spellbound by someone my age who could make things happen just by imagining them. When Bear did it, it seemed possible that all of us could.

"Who's that?" Dad asked, stopping in front of the drawn sign.

"Dad," I said.

A small group of people who were also walking out of the garage turned to stare.

"I left a list for you and Mom on the counter." I lowered my voice. "And all the special editions are in my room. Organized by date."

"I know, I know," Dad said.

"You said you'd watch them."

"I thought I was agreeing to one movie—maybe two. Not the whole BB Gum repertoire."

"*Gun*," I said. "BB *Gun*. And it's just ten films."

"That's a lot of time to spend watching movies." Dad put his hand on my shoulder. His tone was light but the hand was heavy.

I'd thought that Dad would understand, since he knew what it was like to be an artist. Or to appreciate art. After all, he'd been an architect for as long as I'd been alive and spent his weekends building sculptures in the backyard. It was clear I got my creative gene from him, not from Mom, who had been a stay-at-home parent until about two years ago when she went back to school to study law.

"I don't like the language they use." She'd helped me review the registration paperwork in the spring. "They own everything you work on while you're there? That doesn't seem right."

Mom found contracts fascinating. "You can tell a lot about someone by the words they use," she liked to say.

They had all seemed pretty similar to me—a bunch of legalese nonsense.

"They're all about teamwork," I'd said. "You can't own something that's a group effort. And the whole point is to prove to them that you're good enough to be a member of *their* team."

That was my goal, at least. I still had another year of high school, but my secret wish was that I'd prove myself so invaluable during this internship that BB Gun Films—ideally, Bryan Beckett himself—would offer me a position that I could take as soon as I graduated high school.

I knew my parents wanted me to be like my older brother, Zach, who was premed.

"A Jewish doctor," I'd teased him when he declared his major. "How original."

"At least our parents know what that is," he'd teased back.

It was true. They thought all of this was a hobby. They didn't realize that people could actually make a living doing it. They didn't see that it could be more. That *I* could make it more.

I'd tried to show them Bryan's CalTED Talk, but all Mom could focus on was how he had dropped out of CalAn after his freshman year. She'd dropped out of college too, but unlike Bryan, she regretted it. She refused to listen when I told her I didn't need to go to college.

"You can't do your best work if you have a backup plan," Bryan had said.

Even though he never graduated from the school, he'd been given an honorary degree after *A Boy Named Bear* was released.

"Creating is all about risk," Bryan had said. "Taking an exhilarating plunge into the unknown, steadied only by confidence in your own talent. In your ability to land safely."

When I'd first watched his CalTED Talk, it was as if he had taken the things I felt when I drew and put them into words. That video had changed *everything* for me.

We walked out of the parking garage and were greeted by a friendly-faced white woman with a Bear button on her lapel. "You'll be starting in the theater," she said, directing us away from the main structure.

I stared at the big doors longingly. I wanted to get into the studio so badly. I already knew what the theater looked like. It was the only place the press was allowed to go, so I'd seen it in all the videos and interviews and press releases BB Gun Films did. There weren't many available, but I'd watched them all. Studied them. I wanted to go where no one else got to go.

We settled into the theater seats—they were enormous and plush and covered in soft red velvet. If Zach were here, I probably would have said something about how the room felt a bit like a giant beating heart, and then he would have said something gross and anatomically accurate about the biology of an actual human heart. Then I would have socked him in the arm.

Everyone was scattered around alone or in small groups. According to the acceptance e-mail, there were forty-one of us. It seemed like a weird number, but I was certain that there was a reason for it. I was certain that Bryan had a reason for everything he did.

Out of that forty-one, only four of us were going to get the opportunity to direct. I'd been working on my pitch since the moment I read about the internship.

I was ready. I was *so* ready.

I glanced around at the other interns—eager to check out my competition—but the lights dimmed before I could. A white guy with blond hair, at least ten years younger than Bryan, walked out onto the stage. I knew immediately who he was, but I wasn't the only one who slumped backward with disappointment.

"I'm sorry I'm not Bryan Beckett," he said.

We all laughed politely.

"Don't worry—all of you interns will get a chance to meet him tomorrow. I'm Josh Holder, the executive head of story. For all you BB Gun Films fans, you'll know that we do things a little different here than at other animation studios. My role means that I oversee the story teams for *all* the films we have in development."

I *did* know that. I assumed that BB Gun had their own way of doing most things.

"We're so glad to have you here at the studio. In a few hours, there will be a mixer back at the dormitories—sorry, parents, you'll have to say goodbye before then—where you'll have a chance to meet one another before you're introduced to your mentors. Then, tomorrow, you'll be back here bright and early to start your first day as employees of BB Gun Films."

We applauded, excited whispers spreading through the room. It was all happening so quickly. And not quickly enough. I squirmed as Josh continued. Now that I knew what was in store for the next few hours, I wanted to get out of the theater and settle into the dorms.

"For now, we've prepared something to welcome you all to the BB Gun family. Enjoy!"

The lights dimmed. "Welcome!" Bryan's voice boomed through the speakers.

I must have watched his CalTED Talk a hundred times by now, so his voice was as familiar to me as my parents'. I settled back, my fingers curled over my knees.

The film—shot in grainy black-and-white like those old-fashioned movies—opened with Bryan at his desk. I straightened. We'd never seen his office. But before I could get a good glimpse of anything besides his enormous black desk, he was outside the studio gates, walking toward the camera. He was wearing his uniform—black pants, white shirt, and a black tie. He looked like he was outside of time. The film could have been shot yesterday or it could have been shot twenty years ago.

"You're here because you're the best of the best," Bryan said.

I sucked in a proud breath.

"Thousands of students across the United States sent in applications—but we chose *you*. There was something in your reel or your portfolio that showed potential, and here at BB Gun Films, we're all about potential."

I was more than ready to show off mine.

CHAPTER TWO

Last night, while I finished packing, Zach had stood in front of my movie collection, plucking animated films off the shelf and making himself a pile of non–BB Gun Blu-rays and special editions. Mom and Dad each did their own worried-parent pass by my door.

"You can always call if you forget something," Mom had said. "We're only twenty minutes away."

"Uh-huh."

"I know you'll be busy, but if you wanted to come home for dinner, just let me know."

"Mom."

Dad sang on his turn. "'I've got a golden ticket . . . I've got a golden chance to make my way.'"

"We've been over this before," I said.

"Oh no," Zach groaned from the corner. "She's going to monologue."

I'd glared at him. "Charlie got to go on the tour because of luck, not talent, and Wonka hosting a contest to pick a replacement proves that he's a manipulative showman at best. He could have easily passed the factory down to the most senior Oompa Loompa, instead of a *child*. And why didn't he test the business skills of said children versus tricking and torturing them? More importantly, he should have chosen Violet Beauregarde to run the place. She's obsessed with gum, and even puts herself at risk to test a new product. And don't get me started on her being the only person who seems to think there's a problem using Oompa Loompas for . . ."

". . . for what is essentially slave labor," Zach had finished for me. "You know, just because it's a meme doesn't mean it's right."

Dad had walked away half a rant ago. He liked to do that, get me riled up and leave.

I'd stuck my tongue out at my brother. "And just because I've said it before doesn't mean it's not true."

"I worry about your feelings of kinship with someone who turns into a giant blueberry. You do realize she was a bad guy, right?"

"She was misunderstood."

"That's what all bad guys say." Zach had pointed a DVD at me. "And you're not going to make any new friends with that attitude."

"What attitude? My nice, charming one?" I'd given him a sickly-sweet smile.

"You're going to have to pretend to be normal," he'd said, as if I hadn't spoken. "No lecturing people about imaginary characters. No all-nighters over projects that don't even count toward your final grade. No micromanaging Shelley Cona until she cries—"

"That happened *once*! And she wasn't pulling her weight!"

I'd been assigned to do a group project with Shelley, but her on-again, off-again boyfriend kept distracting her. I'd suggested he wasn't worth the effort. She'd said I'd never understand what it was like to be in love. I'd told her that if this was love, I didn't want anything to do with it. Because who had time for that kind of drama? I didn't.

"You have to be a team player," Zach had said. "You have to be able to play nice with others. Or else . . ." I waited as he gathered up all the movies he was stealing from me. "Oompa, Loompa, doo-be-dee-doo," he sang as he left.

I'd thrown a pillow at him.

In his CalTED Talk, Bryan had talked about how animation was all about collaboration. "A successful team works together toward a singular goal," he'd said. "We all contribute to a shared vision."

I didn't like working in teams when I was the only one who cared about the results. That wasn't going to be a problem in this internship.

My roommate had apparently unpacked before heading over to the studio, because when I got there, she was nowhere to be found, but her bed was made and she'd hung things on the wall. I liked her already from the stuff she'd put up—vintage-style posters of BB Gun Films, quotes about art in beautiful graphic lettering, and pictures of her cat.

The dormitories at CalAn were a ten-minute drive from the studio, but we'd be taking shuttles every morning and evening. I had my car—my parents had to sign a waiver to allow me to keep it on campus—but I wasn't allowed to use it to go in between the dorms and the studio.

They were very particular about their rules. I respected that. You had to have rules. You had to have guidelines.

Checking my phone, I saw that I had several messages from Julie and Samantha.

Did you get the director position yet? Samantha had texted.

Are there cute guys? If so, how many? Julie asked. **Please send photos and rankings.**

Or drawings! Samantha added. **Shirtless drawings!**

I laughed, thinking of how they often during the school year they'd request sexy sketches of their favorite celebrities. I'd done quite a few versions of Tom Holland performing Rihanna's "Umbrella" to much acclaim and appreciation.

I didn't mind. In fact, I preferred dealing with guys who could be easily adjusted with pencil and eraser.

I'm here to work, I reminded them, but they understood better than anyone how focused I could get.

Boooooo, Samantha texted.

We want drawings! Julie said.

It wasn't the first summer we'd spent apart. As usual, Samantha would be leaving soon to spend eight weeks at a Jewish summer camp in Simi Valley with limited cell phone service. Julie would be working and taking SAT prep courses. I texted them both an eggplant emoji.

Then I put my phone away and gave myself a once-over in the cheap floor-length mirror hanging over the back of the door. I looked fine. I'd grown accustomed to pulling my hair back in a bun—I'd used to wear it down all the time, but it looked more serious this way. Bryan always had his hair combed back, kind of old-fashioned-like. Wearing my hair this way also kept the wavy mess out of my face and turned out to be a very convenient place to store pens and pencils. Twisting, I checked to see how many I was storing there at the moment. Just two.

I buttoned my blue shirt up one more button and retucked it in to my high-waisted black pants. It was my own version of Bryan Beckett's uniform, which consisted of identical trousers and a variation of the same type of shirt. I relaced my sparkly black

Converse. That was another Beckett-ism—even though his clothing always stayed the same, he favored funky, unique sneakers.

"Wearing the same thing every day clears my mind," he'd said in his CalTED Talk. "It allows me to focus on the work. On my internal process, not my external presentation."

It made so much sense. I still had a closet at home full of dresses and jeans and T-shirts, but since I started wearing a uniform, I didn't have to spend time picking out a new outfit every morning. It made things easier.

There were kids at school who thought I was weird for dressing this way, but most of them also couldn't tell the difference between a Disney movie and a Don Bluth movie. I didn't care what they thought. I cared what Bryan Beckett thought.

I straightened my collar, checked the back of my pants for lint, and headed downstairs. The multipurpose room was already full. My palms were damp as I clasped them behind my back, wondering what would be less awkward—introducing myself to a group of strangers that were already talking, or trying to make conversation over at the snack and beverage table.

At least I knew that we shared a common interest. We were all fans here.

And I wasn't the only one following Bryan Beckett's fashion guidelines. Across the room, a white guy in black pants and a polo shirt beelined for me so aggressively that I glanced back at first, thinking that he was approaching someone behind me that he knew. He was about my height and had dark hair that was slicked back.

"You saw the CalTED Talk," he said. It wasn't a question.

"Yeah," I said.

"'The less time you spend on your appearance, the more attention you can give your art,'" he said. That was a direct Bryan Beckett quote.

"'Be creative with your drawings, not your clothes,'" I said, sharing another Beckett-ism.

"I'm Nick." He held out a hand.

I shook it, hoping my palm wasn't too sweaty. "Hayley."

"I've probably watched his CalTED Talk, like, fifty times," he said.

"Me too."

"It's like, I think I've absorbed all of his wisdom, but then I watch it again and I learn something new." His head bobbed to emphasize his point.

I grinned at him. "Me too," I said, because that was *exactly* how I felt.

I'd tried to explain it to Julie and Samantha, but they weren't really fans. They loved when I shared my drawings, but they didn't understand my obsession—with animation or with Bryan Beckett. This was the first time I'd met someone who seemed to speak the same language as me. More nervousness melted away.

Nick smiled. "No one at my high school gets it," he said. "They used to make fun of me—pretending I was wearing the same exact clothes every day. Like I wasn't even washing them." He snorted and rolled his eyes.

"People at my school don't understand either," I said.

The guys in film club knew about BB Gun Films, and they admired Bryan but thought animated movies were mostly for kids and nerds. We watched a lot of movies about sad middle-aged men, New York mobsters, or blue-collar guys from Boston. Occasionally we'd watched older movies. Classics. About sad middle-aged men who were usually mobsters from Boston.

"They were impressed when I got the internship, though," Nick said. "They made an announcement and everything."

"That's cool," I said. They hadn't done that at my school—I was a little jealous.

"I've noticed a huge uptick in my creativity dressing this way," he said. "I bet it's even more significant, especially for someone like you."

"Like me?"

"I have sisters," he said. "I know how much time girls spend getting ready."

I didn't have a chance to respond because I was suddenly set upon by a pack of the aforementioned species—girls. There were five of them.

"Hey," one said.

She was tall and dressed all in black with short curly hair and brown skin. There was a little diamond in her nose and as she pushed her hair behind her ears, I saw at least three more piercings. For an animation nerd, she seemed pretty cool. In fact, for a *group* of animation nerds, we were all being surprisingly social.

A collection of otters was called a "family." Cats were a "glaring." Lemurs were a "conspiracy." I wondered what the term for us could be.

"Are you Hayley?" the girl in black asked.

Maybe we were a "sequence"?

"Yeah," I said.

The group let out a squeal loud enough to make Nick retreat. I felt a little bad for him as he moved away, casting backward glances toward me.

"We found her," a white girl with glasses said.

From the back of the group, another girl—this one pale and busty—pushed forward and engulfed me in a hug.

"I'm Sally," she said. "I'm your roommate. I'm so glad to meet you—sorry I didn't wait for you in our room, but I was just so excited to explore."

"Hi," I said. Maybe a group of animation nerds could be called a "vector"?

Sally was wearing a top that looked like a watercolor painting. "This place is so cool, isn't it?" she asked. "Caitlin came and found me, and we all went on a tour of the dormitories. I just love it here. It's full of history and inspiration. I feel inspired; do you feel inspired?"

Sally talked fast.

"Yeah," I said.

"Emily knows all their secrets," one of the other girls said. She was white and had bright blue hair pulled back into a ponytail. "Her cousin went here."

Five friendly faces stared at me.

"Cool," I said, a little overwhelmed but in a good way.

A "render." A group of animation nerds was called a "render." If they were all as knowledgeable and friendly as Nick had been, I had a feeling this internship was going to be even better than I expected.

"We're the only girls in the program," Sally said.

I wasn't surprised. I didn't know any other girls that cared about animation. Unless I could drag Samantha or Julie to movie club, I was the only girl there. I was used to being the odd one out. This would be a *very* welcome change.

I glanced around the room and noticed that the other interns were now eyeing us with both interest and suspicion. I recognized the look. I usually saw it when Zach told his friends that I liked animated films.

In his CalTED Talk, Bryan had said that all that mattered to him was talent—he didn't care who had it. Still, I was glad I had been discovered and folded into this little group.

"I think they're going to do some ice-breakers soon," Sally

said. "But they might separate us and I thought we should all get to know each other before they do."

Introductions were made, information coming at me like rapid-fire darts.

Caitlin Gonzalez, with the piercings and curly hair, was from Sacramento, and one of the few girls I'd ever met who was taller than me. Emily Reynolds was the white girl with glasses and long, long blond hair. It nearly came down to her butt. Rachel Goo was Asian with straight dark hair, brown eyes, and incredible posture. She was from Florida, and had a really cool vintage style. Jeannette Conner-White was the girl with the blue hair and a big smile.

Sally Hughes—my roommate—was from Texas. She, Caitlin, and Jeannette would be focusing on animation and special effects—building and polishing the final product. The other two girls, Emily and Rachel, would be studying story with me.

"If animation is the body of a film, then story is the soul," Bryan had said in his CalTED Talk. "They're incomplete without each other."

I noticed, in addition to the intern group being very male-dominated, we were pretty homogeneous as well. Including Caitlin and Rachel, there were only a handful of interns who weren't white. It was hard to tell, but I didn't think there were many other Jewish kids, either.

"Hope you don't mind that I chose a bed without waiting for you," Sally said. "We can totally switch if you don't like it, but I think the beds are pretty similar and I thought it would be better if I was a little closer to the door because I tend to get up early each morning and go for a run. Do you run? We could run together."

I could tell why Sally ran. She seemed to have boundless energy.

If I were to animate her, I'd make her a little blond particle, zipping through space, bouncing off of other particles and lighting them up.

"I usually sleep in," I said. "But I like the posters you put up. I have a few of the same at home." If she was a particle, I was whatever science-thing generated energy by staying still.

"Thanks," she said. "I had a really hard time deciding which posters to bring—I have a few at home that aren't of BB Gun Films, but I thought I might, like, get kicked out of the program if I had some Miyazaki or Laika posters up, you know? I love stop-motion animation—there's something so awesome and tactile about it, you know? I love animation that feels like you could reach out and touch it. Like you could really live in it. I like your outfit."

It took a moment for me to realize that the last part had been directed at me.

"Thanks." I smoothed my hand down the front of my shirt. "And I really like stop-motion animation too," I said.

Sally beamed at me. "What's your favorite?"

Where could I even begin?

"*Coraline* is pretty great," I said, hesitating a little.

Even with some of the guys in film club, when I started talking about my favorite movies, it didn't take long for them to get bored and walk away.

"I *adore Coraline*," Emily told us—and I could swear there was a hint of an English accent there, even though she'd said she was from Montana. "It's so creepy and dark. The Other Mum design is brilliant—how it changes from human to insect-like—the way she gets all stretched out." In addition to the intermittent English accent, she had a flowy, earthy style that made her seem like she belonged in a rose garden.

"What about *Chicken Run*?" Caitlin pulled her hair back, and I could see that she had a big silver piercing going through the top of her other ear. "I love Aardman's style."

"That one's great," Rachel said. Her long, elegant fingers were clasped in front of her neatly buttoned cardigan. She was perfectly put together, except for the smudges of ink on her fingers. The kind of smudges we all had. "Kind of dark, too, in its own way," she said. "I mean, it is about killing chickens and putting them in a pie."

"'I don't want to be a pie,'" Jeannette quoted. She wore cargo shorts and a tie-dye shirt with matching socks. She looked like a really cool camp counselor, with a fading sunburn across her nose to complete the look. I imagined her standing at the top of a mountain with a flag in her hand and a bandanna around her neck. "They're so great with timing," she continued. "Aardman is. Think of everything you get from Gromit's character and he never says a word."

I couldn't help grinning. These were exactly the kinds of things I thought about all the time. Julie and Samantha would watch animated movies with me, but they never talked about them in this way—as if they *knew* them. As if they studied them.

"Your outfit really *is* cool," Sally said.

I stood up a little straighter. "I worried it might come off as being too brown-nosey, but this really is how I dress every day."

"I mean, at least it looks good on you," Caitlin said.

I took it as a huge compliment because Caitlin *looked* cool. With her piercings and her all-black clothes, she just exuded coolness. Like she belonged in a band.

She nodded toward Nick. "He looks like he's trying to *be* Bryan Beckett."

"He's nice," I said.

Caitlin looked skeptical. "As long as he doesn't do the 'Test,' I guess he's okay," she said.

"I loathe the Test," Emily said.

I knew exactly what they were talking about. Before I started wearing my uniform, I was always questioned when I wore my favorite BB Gun Films shirt. It was usually by guys demanding to know if I was wearing it just to impress boys.

"One of my cousins didn't believe me when I told him I'd gotten this internship," Sally said. "He tried to make me list all of the BB Gun Films in chronological order."

A film club guy had done something similar, only he'd made me name an important character from each film. When I'd rattled them off easily, he'd accused me of cheating.

Even though the other guys were still staring at us, I didn't think they'd be like that. We were in this together—united by talent and a love of animation. They were probably just intimidated by all of us. We did look pretty impressive. But we were just artists here. That's what Bryan said.

"Bryan always talks about how important the women on his staff are," I said. "For the last film, they had the female artists sign off on the design for the male lead."

It was one of the few articles that had talked about the behind-the-scenes process, and the reporter had even gotten permission to talk to some of the vis dev artists—the people who helped shape the look and style of each different film.

"I think this is the intern coordinator," Rachel said, and the chatter slowly mellowed out to a hush as two people entered the room.

"Hello." The woman who had greeted us at the theater was

standing with Josh Holder. "Glad to see you're all getting acquainted. For those who haven't met me, I'm Gena Noble."

We all formed a circle around them.

"We thought we'd start off by dividing into two groups—those who are in story and development and those who are in animation. We'll do a few ice-breakers, and get a chance to know each other before your mentors show up and we all head to dinner."

"When I was a CalAn student, the dining hall had the best chicken wings," Josh said. "That's why the place is nicknamed the Wingy-Dingy."

Everyone laughed, even though it was kind of cheesy.

"Okay," Gena said, and looked at her clipboard. "All the animation interns should come with me—the rest of you can stay here with Josh."

I waved goodbye to Sally, Caitlin, and Jeannette.

"Why don't we grab some seats," Josh said.

There were folded chairs leaning against the wall, so I followed the other interns to get one. Before I could, though, Nick reached out in front of me and grabbed two.

"I got you," he said.

"Thanks," I said.

We arranged our chairs in a circle, with Emily on one side of me and Nick on the other.

"We should swap portfolios sometime," he said.

"Definitely," I said. "I'm really proud of mine."

I'd worked nonstop on my submission from the moment I'd read about the internship to the day it was due. My grades dipped temporarily, and I pulled a few rough all-nighters, but in the end, it had been worth it. I was very curious to see what everyone else's work looked like. I wanted to see my competition.

"All right." Josh leaned forward, his hands on his knees. "Why don't we go around the room and everyone can say where they're from, and uh, if they have any siblings and what their favorite animated film is. It doesn't have to be a BB Gun film, but extra points if it is."

He gave us a broad smile to show that he was teasing, but I wondered if anyone was going to say a non–BB Gun film now.

"I'll start. I'm Josh, I'm originally from Seattle, Washington. I have two older brothers, and my favorite film is the one I'm currently working on."

I leaned forward, hoping he'd say more, but he just turned to his right, where a white guy wearing a green shirt told us that he was Keith, he was from Massachusetts, and he was the middle of three boys. We went around the room until it was Rachel's turn.

I could sense the entire group directing their focus toward Rachel, Emily, and me. I tried not to mind, but it felt a bit like we were animals in a zoo. Being watched. Observed. Judged.

"I'm Rachel, I'm from Orlando, Florida, and I have an older sister. My favorite movie is *A Boy Named Bear*."

Emily was next. "I'm Emily, I'm from Helena, Montana, and I have an older brother and a younger sister. My favorite film is also *A Boy Named Bear*."

Everyone had named a BB Gun film—and at least 50 percent of them had been *A Boy Named Bear*. For good reason. I still got little heart palpitations whenever I thought about the movie's opening.

I'd seen it for the first time when I was seven, sitting between Mom and Zach, popcorn on my lap. The theater had stayed dark for a long time—long enough for people to begin shifting in their seats—but I heard it before anyone else. The soft build of music, a low bass that seemed to tremble around my toes before spreading up my body just as the screen flickered, allowing half a second of light at a time. And in the darkness, shapes and shadows. Flashes of color and movement. All too quick to fully register. There was the sound of breathing. Frantic, terrified breaths.

I remember how I'd dug my fist down into my bag of popcorn, squeezing the rubbery kernels between my fingers because I was scared but also too old to hold Mom's hand. The breathing grew louder, the flashes faster, the lights brighter, and then suddenly, the screen was full of everything.

All the images. All the colors. All the brief hints of things we'd seen as the music had built, was now vivid and brilliant in front of us. We'd been in Bear's head. It was a dream, or a nightmare, and it wasn't supposed to be real, but when he opened his eyes, it was.

That was the power of his imagination. It was wild. Uncontrolled.

I'd released the popcorn I'd been holding, the bag all but forgotten in my lap as I'd watched the rest of the movie, my heartbeat never slowing.

Every time I rewatched it, I tried to recapture that feeling. Every time I put pencil to paper I was attempting to re-create what I'd experienced the first time I'd seen *A Boy Named Bear*. It was a special kind of yearning. Loving something so much and being so grateful that it existed, but also hating that I hadn't been a part of it.

It was my turn to speak. But before I could say anything, the door to the multipurpose room slammed open and a tall, broad-shouldered white guy came sauntering into the room.

Like, literally sauntering.

Everyone looked surprised to see him, except for Josh. "Kind of you to join us, Mr. Davis," he said. "Care to take a seat?"

Pulling a chair away from the wall, the newcomer was welcomed awkwardly into the circle. When he sat, he was across from me and he folded his arms, his gaze almost defiant. I found it deeply annoying that in addition to being late and rude, he was exceptionally cute. And kind of familiar.

"Please continue," Josh said, looking apologetic.

"I'm Hayley," I said. "I'm from here, actually."

"From the multipurpose building at CalAn?" the stranger—Mr. Davis—asked, looking at me. His eyes were green.

A few people laughed. I glared.

"From Southern California," I said. "I have one older brother. And my favorite film is *Spirited Away*."

I hadn't meant to say that. But with *Mr. Davis* staring directly at me, my tongue had slipped and I'd said what used to be my favorite film before I'd listened to Bryan's CalTED Talk and got a greater understanding of the incredible creative process happening at the studio.

Everyone was still watching me.

"But I like *A Boy Named Bear* more," I added quickly.

The new guy rolled his eyes.

Next to me, Nick cleared his throat. "I'm Nick, I'm from Maine, and I'm the youngest with two sisters. Obviously, my favorite movie is *A Boy Named Bear*," he said. "It's a complete masterpiece, isn't it? The story—the art—everything about it is absolutely perfect. It totally inspires me."

Everyone nodded. It was exactly what I wished I'd said, but the entire time Nick was speaking, *Mr. Davis* kept his gaze focused on me. I stared right back, eyes narrowed, arms crossed. I didn't like him.

How could he just walk in here—late—as if this was some ordinary internship? Sitting there like he was already bored with the whole thing? There were kids all across the country who would have killed to be in his position. I had been so certain there wouldn't be any Shelley Conas in this group, but apparently I was wrong.

I could only hope he wouldn't be assigned to my team.

I barely heard the rest of the introductions, but just as the green-eyed pain-in-the-ass newcomer was about to speak, Nick sucked in a loud breath of air almost as if he had been drowning.

"I know who you are." Nick pointed an accusatory finger at the stranger. "You're Bear. Bear Beckett."

I stared. We all did. *No. Way.*

Murmurs spread through the group, and Josh closed his eyes, leaning his head back.

The person in question, however, stood up and took a bow.

CHAPTER THREE

t was sheer chaos after that.

Everyone started talking over one another—it was impossible to decipher it all—but to my right Emily and Rachel were basically just saying Bear's full name over and over again like it was a spell of some sort, while someone was shouting that this whole thing had to be a joke.

"We're being pranked, aren't we?" they asked.

Nick was fully staring at Bear, his mouth wide open as if he hadn't expected to be right.

As for Bear, he was still standing, arms crossed, in the center of it all. His eyes had been focused on the ceiling but they slowly swung down and met mine. I hadn't said a word. Hadn't even moved.

We stared at each other and then the corner of his mouth lifted up in a smile. A cocky, *Whoops, did I do that?* kind of smile.

I hated him.

Mostly, though, I was disappointed. An overwhelming, throat-closing, deep-in-my-bones type of disappointment. *This* was Bear? Bored and insolent, he was the opposite of his onscreen persona. *Nothing* about him was magical.

"Okay, okay." Josh pushed up from his seat. "Everyone quiet down." He shot a look in Bear's direction. "Thank you for that,

Bear," he said, making it clear that he was extremely annoyed, but not at all surprised.

They knew each other. Which made sense, if Bear was the son of Josh's boss and the inspiration for the movie that built BB Gun Films. In that way, we all knew him.

Bear shrugged and sat down.

"I would have liked to announce you in a much less dramatic fashion," Josh said. "But since that train has left the station, let's just get it all out of the way. Bear? Would you like to introduce yourself?"

Bear held out his hands, palms up. "I'm pretty sure everyone knows who I am, Josh."

Josh closed his eyes again almost like he was asking for patience. I didn't blame him. Bear appeared to be a grade-A asshole. Who eventually took pity on Josh.

"I'm Bear Davis," he said. "I'm from *here* as well." He could probably mean it literally—who knew how much time he'd spent at CalAn and in the BB Gun studio. "I'm an only child." He looked at me. "And my favorite movie is *Howl's Moving Castle*."

There was a long silence. The introductions were over.

"Why don't you all mingle until the mentors get here?" Josh said before getting up.

No one moved. We stayed in our chairs in the circle, staring at Bear. I purposely turned away, focusing my attention on Emily and Rachel.

"Who do you think our mentors will be?" I asked.

But they were both staring at Bear.

"He's really fit," Emily said.

It wasn't quite a whisper, but everyone had started talking

again, so the room was filled with the sound of dozens of overlapping conversations.

"Not bad-looking at all," Rachel said, twisting her hair between her fingers.

They weren't wrong but I wasn't going to give Bear the satisfaction of having the only three girls in the room say he was cute. He probably knew exactly how attractive he was.

"I knew it," Nick said. "The minute he walked in, I knew it."

The last pictures I'd seen of Bear were from the premiere of BB Gun Films's second movie, *The Grand Adventures of the Frog King*, almost eight years ago. He'd been there with his dad, the two of them dressed identically, white shirt, black pants, and a pair of matching high-tops hand-painted with the main characters from the movie on each side.

Bear had been so young. Short and gap-toothed with closely shorn hair, he'd looked like his cartoon self and yet completely wrong. His shirt had been buttoned all the way up, his wrists scarecrow skinny. His wrists weren't skinny anymore. In fact, his arms, which were folded over his chest, looked really strong.

Not that I cared. I didn't. This internship was too important for me to waste my time even thinking about how cute someone was.

Nick was still talking. "The press isn't allowed to ask Bryan about his family anymore, but there were some articles when *A Boy Named Bear* first came out. No one's talked about him in years—since . . ."

"My parents went to court," Bear said. "Over me."

He had been listening.

Nick went red, but instead of backing down, he just faced Bear. "What are you doing here?" he asked.

I was impressed by his nerve.

"What are *you* doing here?" Bear asked.

"I applied for this internship and beat out thousands of other kids." Nick sat up tall. "Did you? Or did you just go down the hall and ask your dad to add you to the list?"

There was a loud intake of air, as if everyone had sucked in a breath at the same time. I couldn't believe he had just said that. Out loud. But it was what everyone had been thinking.

Bear looked at Nick. "Yeah," he said. "That's pretty much exactly what happened."

No one knew how to respond to that. Thankfully, Josh returned, pushing both doors open. Behind him I could see a crowd of adults. Our mentors.

"Okay," Josh said. "I'm going to call your name and we'll get you all paired off."

Fifteen minutes later everyone had left the multipurpose room except for me, Josh, and, of course, Bear. I thought about how Josh had referred to him when he first came in. And how he had introduced himself. As Bear Davis. Was that his mother's maiden name? Besides being previously married to Bryan, there wasn't much information out there about Bear's mom. I'd looked once, but only under her married name: Reagan Beckett. I made a mental note to look up Reagan Davis when I had the time.

"Hayley, right?" Josh asked. "Sorry about this, but Sloane texted me to say she was running late. She should be here in a few minutes."

"That's okay," I said, casting a sideways glance at Bear, wondering who *his* mentor was.

"Let me guess," Bear said to Josh, answering my unasked question. "You got stuck with me."

Josh was very purposely looking down at his list. "We *will* be working together this summer," he said diplomatically.

Bear was going to work with the executive head of story? That feeling of disappointment returned. His entire presence in the internship reeked of nepotism, and now this? It was completely unfair. Could Bear even draw?

Josh seemed to sense my frustration, and gave me a sympathetic look. "We can either wait with you here or head over to the dining hall—I can tell Sloane where to meet us."

I didn't really want to spend any more time with Bear, but I could see the advantage of getting to know Josh better.

And I was hungry. "We can head to the dining hall," I said.

We started walking across campus but my hope that I'd get to talk to Josh was quickly dashed when his phone rang, and he held up his finger in apology as he answered it.

"Holder here," he said, walking ahead.

Bear and I continued in silence, but I was completely aware of him. He was taller than me, which was unusual and annoying because he seemed to loom over me like a bored, undeserving tree.

"Nice outfit," he said.

I didn't respond—I could tell he didn't mean it as a compliment.

"Reminds me of someone," he said, and out of the corner of my eye, I could see him taping his finger on his chin. "Wonder who."

He was trying to make me feel foolish and I hated that. I sped up, taking long strides to catch up with Josh who was several feet ahead, still talking on his phone. Unfortunately, Bear matched my pace easily.

The quad was big and empty. I tried to imagine how the campus would be during the school year—students and teachers everywhere, instead of just a few high school interns. The soles of my sneakers squeaked along the pavement. They were new and I hadn't thought to check them for sound quality. I walked faster, thinking I could wear them out, but they just got louder and squeakier.

"Is *Spirited Away* actually your favorite movie?" Bear asked.

I ignored him. It felt like a trap.

"The Miyazaki films are pretty great," he said, as if I had answered. "People say that the dubbed versions are better, but I feel like you should be able to watch the movie and read the subtitles at the same time."

I agreed with him, but I wasn't going to say that.

"I could tell you all of BB Gun's secrets," Bear said.

I shot him a startled look.

"Gotcha," he said.

I quickly glanced away.

"Sorry about that," Josh said, putting his phone in his pocket.

"Work stuff?" I asked.

"Don't tell her, Josh," Bear said. "She looks like the type to go to the media."

I wanted to punch him in the face.

As we approached the dining hall, I noticed a petite Asian woman with shiny hair out front. She waved.

"Ah, here's Sloane," Josh lifted a hand. "Hayley Saffitz," he made the introductions. "This is Sloane Li."

Her outfit was incredible. She wore a blue silk jacket over a pair of skinny black jeans, and her glasses were enormous black-and-gold frames that curved up at the ends. Her lips were bright red, and even though she was wearing gold platform sandals, she was still several inches shorter than me.

"Nice to meet you," Sloane said, before giving Bear a knowing smile. "Bear."

"Sloane," he said, returning the grin.

She rolled her eyes, but not in an annoyed way. More out of fondness or familiarity, or both. I was a little disappointed she was being so nice to someone who clearly had no interest in being here. Even if his dad was her boss.

"Shall we?" she asked.

I nodded, eager to get away from Bear. But before I could, he reached out and pulled open the door for me. I darted through quickly, half expecting him to let go of it before I could pass. It was hard to tell if he was a chaotic evil or a neutral one.

"See you around," he said, before following Josh to a far table on the other end of the dining hall. Neither of them stopped to get any food.

"I see you've met Bear," Sloane said as we headed to the buffet.

All the other interns had already loaded up their trays and were sitting, talking to their mentors. I grabbed some mac and cheese, and what looked like meat loaf. Sloane made herself an intricate and massive salad.

"Let me guess." Sloane walked purposefully toward an empty table and I followed. "He made a bit of a scene."

"Yeah," I said.

Sloane laughed. "That kid. He never met a situation he couldn't . . ." She shook her head, and then seemed to really notice me for the first time. "Sorry," she said. "We're not here to talk about Bear. We're here to talk about you." She took a bite of her salad and then pointed her empty fork at me. "I saw your portfolio. Really impressive stuff."

I flushed. "Thanks."

I'd agonized over which drawings to include with my animation sample. I'd only been allowed to include four, which I felt wasn't nearly enough to show the full scope of my abilities. I'd driven Julie and Samantha crazy, eventually setting up a voting bracket with forty drawings to narrow it down. I'd planned to make Zach pick the forty original options, though he only made it to ten before he gave up, because he said I kept questioning his choices.

"You should be able to defend them," I'd argued.

"You should get a life," he'd said.

It was clear now that I had been right and he'd been wrong.

"I can see how BB Gun Films has influenced you," Sloane said.

It was the highest compliment that I could imagine.

"Do you have any other movies that inspire you?" she asked.

I didn't know how to answer—like Josh's request that we name our favorite movie, it seemed inappropriate to talk about other studios here.

"I like a lot of stuff," I said, digging around my mac and cheese looking for noodles. "But BB Gun makes my favorite films."

Sloane didn't say anything, and for a moment I was afraid I'd failed the test.

"They do know how to tell a story," she said.

I nodded. "They're the best."

"Do you have any questions about the program?" Sloane asked. "About what to expect?"

I thought for a moment. "I don't even really know where to start."

She laughed. "Fair enough. This is new for all of us, too. The whole summer-intern thing was a bit of a surprise, to be honest."

"Really?"

She ate some more salad. "Don't get me wrong, I think it's a great idea, but it's definitely not something I would have expected Bryan to suggest."

"Do you get a lot of time with him?" I asked, excited to know more about the man I knew I would eventually work for.

"With Bryan?" Sloane was looking at her food. "Oh, sure. He likes to be involved every step of the way." There wasn't a lot of enthusiasm in her voice. Then she looked up at me and smiled, making me think I had just imagined her lackluster response.

"Let's talk about you," she said. "What do you love about animation?"

My brain seemed to sputter and stall. *What did I love about animation?*

How could I even begin to answer that? It seemed easier to say what I *didn't* love about animation than the other way around. This definitely felt like a test. The panic must have shown on my face, because Sloane laughed.

"Sorry," she said. "I didn't mean to lob the big questions at you right away. Maybe I should start."

I nodded.

"You've seen *Mulan*, right?" she asked.

"Yeah."

"Okay." Sloane held out her hands and closed her eyes. "You know that scene in *Mulan* when she's bathing in the river? When she jumps in the water and throws her head back?"

I knew exactly what she was talking about.

"I remember when I saw that—and I saw the way her hair was animated, how it flicked up and against her face—something inside of me went, *wow*." Sloane opened her eyes. "It wasn't just the rarity of seeing an Asian face in an American movie—though that was really cool—it was how beautifully observed that moment was. How it made her feel *real* to me.

"That's what I love about animation," Sloane said. "The power of those small things. How they can make a character come to life. And knowing that someone made that moment out of nothing— out of pencil and paper—was pretty inspiring. It made me want to do the same." She looked at me, and I knew that she was expecting me to say something equally insightful.

"It's like what Bryan says in his CalTED Talk," I said. "Animation is all about the details." Bryan had said that animators were observers.

Sloane smiled. It wasn't quite as broad as the smile she'd given me earlier, so for a moment, I thought that I had disappointed her.

"That's very true," she said.

I wanted to say more. Wanted to say that I loved animation because it made me *feel* things. That I loved it because I could lose myself in it—watching *and* making it. That I loved it because it was, at its core, the closest thing to magic that I'd ever known.

But even though all of those things were on the tip on my tongue, I found myself holding back because it was too much to say it out loud. Too raw. Too real. Too intense.

It also felt a little childish—thinking of animation as a kind of magic. When Bryan spoke about the work, it was how the process took over—a free-fall feeling. It didn't feel like that—at least not yet. For me, it was all about taking what I saw in my mind and making it come to life. It wasn't about losing control; it was about regaining it. Drawing something over and over again until it fit the image I had in my head. Harnessing something inside of myself.

I worried a little that I was doing it wrong, and I didn't want Sloane to think I was silly or immature.

Thankfully she didn't press any further. Instead, she pushed her plate aside. "I think we're going to make a good team," she said, and smiled.

CHAPTER FOUR

'd never been a good sleeper, but even if I had been, there was no way I would have gotten a decent night's sleep. I texted with Julie and Samantha while Sally went through her nighttime routine. She reminded me a little bit of a hummingbird, flitting around, always moving.

She turned off the light and I stared at the ceiling. There were curtains on our windows but they were thin and gauzy, and lights from the quad outside drew interesting and wavy shapes on the ceiling. Or maybe they were straight shapes and the tiles above were wavy.

Those were the kind of things that got my mind spinning. Things that splintered off into ideas so random and strange that sometimes I'd have to retrace my own thoughts to remember how I got there in the first place.

A lot of good ideas came from that kind of thinking. Lots of good drawings.

At home, if a really great one hit me, I'd get out of bed and draw. I wouldn't be able to do that here—at the risk of waking Sally—and the thought of forgetting something brilliant because I couldn't make a note of it made me a little panicky.

I tried to breathe through it. Zach had said that meditation would be good for me. I told him that he should take his own advice. He was the only person I knew whose obsession with work matched my own.

Sloane and I had talked for almost two hours—through her massive salad and then a towering pile of ice cream upon which she had added whipped cream, cherries, and a spoonful of mochi to. I'd ended up talking so much during dinner that it took me twice as long to finish my meal, and even then, I'd left a lot of it on my plate.

My stomach rumbled a little under my hand, and my mind began to replay the conversation I'd had with Sloane, helpfully reminding me of all the embarrassing moments, like when a bite of meat loaf had fallen out of my mouth while I was talking. Or when I'd called a character from the BB Gun film *The Ultimate Guide to the Universe* "Michael" instead of Matthew. I knew those mistakes would replay in my brain for the next several days, at least.

Sloane was nice, though. She'd been working at BB Gun Films for almost five years in the story department. Before that she'd worked at a few other studios, but she'd been like me—a fan of Bryan Beckett and his work.

"Is it everything you imagined it would be?" I'd asked her.

She'd thought about that for a long time. "I don't remember what I imagined it would be," she'd said.

When my alarm went off the next morning, there was a chai latte sitting on my desk with a Post-it. Sally had told me that she'd already scoped out the nearest coffee place and had offered to get me something after her run.

Today. It begins! was written in curly handwriting, complete with a sketch of MoMo, the sparrow narrator of *A Boy Named Bear.* The quote was one of his catchphrases.

Plucking the Post-it off of my latte, I examined the drawing with a critical eye. It was good—not great. I reminded myself that she had probably drawn it quickly, which would account for MoMo's deflated stomach. He should be twice as puffy and fluffy.

I imagined that Sally would be open to that kind of feedback if we were working together on one of the shorts. Even though I had no idea how the teams would be determined, I'd already mentally drafted her onto mine. We swapped portfolios last night. Quick drawing of MoMo notwithstanding, she was extremely talented. Talented enough that I was glad we wouldn't be competing for the director slot. I shouldn't have been surprised—everyone in the program was here because they'd earned it.

Everyone except Bear. I wondered if he'd even had to submit a portfolio.

"Thanks for the tea," I said when Sally came back, her face flushed and ponytail damp.

"No problem," she said. "I was so excited, I was up even before my alarm went off. I ran into Jeannette, though. She's trying to keep in shape for soccer. The campus is so pretty in the morning— all empty and quiet. If you ever feel like getting up early, we could go for a run together. Or even just a walk if you don't feel like running. There's something really great about getting up before everyone else—like the whole world belongs to you. I get my best ideas when I'm running."

I nodded, still half asleep. Bryan always said that he got his best ideas when he was sitting at his desk with his notebook.

"The blank page challenges me," he'd said in his CalTED Talk. "I like to be challenged."

I felt exactly the same way.

Sally puttered around as I went through my morning routine—throwing on my clothes and twisting my hair into its usual knot. I checked my phone but the only text I had was from Zach. It was a Violet Beauregarde GIF and I ignored it.

I carefully packed my supplies—my best pencils and erasers tucked into their case and a special-edition BB Gun sketchbook. They were almost twice as much as the sketchbooks I used to use, but Bryan had designed them himself. *Animation Stew* had declared it the Tesla of sketchbooks. I'd saved and bought four.

By the time we headed down to the front of the building, the caffeine had fully integrated into my system and I was eager and awake. Emily and Jeannette waved to us from the last row and pretty soon the six of us had taken over the back of the shuttle.

"I couldn't sleep, I was so excited." Caitlin draped her elbows over the back of my seat. She was wearing all black again, her hair pulled back in a ponytail that revealed that the sides of her head were shaved.

"My dreams were all animated," Rachel said. Her look was a total contrast to her roommate's, all pastel colors and rows of neat little buttons down the front of her shirt and skirt.

"What do you guys think of the dorms?" Sally asked.

"They're nice," Emily said. "But I was thinking of getting a plant or two to spruce things up. I cannot abide a room without greenery."

Everyone laughed at the dramatic turn of phrase.

"Just don't turn it into a jungle," Jeannette said.

"Have you guys thought about what you're going to do for your director pitch?" I asked.

Rachel shook her head, ponytail flapping. "No idea. But we have until Friday, right?"

"Yeah," Emily said. "That's plenty of time."

I nodded, but felt a twinge of judgment toward the two of them. If they didn't have anything, it was *definitely* not enough time to put together a pitch worthy of BB Gun Films.

"It would be really cool to work on the same project," Sally said to me.

"Your MoMo drawing was really good," I said.

She beamed, and I figured I'd save the constructive feedback for another time.

The shuttle dropped us off inside the gate. Gena was waiting for us like she'd been yesterday, only this time she was armed with a large box overflowing with lanyards.

Nick and his roommate, Karl, were standing nearby. Both of them were wearing polo shirts—Karl in jeans, and Nick in black pants that were just a little too long for him. In my mind, I pictured the three of us in a row—three variations on Bryan Beckett. I personally thought I looked the least like an exact imitation. I still had my own style.

"Our IDs." Nick motioned to the box of lanyards. "My mentor said we'll get temporary ones for the week and then real ones for the rest of the summer. Like they do with all employees."

I kept waiting for the doors of the studio to open and for Bryan Beckett himself to appear. For some reason, every time I imagined it, he was eight feet tall, even though I assumed he was normal height. Maybe a little taller, if Bear was any indication.

Once we were all gathered, Gena began calling out our names, and passing out IDs. I immediately put the lanyard around my neck and examined the card—it was heavier than I expected, with the BB Gun logo on one side and a bar code on the other.

"This is your key to getting around the studio," Gena said. "If you don't have it, you can't use the elevator—or the stairs—and even then, there are parts of the building that are restricted."

"Is it true we have to turn in our phones every day?" Nick asked.

"Good question, Mr. Cunningham," Gena said. "I was just about to discuss that."

"Way to come out swinging, man," someone said.

I knew immediately it was Bear. There was a huff of laughter, and I glanced over at Nick to see that his neck and cheeks were red. He didn't look back, just kept his attention focused straight ahead at Gena, ignoring Bear.

I wasn't proud of myself, but I'd googled him last night. As Bear Davis. Just to see what I could find.

"Mr. Cunningham is correct," Gena said. "You will all be required to surrender your phones at the beginning of every day. Or you can leave them in your dorm room if you'd like."

There wasn't much online—Bryan's desire for privacy had clearly extended to his son—but I learned that Bear went to a fancy private school in the Valley, not too far from my own public school. He was on the soccer team. There were a few pictures of him. In shorts. Running. Kicking things. Drinking Gatorade.

I knew of the school and the types of kids who went there. A lot of his classmates were the sons and daughters of actors or musicians. Nothing I'd seen had indicated that Bear wasn't anything more than a spoiled rich kid with a famous father.

"We're going to head inside in a moment," Gena said. "You'll be given the standard NDA that all employees sign. Know that if you don't sign it, you won't be going any further—in the building or in the program."

On that ominous note, we were allowed in. Still, I could feel excitement vibrating from the bottoms of my feet through my hands and up to the top of my head. Today. It begins!

The lobby was like the ones I'd seen in extremely fancy hotels on TV. The floors were shiny, the ceilings tall. I tried to take in everything at once, from the enormous round desk to the four security guards who sat behind it, their faces bathed in the glow coming from their screens. Everything was white and round and felt like a cross between a spaceship and a museum atrium.

"You can check your phones here." Gena gestured to the desk. "If you line up, this will go faster."

We scrambled into four untidy lines.

"It's like we're in the beginning of some sci-fi movie," Sally whispered. "Where they're going to put a computer chip in the back of our neck or our arm or something and the audience finds out later that we're all part of some mind-control experiment. Or that this whole thing has been nothing more than a dream."

I looked at her.

"This is intense," she said.

I squeezed her arm. "I know."

We were all whispering. We probably didn't have to, but the last thing I wanted was to say something and have it bounce around the room like an endless echo.

"Did you know about the NDA?" she asked. "What do you think it says?"

I shook my head. "All I know is that there were rumors."

"Right. I mean, I'm sure it's standard. They wouldn't ask us to sign something illegal, right? Are you going to sign it?"

"Are you not?"

The idea of getting this far—getting inside the building and then leaving without having seen the rest of the studio, or Bryan Beckett himself—was unfathomable to me.

Sally didn't have a chance to answer because it was her turn to hand over her phone. She waited for me to do the same and then we followed the stream of interns through a set of double doors. We stayed close to the other girls.

The conference room was immediately to our right, but I caught a glimpse of an enormous mural painted on the hallway that veered off to the left. It was colorful and seemed to portray multiple characters from the BB Gun Films universe, including Bear.

A few years ago, someone online had taken to drawing adult versions of animated characters who we'd only seen as children. They'd all been slightly sexualized—Lilo from *Lilo & Stitch* as a curvy young woman, wearing a lei and coconut bra. Boo from *Monsters, Inc.* wore an oversize T-shirt the pattern of Sully's fur, her black hair in messy pigtails, her legs exposed.

There had been a grown-up version of Bear as well. Whoever had done the drawings had apparently believed in equal-opportunity objectification, because adult Bear had been drawn in the same outfit he'd worn in the movie, namely a loincloth fashioned out of leaves. Only instead of an appropriately rounded tummy and thin, preadolescent arms, Bear had been given a six-pack, chest hair, and broad, bronzed shoulders. His face had been aged up as well, squaring out his jaw and giving his grin a wicked twist.

It was one of the images that had come up when I googled him. I'd thought about sending it to Samantha and Julie as a joke of sorts, but now that he was a real person, looking at it had made me feel weird. Like inappropriate weird.

I took a seat at the conference table, the NDA laid out in front of me. To my side, Sally coughed and gave my leg a jab. I looked up and found that once again, Bear was sitting across from me. He had put his fricking feet up on the table and was leaning back, his arms crossed. There was a smile on his face.

As much as I hated to admit it, whoever had drawn it had done a pretty damn good job imagining what he'd look like grown up. The jaw was there; the grin, too. I could only imagine how accurate the rest of the sketch was. Before I could stop myself, my gaze dropped downward. He was wearing a gray T-shirt and jeans and they all fit him well.

I hadn't been able to find any social media accounts for him. Either they were set to private or they were under another name. Or he just didn't have any.

"He's staring," Sally said.

"He's trying to annoy me," I said, but I said it just as the room had gone silent.

Everyone heard. Bear touched a finger to his forehead and gestured toward me—tipping an invisible cap. I slid down in my seat and stared at the NDA. Mom would have been able to explain it to me. She probably would advise me not to sign it—just like she'd done with the paperwork that had come with my acceptance letter. But I hadn't come this far not to.

Next to me, Sally nibbled on her bottom lip, her pen hovering over the paper. She touched the tip to the NDA, removed it, touched it again, and eventually wrote her name in the same curly handwriting she'd used on the Post-it she'd left on my chai latte.

Pretty soon, I was the only one who hadn't signed. I didn't know why I kept trying to decipher it—I just knew Mom would have been disappointed if I didn't look over every single word.

"Ms. Saffitz?" Gena asked. "Do you have any questions?"

Everyone was looking at me.

"Sign it, Saffitz," Bear said. "It's only a contract with the devil."

I noticed that his NDA was still pinned underneath his boot.

"Bear," Gena said, patiently, firmly.

"Sorry," he said. "I meant a contract with the four-time Academy Award–winning devil."

He kicked his feet off the table and grabbed a pen. With a big, dramatic sweep of his arm, he signed the paperwork.

"Ta-da," he said.

Clenching my jaw, I put my signature on the bottom of the paper and passed it to the front, where it was added to the pile.

Gena smiled. "Now I can officially welcome you to the BB Gun family."

"Wait a minute, Gena," a voice behind us said. "I'm pretty sure that's my line."

We all turned to the other side of the room, to find a door—where a door hadn't been before—opening out of the center of the wall. A man stood there, not eight feet tall like I had imagined, but very, very tall. He was wearing black pants, a white shirt, and a black tie. His shoes were neon-green sneakers.

"Welcome," Bryan Beckett said. "We're excited to see what you can do."

CHAPTER FIVE

I t was a little like seeing a movie star in real life. Someone I recognized—someone I felt like I knew—but didn't really know at all. He looked exactly how he had in the video from yesterday, except close up I was able to see that his dark hair had quite a lot of gray in it. There were lines fanning out from the corner of his eyes but I could easily imagine Mom describing him as "a total hunk," as she embarrassingly did when referring to celebrities she thought were cute. He looked like Bear and not like Bear. Same jawline, different eyes. Different smile, too.

Like a school of fish, we followed him through the hallways of BB Gun Films. It was hard to know what to concentrate on—a tour of a previously unseen animation studio that had shaped most of our childhoods, or the man who had inspired those stories.

I'd decided to focus on Bryan himself, nearly elbowing my way to the front of group. At some point, I'd left Sally and the other girls behind.

"I founded BB Gun Films because I wanted to tell the type of stories I wasn't seeing out in the world," Bryan was saying. His back was to us, his strides long and quick as he moved through hallways he could clearly navigate in his sleep.

"Most people think that animated movies are for children,

and most people think that children are stupid." He turned to face us. "But you're not stupid, are you?"

"We're also not children," Bear said.

His father ignored him. In fact, the two of them had barely acknowledged each other. I didn't want to care, but I was confused. If Bear disliked his father—referring to him as "the devil" seemed to indicate as much—why was he doing this internship? When Nick had accused him of getting the whole thing essentially handed to him, Bear had only confirmed everyone's suspicions.

Bryan was still talking. I pushed thoughts of Bear out of my head and listened, trying to absorb as much of his wisdom as possible. If I were to animate myself, I'd be a giant sponge, squishing behind Bryan, soaking up his droplets of words as we walked.

"I wanted to create movies that appeal to a child's innate creativity, but also entertain the parents who would have to go watch it with them. I wanted to remind them of their own curiosity," Bryan said. "Sadly, we seem to grow out of it the older we get. You all don't realize how lucky you are to be able to hold on to some of that wonder."

The hallway ahead seemed to clear magically. When employees saw us coming, they quickly ducked into offices or cubicles. Bryan didn't seem to notice, his pace never faltering.

"I grew up watching princess movies where furry little animals broke out into song and villains were identifiable the moment they appeared onscreen, twirling a mustache or wearing a black cape," he said.

Nick had also pushed his way to the front of the group and was standing next to me, his head bobbing in agreement. We were two sponges, taking it all in.

"I wanted to create movies with nuance. With depth," Bryan

said. "I wanted the heroes to be villainous and the villains to be redeemable. No more fairy tales. No more musicals."

I knew the kind of movies he was talking about. I liked those movies. At least, I thought I did. Maybe I needed to rewatch them—maybe I needed to look through Bryan Beckett's eyes. I needed to see what was wrong with them. How I could do better.

"I built my career on creating complicated stories—crafting vibrant worlds and sympathetic but complex characters. With each film, I want to push the limits of filmmaking—of story-telling. Every new project is a chance to improve. To astonish."

Bryan halted so abruptly that we all had to stop as well. My feet got bunched up beneath me, and I began falling forward. I put my palms out, prepared to hit the floor, but before I could, a hand on my arm yanked me upright.

"Careful," Bear said. His voice was in my ear. His tone wasn't cocky or arrogant, and he let go of me almost as quickly as he had grabbed me. He ducked his head and I did the same. A *Thanks for saving my ass* nod. Then, I stepped away from him. Refocused.

"Do you know how lucky you are?" Bryan asked. "You have the most powerful weapons in your arsenal right now—curiosity and determination. You can do anything—*anything*!"

I felt like a soldier, preparing to go into battle, with Bryan as our commander.

"There are no limits to your imagination," he said. "Challenge yourself. Surprise yourself. Each one of you is capable of extraordinary things." He was looking out at all of us, but I knew he was speaking to me.

"This is where I leave you," he said, and gestured toward the back of the group. "Gena."

The internship coordinator wove her way through the pack. "Thank you, Bryan."

"Looking forward to seeing your pitches," he said. "Impress me."

And then he was gone, long strides taking him down a hallway and out of sight. I stared at the place he had just vacated. *That was it?* I wanted more. More time, more guidance, more advice.

"Inspiring, isn't he?" Bear asked.

I glared at him. Even though it had been brief, it *had* been inspiring. And now I just wanted to impress him even more.

"Your father is a very busy man," Gena said.

Bryan *was* running an entire studio. We were lucky to have any time with him at all.

"We'll be returning to the conference room for orientation, which will last for the rest of the morning," Gena said.

There was an audible ripple of disappointment.

"It's standard for all new employees," Gena said.

We puffed up a little at that—it was such a thrill to be referred to as "employees."

"Your mentors will come take you to lunch and then you'll be shadowing them for the rest of the day."

With a wave of her hand, we were off, following her down the enormous staircase at what seemed to be the center of the building. I wanted to memorize this place—wanted to know everything about it.

"In addition to working with your mentors and on your short films, you'll also get the chance to learn how our pipeline works," Gena said. "Starting next week, you'll be having Wednesday lunches with different department heads, and we've divided you into five smaller groups so you'll get more one-on-one time."

We made it back to the enormous conference room where shiny plastic folders were now laid out in front of each seat. Inside were several informational packets, a phone registry, and thankfully, a map of the studio. I studied it, discovering that in addition to the theater and the main building, there was a large cafeteria on the other side of the campus and several smaller bungalows in between.

"If you look inside your packet, you'll find a piece of colored paper with a number on it—that's your group for the lunchtime lecture series. There's also a schedule included."

I found a green piece of paper with a number one. Sally, sitting next to me, pulled out a blue square with a two. Looking down the long table, I saw that Caitlin also had a blue piece of paper. She saluted Sally. None of the other girls were in my group.

Bear didn't bother opening his folder.

"Lots of rules," Sally said. "Guidelines for everything, it seems. Look at this, it says that clothing isn't optional. I wonder why they had to put that in the manual. Do you think it was a problem before?"

She was flipping through one of the thick, stapled guides labeled EMPLOYEE CONDUCT. I was focused on the double-sided sheet of paper that outlined the pitch process.

"Interns will be expected to present a five-minute pitch, which includes artwork and a proposed story synopsis, twice. First to the BB Gun Films brain trust and secondly *to Bryan Beckett himself.* The brain trust will offer feedback, but the final decision will be Bryan's alone."

We were going to be pitching directly to Bryan? And he'd be

the one choosing the directors? My hands went numb, but my heart sped up. I was overwhelmed with a desire to run back to the dorms to perfect my pitch. I'd suspected that Bryan would be involved in determining who would be leading the short films, but to see his exact role spelled out so clearly had me feeling both terrified and exhilarated. No matter what, I was guaranteed one-on-one time with Bryan. I was going to be able to present my idea directly to him.

Getting the internship wasn't enough. Getting the chance to direct a short would prove to my parents that I could do this. It would show them—and Bryan—exactly what I was capble of. That I belonged here.

Confidence surged through me. My idea was good, I knew it was. It was well-thought-out and beautifully designed and absolutely perfect for BB Gun Films. It just needed a few tweaks so it could be perfectly tailored for its now-intended audience.

I was going to knock Bryan Beckett's socks off.

Sloane was waiting for me outside the conference room when it was time to break for lunch. She was wearing the same black-and-gold glasses from last night, her hair pulled back in a sleek pony-tail. Her dress was a green graphic print that buttoned down the front, with big pockets on either side. I tucked my orientation folder into my bag, next to my sketchbook, and followed her down the hall. We walked by the mural, and I slowed to take it all in.

It was beautiful—a dreamy, colorful interpretation of all the notable BB Gun characters—each of them in action poses. All of the movies had had their own distinct style, but the artist of the mural had found a way to fit them all into the same universe, tweaking and adjusting each to fit more neatly with the other.

"This is so cool," I said to Sloane.

"Thanks," she said. "I drew it."

I turned toward her, my eyes wide, mouth hanging open. She laughed.

"You drew this?"

She nodded.

"How long did it take?" I wanted to reach out and touch it, but stuck my hands in my pockets to keep from doing exactly that.

"The initial design took a month or so," she said. "Approval took another month. I think I got the actual painting done in two weeks."

"It's . . . wow." We continued walking, but I kept twisting my head to look at the mural.

"Why is it down here?" I asked as we turned the corner. "Shouldn't it be where more people can see it? Like in the theater?"

The lobby of the theater had been decorated as well, but the mural wasn't nearly as good. That one had been done by Josh—I knew because there was a plaque next to it.

Sloane shrugged. "You'd have to ask Bryan."

She pushed open a door, and suddenly we were outside. I squinted. Even though I'd grown up in Southern California, the heat could still surprise me. It was a bright, cloudless day and I peeled off my cardigan, already too hot. Luckily, we didn't have to walk far before we were shielded by a canopy of leaves.

Unlike the front of the building, which was colorful and bright but consisted mostly of the theater and a parking lot, the rest of the campus was lush and beautiful—almost like a botanical garden. There were trees everywhere, flowering bushes, and vines climbing up the sides of the building. Everything that wasn't green was painted in soft, warm beige tones and there was even a small stream running between us and the cafeteria, complete with a wooden bridge to cross. I knew there was a freeway nearby, but I couldn't hear it. All I heard was the gargling of the water and the chattering of birds.

"Wow," I said.

Sloane—who hadn't stopped—glanced back and grinned. "There are even some ducks that hang out by the stream," she said. "We get ducklings in the spring."

"Really?"

"Yeah—that's the reason there's always a duck in our movies."

I felt like my brain was going to explode with all this new, unexpected information. Because there *was* always a duck in BB Gun films. Plenty of people had noticed—there was even a Twitter account that tracked all the appearances of said ducks—but I had never imagined that this was the reason.

"The story department likes to come out here and sketch them," Sloane said as we walked over the bridge. "It can be a nice break if we're in crunch mode."

I kept an eye out for the ducks but didn't spot one. It would have to happen before the end of my internship, though. I'd make sure of it.

The cafeteria looked a lot like the CalAn dining hall (or the "Wingy-Dingy," as Josh had called it), only bigger and with twice as many options. There were signs at the end of every buffet, with vegetarian, gluten-free, and other dietary options clearly labeled, plus a massive salad bar.

"What looks good?" Sloane asked.

"What do you usually get?"

"Depends on my mood," she said, and grabbed a tray. I did the same. "Sometimes I go for the healthy option, but since I had a salad last night, I think I'll load up on carbs," she said, leading me to one of the stands where a Black man was standing behind multiple pots of pasta.

Dreadlocks peeped out from under his chef's hat. Just like the intern class, there were only a handful of mentors that weren't white, and I hadn't seen much more diversity on our brief tour of the studio.

"Hey, Ron."

"Sloane! What can I get you today?"

"Penne with pesto and chicken, please," she turned to me. "What about you?"

"I'll have the same." I was overwhelmed with options. "Please."

"Is this your mentee?" Ron asked.

"Hayley Saffitz, meet Ron Austell."

I waved.

"How do you like the place so far?" Ron asked as he threw a cup of pasta into a hot pan before adding some fragrant green sauce and sliced chicken.

"It's amazing."

"She's a fan," Sloane said.

"Aren't we all?" Ron asked. Something in their tone made it seem like they were having two conversations at once. Ron plated our pasta and passed it over. "Nice to meet you, Hayley," he said. "I'm sure I'll be seeing you around."

Following Sloane's lead, I took my tray and added a piece of bread. We went to get beverages next—a row of machines that had everything from soda to iced tea to coffee. I thought about getting a root beer but saw that Sloane was drinking iced tea, so I got that instead. I glanced around for registers but didn't see them.

"It's all free." Sloane led us outside. "One of the perks of working here."

"Wow." I was saying that a lot today.

There was a small table overlooking the stream, and I took the chair closest to the water, hoping that one of the ducks would swim by while we were eating. Even though I knew they would probably look like ordinary ducks, I couldn't help imagining them as bigger, brighter, fluffier than the average duck. As if just being around all this magic and creativity would make them visibly different.

I felt a little different being here.

"What do you think of the studio so far?" Sloane tore off a piece of bread and dipped it into the excess sauce on her plate.

I'd just taken a bite of the very, very good pasta, so I had to nod and chew. "It's really cool," I said once I had swallowed. The food was good, too. "Bryan gave us a tour this morning."

Sloane lifted an eyebrow, and for a moment I wondered if I should be referring to him as Mr. Beckett. Then she smiled and I relaxed.

"How was it?" she asked.

"Interesting." I took another bite of pasta. "I mean, the tour itself was confusing, but he told us all about his reasons for starting the studio, which was really awesome."

Sloane laughed. "Yeah, it's pretty easy to get lost," she said. "When I first started, I always seemed to end up in the layout department, no matter which way I turned. My mentor used to joke that I had a crush on someone there." She made a face. "I didn't."

"You had a mentor?" I asked.

Sloane nodded. "Monica," she said. "They assign mentors to all the new employees—it helps people acclimate quicker. It's a great model. She retired about a year ago, but she taught me the ropes when I was starting out." She smiled at me. "Don't worry, after a week or so, you'll get the hang of it."

"I was reading the orientation stuff"—I pulled the folder out of my bag—"and it said that Bryan is going to be determining who will be directing the shorts."

Sloane scanned the printout. "Seems about right," she said. "Any ideas for your pitch?"

"I've been working on it for weeks." I put my sketchbook on the table. "It's ready to go—I just need to make a few adjustments now that I know I'll be pitching it one-on-one to Bryan."

"Do you want some help?" she asked.

It was exactly what I had been hoping for. I'd had numerous art teachers over the years, all of whom had been helpful and encouraging, but they hadn't known anything about working in animation. Sloane's feedback would be invaluable.

"Would you mind?" I opened my notebook and took out a pen.

Sloane looked down at my supplies. "Ah, the special-edition series," she said.

I touched a hand to the page, self-conscious all of a sudden. "They're good notebooks."

It came out more defensively than I intended.

"Only the best for Bryan," Sloane said. "Let's take a look at some of your ideas."

The brief tension faded as I flipped through the pages, looking for something to show her.

"I mean, if you could just tell me a little bit more about what Bryan likes or doesn't like, that would be really helpful."

Sloane leaned back and crossed her arms. A smile began to curve at the corner of her lips. "You know exactly what you're doing, don't you?" she asked.

I didn't know how to respond to that, though it sounded like a compliment.

"I'm going to be one of the directors," I told her.

"All right, then," she said, openly grinning now. "Let me see what you've got."

CHAPTER SIX

The next morning, bath caddy in hand, I shuffled my way to the shared bathroom, where I opened the door to a flutter of activity.

"You're awake!" Sally said. "We missed you last night. We started a mini marathon after the movie—it was really fun. I think we're going to continue it tonight if you want to join— Jeannette has all the movies on Blu-ray."

I felt a twinge of regret. After our first day, I'd headed back to the dorms, wanting to incorporate Sloane's input while it was still fresh. The others had gone to a screening of *A Boy Named Bear* in the multipurpose room. It wasn't that I didn't want to spend time with them—I just *had* to get the pitch right. I hadn't even texted Samantha and Julie, even though I'd had messages from both of them. But I knew they'd understand. They knew how important this was. It was my one shot to impress Bryan. To make everything happen the way it was supposed to.

"Every moment that isn't spent creating is a wasted moment," Bryan had said.

Even though there were six of us, the bathroom was huge— clearly meant to accommodate an entire floor. I washed my face, the cold water doing a lot to wake me, the overlapping conversations beginning to pierce through my morning haze.

"How was your run?" Caitlin asked.

"Good," Jeannette said. "There's a park nearby, so Sally and I did some laps."

"I can't believe how dedicated you are." Rachel brushed her hair. "When I quit ballet, I *really* quit ballet."

"I can't quit soccer," Jeannette said. "They'd have to cut my feet off. And even then I'd find a way. I just couldn't do this *and* soccer camp, but I have to stay in shape."

"I don't like running *that* much," Sally said. "But it definitely helps keep me focused."

"That's how I feel about music," Caitlin said.

"When are you going to play us some songs?" Emily asked.

"Yeah, when do we get a private Caitlin Gonzalez concert?" Rachel asked.

Caitlin grinned. "I *do* know how to play the *Spider-Man: Into the Spider-Verse* theme."

It was hard to imagine how the other girls had time for anything that wasn't animation-related. My parents always worried I wasn't well rounded enough in my interests, but I also knew they were mostly concerned with how those interests would look on a college application.

Animation was my whole life, and I liked it that way.

Still, it made me feel a little like I was on the outside, even here, even among other girls who liked the same things that I liked. I just seemed to *care* more. It wasn't a hobby or something I did for fun like guitar or soccer. This was my future. It was everything.

I twisted my hair back into a bun and listened as the conversation shifted to our mentors.

"Amber said she'll show me concepts for the project that's

coming out in two years," Rachel said. "She's already been working on it for six months."

"Vicky worked on the very last shot that got approved for *Mountains of Manhattan*," Jeannette said, referring to the latest BB Gun Films release.

Each not-so-humble brag about our mentors was met with an approving "ooooh" from the group. Everyone seemed thrilled with the mentor they'd been assigned to, and I was no exception.

I brushed my teeth and watched everyone get ready. Rachel had her hair pulled back in a glossy ponytail, the ends of it perfectly curled—giving her a major Disney-princess vibe. She'd mentioned that she, her girlfriend, and her sister would go to Disney World for Dapper Days, where everyone dressed up in vintage-style interpretations of Disney characters. Even now, her outfit looked a little like an updated Elsa with an ice-blue circle skirt and white high-necked blouse. She also seemed the most likely of all of us to have a furry animal sidekick. My imagination whirred, taking the other girls in. If Rachel was the most Disney-esque, then what animation studio would the other girls represent? It was a little like taking one of those online quizzes, only I was creating it as I went.

Jeannette with her Megan Rapinoe jersey and colorful sneakers reminded me a bit of DreamWorks films—playful and energetic. A little all over the place, but in a good way. Caitlin was definitely a Laika girl—indie and offbeat—with her half-shaved head and myriad of piercings. She also knew a lot about obscure animated films I'd never even heard about.

Emily reminded me of the Aardman films, with her irreverent humor and a tendency to say random words with a British accent despite the fact that she was definitely not British. Her style was

a little wild and free, with her long hair and flowy skirts. She was also the only other girl who preferred tea to coffee.

It wasn't a perfect analogy, but I could see Sally as a Pixar film. Fast-moving and funny, but with an emotional side. It seemed like she felt all things in big ways. Sloane would be the Miyazaki films—next-level kind of work. I thought about the mural she had done—how epic it was.

Of course, I cast myself as BB Gun Films. Clever. Thoughtful. Capable of great things.

Sally looped her arm through mine as we left the bathroom and headed back to our room, her in her robe, me still in my pajamas. "I hope I didn't wake you when I came back last night," she said. "It was kind of late, but I tried to be quiet. Did you get your work done?"

I nodded. "Going to try to do a little more this morning."

"You're so focused," she said.

I shrugged, pleased, but a little surprised that *she* seemed so amazed by my dedication. I'd thought that everyone in the program would be just as committed as I was. Then again, she was probably enjoying the downtime. We'd all be extremely busy once the shorts started—no time for long dinners and movies afterward.

"Art is work," Bryan had said in his CalTED Talk. "And it takes sacrifice. You only have so much time. Do you want to look back and regret the things you never made?"

I didn't want the girls to think I was antisocial. I *wanted* to spend time with them, I just had to make some sacrifices. And even if I wanted to relax, there was no way I could. When I was focused on something, it felt like my brain divided itself into two parts. One part was constantly sorting through ideas, looking for solutions, making changes. It never stopped spinning. The other half of my brain was left to deal with everything else. School. Friends. Family.

Zach told me it was physically impossible for a brain to separate into factions, but that I should donate said brain if I was convinced I was special.

Last night, Sloane had explained that once the directors were chosen, the rest of us would be given roles similar to a full-length animated film.

"You'll only be ten people per team, but you'll have a head of story, a head of animation, and a head of special effects. Everyone reports to the director, but the heads of each department will have a say in how work is divided up," she'd said. "You'll also have PAs—production assistants—to handle the scheduling side of things."

According to Sloane, there wasn't another animation company in the United States—possibly in the world—that had an internship as hands-on and focused as this one was.

"Bryan doesn't do things halfway," she'd said.

Across the room, Sally was curling her hair—there was the slight smell of burning—while I sat down at my desk to do a little more work.

"Can I put on some music?" Sally asked. "I call this my 'Hero's Journey' mix," she said when I nodded.

I immediately knew the track. It was "Almost There" from *The Princess and the Frog*.

"I love this song," I said.

Sally grinned at me before showing me her phone. "It's hopelessly nerdy, but I figured that if I can't be nerdy here, then what's the point?"

I looked at the playlist. It was all the best hero ballads from animated movies—like "Journey to the Past" or "When Will My Life Begin."

My head started bopping, my shoulders swaying. I'd sung along to all these songs in my bedroom—arms outstretched, belting everything off-key. It was tempting to do that now. Behind me,

Sally was humming along. I had a feeling she'd join in if I started singing.

Then I remembered that Bryan had told us how much he hated animated musicals. The songs seemed to sour in my eardrums as I heard how cheesy and cliché they were. I was annoyed at myself for liking them.

Sally shimmied along in the background as I tried to focus on my work, doing my best to ignore the music. Trying to clear my head. After finishing with my sketches, I got dressed—a white shirt with little black polka dots and red Vans today—and sat at my desk, my sketches stacked neatly in front of me. When I started experimenting with wearing the same thing every day, I'd expected Mom to be disappointed—after all, we used to have a lot of fun going shopping together—but instead she'd helped me settle on the perfect outfit.

"What do you think?" Sally had on a pair of jeans and a black top with floaty, sheer sleeves. "The yellow sweater or the orange one?" She held out the two options.

"I like the yellow," I said.

"I don't think I could wear the same thing every day," Sally said. "Sometimes I even change my clothes after school just to mix things up. I get bored really easily. But it seems to really suit you."

"Thanks," I said. "My mom thinks I look like Katharine Hepburn."

It had been the ultimate compliment coming from her. She'd even helped me find shirts that weren't see-through and flimsy like most women's button-downs were. When it was cold, I usually added a cardigan. The whole thing had a bit of a vintage vibe to it, which made it seem a little less like full-on Bryan Beckett cosplay.

"I'm so nervous," Sally said. "What if they realize I'm terrible and throw me out of the program?"

"They won't," I said. "Your work is really good."

She'd shown me the animation test she'd used for her application. It had utilized shadow puppets—black over a pale indigo background—and the effect was beautiful and eerie. She had the puppets pinned up on her bulletin board and every morning she put them in different poses. At the moment, one of them was standing on its head, while the other was balancing on the first one's feet.

Sally leaned close to the mirror, putting the finishing touches on her eyeliner. "What do you think?" she asked. "Are they even?"

Even though I had basically gotten this internship based on the things I could do with a pencil, I was still in awe of the perfect, identical swoops of black that Sally had applied to the corners of her eyes. I'd yet to master eyeliner.

"They look great," I said.

She beamed and shoved her sketchbook into her bag. "Okay. Let's go!"

Sloane's office was small and full of stuff. Yesterday, we'd spent most of our time outside or around the building, but today she had cleared off a space for me in the corner.

"Sorry about the mess," she said.

In Bryan's CalTED Talk, he'd spoken about the importance of having a clean and clear working space. "Clutter on your desk only leads to clutter in your brain," he'd said. "You can't create if you're distracted."

He spoke a lot about distractions. How one had to get rid of them in order to work.

My desk at home—and in the dorm—was spotless. I couldn't imagine how Sloane managed to get anything done in this space—everything was covered in drawings. They were taped up on the walls, several pieces of paper stuck on top of one another, others sliding down to the desks and bookcases, which were crammed full of books. There were even sketches on the floor, and when I rolled my chair back, I ran over a couple of them, the crinkle of the paper making me cringe.

"I'm so sorry." I tried to free the paper from the plastic wheels of the chair. To my great horror, I ripped one sheet in two.

Zach had once spilled an entire can of soda on my sketchbook and I'd screamed so loud, Mom thought I'd cut my finger off.

"Oh, don't worry about it." Sloane took the two ruined halves of her drawing from my hands and smoothed them out on her desk. Then, with a piece of Scotch tape, she reconnected them and tacked it back onto the wall. It stared at me, looking like a gaping wound held together by a single stitch.

"I know it's a lot," Sloane said. "But it's the only way I can work."

I eyed the chaos suspiciously.

Sloane sat. "I've been thinking about your pitch."

I immediately perked up. "Me too." Reaching into my bag, I pulled out the sketches I had worked on last night and this morning. "I think you're right about making sure everyone knows what a golem is."

"These are great," she said, looking at the drawings I handed her. "This is the one you should start with." She pointed to one of my favorite images.

It was the sketch that had inspired the whole thing. Miriam—

the hero of the story—was standing next to a giant man made out of mud wearing a vest and torn pants. It was a pose loosely inspired by *Butch Cassidy and the Sundance Kid*—one of my dad's favorite old movies that he had made me and Zach watch growing up. Both characters had cowboy hats and stood with their hands on their hips. There were flowers and other green things sprouting out of the golem's wide shoulders. I'd been playing around with contrasts when I drew them—using simple, bold lines with the golem while Miriam had a sketchier feel to her. In the story, despite the golem's physical strength, Miriam was the strongest of the two. I liked the idea of putting together characters that looked the opposite of how they'd usually be perceived. Miriam had a grim look on her face, but the golem was smiling.

"It conveys the central theme of the story perfectly," Sloane said. "The way that the mystical and the familiar exist together in this world."

I released a satisfied breath—it was exactly what I had been aiming for.

"I think you should lean into that even further." Sloane sat back in her chair, her pencil against her chin. "Maybe even see if you can incorporate it into your title. We want to know exactly what we're getting into from the very beginning."

Right now, the project was just called *The Golem*. I wasn't very good at titles, so I tended to name everything exactly what it was.

Sloane was slowly spinning in her chair now, her fingers tapping together like a villain in a comic book. "Hmm, hmm," she said. "Hmm."

I sat there, notebook open, pencil poised. Was this how Sloane's creative process worked? Spinning and humming? When I needed ideas, I sat at my desk, feet on the ground, staring at the blank wall. Sometimes I put some music on and just started drawing. It's what Bryan did.

"Golem. Golem. Golem," Sloane was now saying. "Cowboy Golem. Farmer Golem."

I wrote it all down.

"Golem on the Prairie. Little House Golem. Adventure Golem."

This went on for a while, Sloane spinning, me recording all her thoughts. Then she grew silent, her chair still rotating, with her staring off into the distance. While she did that, I let my pencil wander.

I still hadn't seen any of the famous BB Gun ducks, so I did a few sketches of how I imagined they would look. I made them fancier than the average duck, their feathers fluffier, their eyes shinier. I drew them hiding under the bridge, imagining that they had their own world under there—a little duck town.

Suddenly Sloane stopped and faced me. "I don't know," she said. "I think we'll need to marinate on that some more."

I looked at the clock. We'd been marinating for an hour. I felt a rush of panic—an hour wasted trying to think up a title! I didn't have that kind of time. This pitch had to be perfect.

"Want to go for a walk?" Sloane pushed up from her chair.

I didn't—I wanted to find a quiet, clean conference room and work, but Sloane was my mentor and I wasn't exactly sure if I was allowed to say no to things she suggested.

Sloane was wearing a gauzy blue vest decorated with little sparkling crystals over black jeans and a black shirt. It swayed from side to side as we walked down the hall, a floating constellation.

She waved at open doors, and occasionally people popped their heads up from their cubicles like little gophers to greet her.

"Hey, Flores." Sloane all but swung into a nearby office. "Question for you."

Inside was a bespectacled guy with brown skin in a plaid shirt, a little older than Sloane. His hair was curly on top, shaved close on the sides. It was black with little twists of gray throughout.

"Hit me," he said.

"What do you imagine when you hear the word 'golem'?" she asked. "We need a title."

What was she doing? Why was she telling some random guy about my pitch? I hadn't even told Sally about it—I wanted it to be a complete surprise to Bryan and the brain trust.

"Hmm." He leaned back in his chair. "Golem. Like the fictional creature?"

"The one and the same." Sloane was bouncing on her feet, back and forth, more like she was playing a sport instead of spitballing in an animation studio.

"Big," he said. "Made of mud."

"Ooh, mud, yeah." Sloane snapped her fingers. "Good. Really good."

"Mud Man," he said. "Dirt. Clay. Dust."

Sloane was nodding. I wasn't sure if I should be writing all this down.

"Dust to dust," he said.

"Exactly," said Sloane. "Exactly."

"The Incredible Shrinking Dust Man," he said.

He looked at Sloane. Sloane looked at me. I wrote it down.

"Not exactly what you're looking for, right?" he asked.

"Still helpful," Sloane said. "Oh, this is Hayley, by the way. Hayley, meet Isaac Flores, storyboarding savant."

Isaac pushed his glasses back. "Ah, the intern. Welcome."

"Nice to meet you." I waved.

"Sloane's the best," he said. "You're in great hands."

Sloane fluttered her fingers in his direction. "You have to say that."

Before Isaac could respond, we were on the move again.

"He's the head of story on the next feature," Sloane said. "Just below Josh in the story department hierarchy."

That was a little strange, since Isaac seemed at least fifteen years older than Josh.

We passed by an open conference room. Sloane backtracked immediately.

"Boys," she said, leaning against the open door. "Working hard?"

I peered in to find Josh and Bear sitting at the conference table. Well, Josh was sitting, leaning over a pile of papers, while Bear had his feet up on the table, his head tilted back as he stared at the ceiling. His chair was perched precariously on two legs. Too precariously, because when he glanced up and saw me and Sloane, he leaned back and went down, his feet practically flying over his head.

He immediately scrambled upright, brushing his jeans off.

Josh's eyes were closed and he was shaking his head, his lips pressed together. It was hard to tell if he was annoyed or trying not to laugh.

"Men," Sloane said. "Always falling at my feet."

"What are you two up to?" Josh asked.

For one horrible moment, I thought that Sloane might tell them the same thing she'd just told Isaac. It was bad enough that she was telling other BB Gun employees about my film, but it would be a disaster if she told my direct competition about it. I pressed my sketchbook hard against my chest, feeling it dig into my breastbone.

"We're just brainstorming Hayley's project." Sloane put her hands on my shoulders. "She's going to blow your boy out of the water."

Josh looked down at the pile of papers in front of him, and then at Bear, who had righted his chair and sat back down at the table. "She can try," he said, but it didn't sound like he had much faith in Bear.

Confidence surged through me. I was going to get one of the four directing slots. I just knew it.

"How are you guys doing?" Sloane asked.

"We've decided I'm just going to wing it," Bear said.

"We have not—" Josh started, but then seemed to give up. "Where are you guys headed?"

"I thought we'd get some ice cream," Sloane said.

"Great idea." Josh pushed back from the table. "Come on, Bear. I think we need a break."

"I think *you* need a break," Bear said. "I could do this all day."

As Josh ignored him and gathered up his things, I tried to communicate my displeasure to Sloane. Silently. But she wasn't paying attention. Instead, she walked ahead with Josh, leaving me alone with Bear. Why did this keep happening to me?

We were met by the dry heat of summer as we headed outside. Despite my annoyance at Bear and my frustration that I'd accomplished absolutely nothing today, I could still appreciate the sunshine and the respite from the frigid studio air. My skin felt like it was thawing as warmth spread through me.

Bear was whistling something under his breath. It took a moment before I realized it was "Oo-De-Lally" from *Robin Hood*. Apparently, he and Sally had similar taste in music. I also wouldn't be surprised if he liked it just out of spite. I didn't understand his relationship with his dad. Even though I had a hard time imagining what it was like to be Bryan Beckett's kid, I was pretty certain I'd be a hell of a lot more gracious than Bear was.

"Your pitch is about ducks?" he asked.

I was confused until I realized I'd lowered my sketchbook, giving him a pretty clear view of the page. At the drawings I'd been doing in Sloane's office.

"They're good," he said.

I pulled it back against my chest. "I *know*."

I was annoyed that he seemed surprised.

"You *do* have something prepared," I deflected. "Right?"

The thought of going into a pitch *this* important and just "winging it" made me a little nauseous. I imagined a duck going into the pitch meeting and flapping at the brain trust. A duck's version of "winging it."

"Thought you'd be thrilled," Bear said. "Less competition for you."

"What's the point in winning by default?" I asked. "I want to know I'm the best."

I turned and found that Bear was staring at me. I couldn't read his expression. Was it awe? Or intimidation?

He laughed. Nope. Neither of those.

I didn't say anything, and he widened his eyes in mock amazement. "Oh my god. You believe that. You believe that talent actually matters." He shook his head. "Wow."

I sped up, but he just matched my pace.

"You know, it's kind of cute that you think that's how this will work," he said.

Anger boiled up inside of me. Cute? What a condescending asshole.

I faced him. He stopped short, his feet almost touching mine. He was way too close, but neither of us moved. I wasn't going to back down if he wasn't.

"How will it work, then?" I asked.

He gave me a long, assessing look. "It will work the way it always does," he said. "The way it always will."

"Guys?" Sloane asked.

I turned and found her and Josh waiting by the entrance to the cafeteria.

"Ice cream?" she asked.

I put a smile on my face. "Sounds great."

CHAPTER SEVEN

I used all my available free time to work on my pitch. When I wasn't at the studio, I was in the library on the CalAn campus or in my room. Even though I knew the other interns were working on their pitches, the only person I ever saw in the library was Nick.

We each had commandeered our own sides of the building—I liked the big table underneath a row of round windows—while he seemed to prefer the desks in the back. We'd wave to each other, but for the most part, we were focused on our own work.

I had a feeling that Nick was going to be the pitch to beat. Even though I still stayed later then he did each night, his dedication seemed to match mine. I respected that. Unlike Bear, who never appeared to be working. I did my best to ignore him, but it wasn't easy. He wasn't in the library, but somehow, he always seemed to be everywhere else—reading by himself at a table in the dining hall, or listening to music out on the quad. Sally even mentioned that she'd seen him out running in the morning. Always alone.

The day before the pitch, Sloane and I were in her office. I had just shoved my hand into a bag of chips when someone appeared in the doorway. It was Bryan.

I hadn't seen him since our first day, when I'd been just one of the forty unfamiliar interns following him through the halls of BB Gun Films. It was unlikely that he had noticed me then, and he didn't seem to notice me now, his attention focused on Sloane.

"Just wanted to stop in and say how impressed I was with the work you did this week," he said. "The forest dance sequence turned out great."

"Thanks," Sloane said.

"You and Josh really nailed it."

I'd gone totally still when he appeared, but for some reason, my hand hadn't gotten the memo and chose that moment to get caught in the world's noisiest chip bag. The rustling is what caught Bryan's attention, and he turned toward me.

It was like that moment in *Ratatouille*, the camera zooming in fast to capture my frozen, deer-in-headlights look. I had a weird impulse to wave. Thankfully, I did not. My hand was still stuck.

"Working on your pitch?" he asked.

I nodded, wondering if I should say something. Or do something. How would he react if I just whipped out my sketchbook?

"Looking forward to seeing it," he said, before turning back to Sloane. "Keep up the excellent work. You really have a great handle on Hazel as a character."

He gave the doorjamb a very dad-like knock, as if he couldn't really figure out what to do with himself at that moment. *Rat-a-tat.*

"All right, then," he said. "I'm expecting to be impressed tomorrow."

He said this to me.

"Yes, sir," I said.

Sir? His eyebrows went up at my formality. I wanted to die.

After he was gone, I extracted my hand from the salty, noisy chip bag and let out a groan. Sloane could barely contain her laugh.

"Well," she said. "At least you've faced him one-on-one. Tomorrow should be a snap."

The next morning, I got only twenty minutes with Sloane before all the eligible interns were called down to the adjoining conference rooms. We'd be pitching to the brain trust first and then to Bryan immediately after. You'd enter one door and leave from another.

It was alphabetical so I was going to be one of the last to present. I didn't mind—in fact, it played into my fantasy of Bryan offering me the directing position right on the spot. If he'd seen all the other pitches by the time I arrived, then he would know for sure that I deserved the opportunity.

"I wish that you could just wait here," Sloane had said while straightening my collar. "But Bryan tends to have a flair for the dramatic."

It did feel dramatic, twenty-one of us story interns sitting or standing in the hallway outside the conference rooms. Occasionally, an employee would pass and give us all a sympathetic smile.

I wiggled my toes in my shoes. Before leaving my phone in my room that morning, I'd texted a picture to Julie and Samantha of the good-luck socks they'd bought me. I knew I'd get back tonight and have a dozen messages, though by that time, the conversation would have moved on to something else.

My parents hadn't texted me—I was pretty sure they'd forgotten today was the day and I hadn't reminded them—but Zach was taking a lot of pleasure in sending me Willy Wonka GIFs in the middle of the night.

I stood against the wall, my sketches in their case, tucked behind my legs. Every few minutes, I would lean back to feel the leather case against my knees—worried, irrationally, that they'd collapse and I'd have to go into the pitch with bent drawings.

Both Emily and Rachel were on the other side of the hallway, sitting on the floor across from each other, going over their notes. I'd done the pitch for Sally last night, who'd told me that it was better than Emily's, the only other pitch she'd seen.

"It was fine," she'd said. "But not as unique as yours."

I was 95 percent sure my idea was brilliant. The 5 percent kept me up at night. It drove that unrelenting, divided half of my brain.

Sloane and I had finally come up with a name for my short film: *Golem Goes West*. It was simple and precise and completely right. Immediately, it told you that the story was both ordinary and extraordinary. There was a hint of fear, but also humor.

The door to the conference room opened and everyone stopped what they were doing, the tension in the hallway immediately going to eleven. Yvett, the PA who would be escorting us, poked her head out.

"It'll just be a few more minutes," Yvett said before disappearing back into the conference room.

We all relaxed—but just a little.

"Are you ready?" Nick stopped in front of me. He had been pacing the hallway for the last ten minutes.

"Yep," I said. I didn't really want to talk. I wanted to focus.

"Me too." He glanced down at my portfolio. "How big are your images?"

"Sixteen by twenty."

"Huh," he said. "Mine are eight and a half by eleven." He'd left his drawings against the wall across from me. The images were faced away.

"It didn't say how big they had to be," I said.

Secretly, I thought his were way too small. Sloane and I had debated between sixteen by twenty and eighteen by twenty-four, but eventually decided that based on the size of the room, sixteen by twenty would be fine.

"You want them to be easy to read but you don't want to have a hard time moving them around." She'd even lent me a case to keep the drawings from getting bent.

"What's the title of your project?" Nick asked.

"You'll find out when they announce it," I said.

"That's funny." He looked down the hall to where Bear was. "Did he tell you his pitch?"

"No," I said.

"Huh." Nick looked surprised.

"Why would he?"

Nick shrugged, and stared at Bear again. He was sitting on the floor, hands draped over his knees, head back against the wall. He could have been sleeping, for all I knew. Unlike everyone else, he didn't have a stack of poster board. Instead, on the floor next to him was a thin pile of paper, some of it wrinkled.

"You know, he has his own room in the dorms," Nick said. "Guess his daddy decided he didn't need a roommate."

I hadn't known that, but I wasn't really surprised. Bear seemed to be the odd man out in our group, in a way that felt increasingly intentional.

The door opened again, and Yvett's head appeared.

"Bear Beckett," she said. "You're up."

There was a loud sigh from the end of hall, and we all watched as Bear slowly pushed himself up from the floor and ambled toward Yvett. As he passed, he glanced over at me.

"Quack, quack," he said, and then disappeared into the conference room.

I rolled my eyes. He probably still thought my pitch was about ducks.

Even though each presentation was limited to five minutes, it felt like hours between when Bear was called and when he emerged from another door at the end of the hallway. He looked none too worse for wear when he came out, whistling "When You Wish Upon a Star," his hands shoved in his pockets, his messy stack of paper tucked under his arm, as he walked away.

"Nick Cunningham," Yvett said.

Nick, who had started pacing again, bolted toward his drawings, reached for them, dropped them, reached for them again, dropped them again, and finally managed to gather them up in his arms. I hoped that they were all still in the right order. I felt a twinge of secondhand nervousness on his behalf.

"Good luck," I said.

"Thanks," he said, clutching his drawings with white knuckles.

"Ready?" Yvett asked.

Nick took a deep breath. "Yep." He was pale. I hoped I didn't look as anxious as him.

She held the door and he marched in there like he was preparing for battle. Or a firing squad. Minutes ticked by. When Nick finally appeared, he was swarmed by the other waiting interns. I stayed where I was. I was curious about what had happened but I also didn't want to let it distract me. I listened with one ear.

"What was it like?"

"Did they ask anything?"

"Did *he* say anything?"

Now that Nick was done, I could see his confidence returning. His color had improved and he addressed the other interns with ease—fielding questions like a politician at a town hall.

"It was all a blur," he said. "The brain trust had a few questions, but I was prepared. And Bryan didn't say anything, but I expected that. Remember his *Vanity Fair* article?"

I knew exactly what Nick was talking about. "I'm not a fan of false praise," Bryan had been quoted as saying. "Words are meaningless. Actions are all that matter."

I'd read that when comedians auditioned for SNL, the people they were auditioning for were instructed not to laugh. I assumed it was for the same reason. That if they liked you, they'd hired you. And if Bryan liked my work, he'd pick me to direct one of the short films.

"My mentor says that we shouldn't expect much from Bryan as a response," one of the other interns was saying. "I guess he's known for his poker face."

I revised my fantasy of him applauding after my pitch. Instead, now, I just imagined him standing and extending a hand for me to shake.

Sloane had mentioned that the brain trust might ask questions. I'd told Emily and Rachel, so they'd be prepared as well. Because I'd meant what I said to Bear—I wanted to know I was the best. I didn't need to sabotage anyone to prove that.

Slowly, Yvett made her way down the list of us, and the hallway began to empty out. Soon it was just me, Emily, and three other interns.

"Karl Randolph," Yvett said.

Emily would be next, and then me. My fingertips were ice-cold as I pressed them against my palms. My mouth was dry, my armpits were damp, and I couldn't tell if I had to go to the bathroom or not.

"You're going to do great," Emily said, and put a hand on my shoulder. She was trembling a little.

"You too," I said.

We were both leaning against the wall, staring at the closed door.

"They wouldn't laugh at me, would they?" Emily asked. "Like, if I made a mistake or my pitch was bad—they wouldn't laugh, right?"

I shook my head. "No, they wouldn't do that."

But I hadn't even considered it. Except for Nick, no one else had stopped for a postmortem, looking either relieved or a little shell-shocked. No tears, though. When Rachel had finished, she'd seemed somewhat dazed, but managed a thumbs-up in our direction before heading back upstairs.

"They wouldn't do that," I repeated, hoping that it would make it true.

"Yeah," Emily said. "That would be mean. And we're just interns. Why would they do that?"

"Exactly," I said.

"Emily Reynolds," Yvett said, and both of us jumped.

With wide eyes, Emily turned toward me. "Wish me luck." She gave me a quick hug.

"You'll do great," I said.

She nodded and followed Yvett into the conference room. The slam of the door behind her felt final. Ominous. I let out a deep breath.

I was going to be fine. I'd practiced my pitch a million times. I could do it in my sleep. I could do it upside down. I could probably do it backward if I needed to.

My heart was pounding in my chest and I really couldn't decide if I needed to go to the bathroom or not. It didn't matter—there wasn't time anyway. If I had to go, I would have to hold it for the next twenty minutes—through Emily's pitch and my own.

When Emily finally emerged, I barely had a chance to catch her eye before Yvett was calling my name. I managed a furtive wave before I gathered up my drawings and followed Yvett into the conference room.

I was glad Sloane had suggested practicing in the space, because when I walked in, I knew exactly where I needed to go.

"This is Hayley Saffitz," Yvett said. "Hayley, if you have drawings, you can place them on that stand, or hold them. Whatever you'd like."

Sloane had prepared me for that as well.

"Thank you," I said, quickly unzipping the portfolio and placing my foam-board pictures on the easel in the middle of the room. The first board was blank—Sloane and I had decided not to give anything away until I was ready to speak.

There were six people sitting behind a desk, facing me. I recognized Josh, but everyone else was a stranger. All of them were men, wearing either suits or T-shirts, though it was hard to see too much of them. Most of the lights were focused around the easel, where I was expected to stand.

"You have five minutes, Hayley," Yvett said. "Whenever you're ready."

I removed the first board, revealing the title.

"My pitch is called *Golem Goes West*," I said.

I heard people shifting in their seats, and when I glanced up, I saw that at least two people had leaned forward. That gave me a surge of confidence, and I continued—the entire thing flowing from me, perfectly and without any missteps. When I was done, I felt as if I had run a marathon, my heart pounding, my skin hot.

"Thank you, Hayley," Yvett said. "Any questions from the board?"

"Could we see the picture of the golem again?" one of the members of the brain trust asked.

I put the corresponding foam board back on the easel, making sure to keep all of my images in order. Even though I knew this pitch had gone well, I still had to do it again and even better, if possible.

"Your story takes place during the Gold Rush, is that correct?" another one asked.

"The 1850s, to be exact," I said.

I saw some nodding heads. "And golems existed then?"

"Well, golems are fictional creatures," I said. "But the most famous golem story occurred in the sixteenth century, so we've been aware of them for a while."

There was a slight chuckle from the brain trust. I was so thankful that Sloane had prepared me for questions like these.

You need to know everything about your material, she'd said. *Be the authority.*

"Thank you, Hayley," Josh said. "Very impressive work."

I beamed. "Thank you," I said.

I gathered up my things, trying to balance the poster board and the empty portfolio. That was one thing I hadn't practiced and I felt awkward trying to hold both at the same time. I scooped the drawings up under my arm and held the leather case in my hand.

"Good luck," Josh said.

I nodded and followed Yvett to the door on other side of the room.

She opened it and led me in. "Bryan?"

He was sitting there, in a room almost identical to the one I'd just been in, behind a similar desk. I couldn't be sure, but it seemed like this space was a little darker, because it was even harder to see him than it had been to see the brain trust.

"This is Hayley Saffitz," Yvett said.

I put my pictures on the easel, feeling a bit of déjà vu. I mentally gave myself a slap; I had to be just as good—if not better—than I'd been a few minutes ago.

Bryan didn't say anything.

"Whenever you're ready," Yvett said. I wondered if she was going to be tired of saying that by the end of the day.

"My pitch is called *Golem Goes West*," I said.

This time, however, there was no shifting, no leaning forward as I revealed my first drawing. In my mind, I stumbled a bit, but thankfully my mouth didn't.

"This is a story about a girl," I said. "And a golem. Miriam has traveled to America with her family during the Gold Rush, but instead of opportunity, they've been met with hardship and tragedy."

I spoke, telling Bryan the story of a girl who had lost her parents and gained a golem—a friend she doesn't want and believes she doesn't need. Together, the two of them travel across the country, looking for her brother.

"And when Miriam reaches out her hand to the golem, she discovers that he has returned to his original form—his journey over, just as hers is beginning." I revealed the final image—of Miriam sitting in the wagon that carried her and the golem to her brother's home—her hand full of dust.

There was silence. I cast a look at Yvett, who then glanced over at Bryan.

"Thank you, Hazel," he said.

A dismissal. I gathered up my things and followed Yvett out.

"Thank you so much," she said. "Really good job."

I hadn't heard her say that to anyone else.

"Thanks," I said, but she'd already closed the door.

I stood there for a moment. I'd been prepared for Bryan to say nothing, so I knew I shouldn't be disappointed. The handshake fantasy had been just that, a fantasy. My pitch *had* been good. I hadn't stumbled over any words, and none of the poster boards had gotten stuck together. I'd done my story justice. That was all I could hope for.

It wasn't until I was halfway down the hall that I realized that Bryan hadn't gotten my name right.

CHAPTER EIGHT

To mark the end of our first week in the program, BB Gun Films held a little banquet for us in the cafeteria on Sunday night. It was a chance to mingle with employees who weren't part of the internship and would be where Bryan would announce the projects that had been chosen.

I kept telling myself it didn't matter that Bryan hadn't remembered my name. There were forty-one of us, after all. As long as he remembered my pitch, that was all that mattered.

"Bet you wish you packed a dress," Mom said. "You know, there's still time—I could bring one over if you'd like."

I wasn't going to admit it to her—because she *would* drive to campus—but I did sort of wish that I had packed something other than my uniform for an occasion like this. Sally and all the other girls had been in the bathroom for the last hour getting ready, and each of them had come by the room at least once to get my opinion on which of their multiple dress options they should wear tonight. Every time the door swung open, I got an earful of the Disney music they were blasting down the hall.

I felt separate from them. Distant. Different.

"It's okay." I shifted my phone to my other ear. "I have my bow tie. And nice shoes."

"Your oxfords?" Mom asked. "I do like those shoes."

"Yeah," I said.

"We missed you at Shabbat dinner," she said.

It was a tradition—having family dinner every Friday night. We weren't religious—we didn't even go to temple anymore—but I think Mom liked the ritual of lighting candles and saying prayers.

"I guess I should start getting used to it," she said. "After all, it won't be long until you're off at college."

The college talk again. Acting like it was a foregone conclusion. Bryan went to college because his parents had wanted him to as well.

"But it wasn't long before I realized that my time—and talents—were wasted in a classroom. It was stifling me," he'd said in his CalTED Talk. "I got my first job as a story artist less than a month after dropping out."

I'd been a little surprised the college hadn't edited that out.

"Uh-huh" was all I said to Mom.

"How is the internship going?" she asked. "You seem like you're busy."

"Yeah," I said.

"Are you learning a lot? Making friends?"

"Uh-huh."

"'Nooooooo . . . ooooooooooone . . . fights like Gaston!'"

Caitlin had just appeared in the doorway, holding up two dresses—one black and one gray. I pointed to the black one. She held out the gray one—*Do you want it?*

I shook my head and mouthed *But thanks*. She was the only one as tall as I was, but we weren't remotely the same size. I didn't have the curves to pull it off. The door closed behind her, cutting off the music.

"Do you want to talk to Zach?" Mom asked, calling out to my brother before I could respond. "Zach! Your sister's on the phone!"

There was a muffled shuffle and then he came on the line.

"You didn't have your DVDs organized in any particular way, did you?" he asked.

He was joking. I was pretty sure.

"Stay out of my room," I said.

"Sharing is caring," he said.

"Dad will be disappointed he missed you," Mom said when she got back on the phone. "Maybe you could call back in an hour or so."

"That's when the banquet is," I said, even though I'd told both my parents—numerous times—that they'd be announcing who would be directing the shorts tonight.

"Of course," she said. "You'll tell us how it goes?"

"Yep."

Hanging up, I sat on my bed and laced up the oxfords I'd found at a secondhand store last year. They definitely made my uniform look a little fancier than usual. I checked my tie—the knot had taken me twenty minutes—but it looked good too. I'd decided to forgo my usual bun, so my hair was down. I pushed it back over my shoulder and then brought it forward, unable to decide which looked better. No matter what I did, my brown mass of waves just seemed to sit there.

I'd felt a little unmoored ever since Friday. Before, when I was focused on the project, there hadn't been enough hours in the day. Now, the hour until dinner at the studio seemed to stretch out forever. I didn't know what to do with myself. I thought about texting Samantha and Julie, but none of us had been great about keeping in touch these past few days. My phone buzzed.

Zach had sent me an Oompa Loompa GIF. I texted him back: **Thanks, Dr. Saffitz, MD.** I knew he'd hate it.

"It's redundant," he always told me. "Say 'DR' *or* 'MD,' not both."

Sally swanned into the room wearing a pale blue dress and black heels. She fell dramatically onto the bed. "How do I look?" she asked, hand against her forehead, eyes closed. "Do I look fabulous? I feel fabulous. Extremely fabulous."

"You look *extremely* fabulous," I said. "What about me?"

I felt underdressed compared to her, but when her eyes popped open, she grinned.

"You look great!" she said. "*Very* Hepburn-esque. Like, I could totally see you bantering with Cary Grant, all like—" She sat up, shuffling her shoulders a little like she was having a conversation with someone. "You *don't* say. You don't *say*!"

I laughed. "Thanks." I looked at my feet. "Sally, do you think . . . do you think you could help me with some eyeliner?"

She let out a squeal. "I would love to!" She grabbed her makeup bag and directed me to sit down on the bed next to her. "Can we do something more than just a regular wing tip? Something fancy and different? Please?" she asked, holding up a sparkly gold liner. "It will look so gorgeous and dramatic on you. Maybe a red lip, too?"

It reminded me a little of Sloane's style—her gold glasses and bold lipstick. That was *exactly* the kind of energy I wanted to harness going into tonight.

I closed my eyes. "Do your best," I said.

The studio looked different at night. There were all these twinkly lights in the trees that I never would have known were there, and they all conspired with the dense foliage to give the illusion of a fairy ring. I knew that Bryan would never call it something so fanciful, but it was still beautiful.

Looking around, I felt a little less out of place than I had getting ready with the girls. Most of the guys were wearing the same thing they always did—a few of them had thrown on jackets, but there were one or two wearing hoodies and flip-flops. The same went for the male employees. It seemed like most of the women at the studio dressed nicely—like Sloane, they wore colorful dresses and did impressive things with their hair—while most of the guys wore cargo pants and sneakers. There were a few who followed Bryan's uniform, but they never looked quite as good as their boss.

The studio cafeteria was different tonight. All of the buffet bars had been rolled off to the side and in their place were round tables covered in tablecloths and decorated with fancy flower arrangements. There were nice plates and very shiny silverware. We were all given yellow bracelets when we entered, which would keep the waiters from serving us alcohol, something some of the guys were already complaining about.

I didn't care. This was already the fanciest party I'd been to in my life and I didn't need a drink to enjoy it. In fact, I'd rather be clearheaded when they announced my name. I wondered if Ron was in the kitchen, helping with the food.

"Hey, Hayley." Nick appeared out of nowhere. "You look . . . different," he said.

I couldn't tell if it was a compliment from the way he was squinting at my face. Suddenly I felt self-conscious about the lipstick Sally had applied. I wore makeup sometimes but usually more subtle stuff. Sally had definitely gone for dramatic. I'd liked it when

I saw it in the mirror back at the dorms, but now I wasn't sure. Was it too red? Too bright? Did it make my mouth look like a clown mouth?

Nick was wearing his usual white polo shirt and black pants, but he'd added a tie as well. I was close enough to see the metal clip that attached it to his shirt.

"How'd your pitch go?" he asked.

"Good," I said. "Yours?"

"Fantastic," he said.

He was still staring at my mouth. I ran my tongue over my teeth, wondering if I had gotten lipstick on them.

"You look like Sally," he said.

"Thanks," I said. "She did my makeup."

He nodded as if that explained something. We just stood there for a moment, him bobbing his head, me waiting for him to walk away so I could check my teeth.

"Well," he said, and swayed forward. "Good luck tonight."

"You too," I said.

He walked off, and I reached for my phone so I could use the camera to look at my makeup before remembering that I'd left it at the dorms. I'd just have to go to the bathroom or find one of the girls, who could tell me what was wrong with my face.

"Hey, Saffitz," Bear said.

I jumped, putting my hand up to my mouth. If I had red lipstick smeared all over me, I really didn't want Bear to see it. He glanced at my hand and gave me a weird look. I had expected to see him in his usual well-worn jeans and gray T-shirt, but to my surprise he was wearing a nice button-down shirt and dark jeans.

"Cool tie," he said.

"Thanks," I said.

"Good luck," he said, and walked away.

"Is there something on my face?" I found Sally in the crowd. She peered at me. "No, why?"

"Anything on my teeth?" I bared them for her.

"Nope," she said. "You should let me do your makeup more often. You have such big eyes—makes it easy to do fun stuff with eye shadow. It looks really good."

I relaxed, and the two of us wove through the crowd until we found a mostly empty table. Across the room, I saw Bear sit down at a table with his dad and Josh.

"Did you hear anything about his pitch?" Sally asked, her eyes following mine. "I overheard Nick and Karl talking about how they both nailed it, but they didn't say anything about the pitch itself. Did they tell you how it went?"

I shook my head. "Not really."

Sloane had sent me a text before I left the dorms, apologizing profusely but saying a family emergency had come up and she wouldn't be able to make it. **We'll celebrate tomorrow**, she'd texted, complete with lots of horn and confetti emojis.

Sally's mentor—Maurene—joined us, and it wasn't long before the rest of the girls found our table. I was a little disappointed that Sloane wasn't there, but everyone else's mentors made a point to include me in their conversation.

"How did you feel about your pitch?" Maurene asked. She was wearing a beautiful linen sheath dress, her dark hair brushing the top of her shoulders. "I heard it was very unique."

"I waited until after the pitches started before I told her," Sally said. "I had to tell someone. I'd never heard of anything like your story before—I wanted to know if Maurene had, but she hadn't. You're not mad, are you?"

I shook my head. I knew it would be silly to be mad at her, especially since she had been saying nice things. And she was right—the pitches were over—whatever was done, was done.

"Thanks," I said to Maurene. "I think it went well."

"I wish I had your confidence," Rachel said. "I was so nervous, my hands were shaking."

"I dropped my cue cards," Emily said. "Totally bungled it."

"During the pitch to the brain trust or to Bryan?" Jeannette asked.

"Bryan!" Emily wailed.

Everyone at the table sucked in a sympathetic breath. I was glad I'd chosen to memorize mine instead of relying on cue cards.

"It's okay," Emily said. "I'm just glad it's over."

Except it wasn't over. It wouldn't be over until they announced the four directors.

It was then that I realized that everyone at our table was a woman. Looking around the room, I saw a few more women—like Yvett—but they all seemed to be sitting at the PA table in the corner. The exceptions were the two seated with Bryan—Gena and a white, brown-haired woman I didn't recognize.

It made sense, I supposed. I spent most of my free time with the other girls in the program and all of us had female mentors. And we weren't the only ones grouped together in a certain way. The room was a sea of white, male faces except for our table, the PA table, and one other, where the few interns and mentors of color were seated. I spotted Isaac among them, even though I was pretty sure he wasn't part of the internship. He waved and I waved back.

Dinner was served, but I ate without really tasting anything. I kept looking over at Bear's table, at his dad, searching his expression for anything that might indicate what he was thinking. Part of me wanted Bryan to look over here. Part of me thought it was better if he didn't.

Finally, our food was taken away and Bryan got up from his table and walked across the cafeteria to where a microphone had been set up.

"This is it," Sally said. "Are you nervous? I'm nervous. I'm nervous for you. But it's going to be fine. It's going to be great."

I looked at her and she held up her crossed fingers.

"Welcome," Bryan said. "I want to thank everyone for joining us tonight, to officially welcome our first class of BB Gun interns." There was a ripple of applause. "Within this first week, I have been blown away by the talent demonstrated by this group of young people," Bryan continued. "They're clever and inventive and creative. If they truly are the next generation of filmmakers, well, let me tell you, I'm not worried about the future of the medium at all."

There came more applause. Bryan smiled and looked around the room, his eyes eventually landing on Bear, who was staring down at his hands.

"As you all know, the culmination of this internship will be the screening of four short films. It is my absolute honor to announce the names of the four interns that will be at the helm of these projects."

He pulled a list out of his pocket. I leaned forward.

"I have to tell you," Bryan said, not looking at the list. "It wasn't easy choosing just four. The caliber of talent in this group is"—he mimed an explosion on the side of his head—"mind-blowing."

People laughed.

Finally, Bryan unfolded the piece of paper. "Join me in congratulating our four newest directors and their projects: Nick Cunningham directing *Jack and the Beanstalk*; Jeff Oliver directing *Salt for Stars*; Eddie Lassen directing *Nite Time Somewhere*; and Bear Beckett directing a currently untitled project. Congratulations to you all."

CHAPTER NINE

I sat there, stunned, not fully comprehending what had just happened. I . . . hadn't been chosen?

Everyone around me was applauding, but how was that possible? My name hadn't been called. This couldn't be right. There had to be a mistake.

"Oh, Hayley." Sally's voice broke through the hum that had started in the back of my head, slowly moving forward. "I'm so sorry."

I stood abruptly. People stared, but I didn't care. I walked away from my table, across the main floor of the cafeteria, and out the door. I didn't stop until I came to the bridge.

Where were the ducks? I still hadn't seen any ducks.

I looked down at the water, the stream moving beneath me. My hands were numb. My ears were numb. My teeth were numb. Was that even possible? Could teeth go numb?

I didn't understand. My pitch had been incredible. It had been perfect.

I didn't know anything about Jeff or Eddie's pitch, but I also knew that neither of them were story geniuses. I'd overheard Jeff ask Eddie what a deus ex machina was, before listening to them both reach the conclusion that it had something to do with machines in sci-fi stories. And Nick's pitch was *Jack and the Beanstalk*? What happened to Bryan's hatred of fairy tales? He'd been very specific about that.

And Bear. With his crumpled-up pile of notes and his joke that I was pretty sure wasn't a joke at all about not preparing. Bear's project didn't even have a title. Sloane and I had agonized over mine for days.

All for nothing.

"Hayley?"

I turned and found Sally, Caitlin, Emily, Jeannette, and Rachel all standing next to the bridge, wearing identical expressions of concern.

"Are you okay?"

I shook my head. They came over to me, forming a protective circle.

"I'm really sorry." Sally rubbed my back.

"I don't understand," I said. "I don't get it."

"It just didn't work out this time," Caitlin said.

I stared down at the water, the twinkly light from the trees reflecting in the soft ripples of the current. "My pitch was good," I said.

My hands were wrapped around the bridge's railing.

"It was," Sally said. "But maybe, I don't know, maybe Bryan wanted something different."

I shook my head. "No, my pitch was good."

There was silence and I could sense the circle expanding a little. All of them taking a step back from me. I knew I should stop talking, I knew this wasn't going to change anything, but I couldn't help myself.

"My pitch was good." I pressed my palms against the railing.

"You're not the only one who's disappointed, Hayley," Emily said.

I turned toward her. "My pitch was better than yours, Emily," I said, the words spilling out before I could stop them.

Emily's eyes widened.

"Stop it," Sally said.

I knew I needed to listen. I knew I needed to shut up—but I couldn't. It all just kept coming. "You said it was. You told me mine was better," I said. "That's what you said."

There was a collective gasp. I'd gone too far, and I knew it.

"You're being a prat," Emily said. "Both of you."

"Emily, I—" Sally said, but Emily had already turned and run back into the cafeteria.

I faced the other girls. Their expressions were a combination of shock and disappointment. Caitlin, though, her lips were pressed together in anger.

"We all know that you think you're better than us," she said.

Everyone else looked at the ground, Sally included.

"You think that because you dress like Bryan Beckett and you've memorized his CalTED Talk and you're too busy and special to care about things like this." She gestured toward herself—her dress, her makeup. "You think that makes you better than us. It doesn't. It just makes you a bitch."

Thankfully, all the words that were tumbling around my head stayed there this time. Because she was right. I did think I was better than them. It was an awful realization and an even worse feeling.

Caitlin turned and left. The rest of the girls followed. It was just me and Sally now.

"You sound like a sore loser," she said.

"It was a good pitch," I said, unable to help myself.

She sighed, and walked away from the bridge. Then she paused, and turned once more to look at me. "I guess it just wasn't good enough."

All the girls caught the first shuttle back to the dorms. No one saved me a seat so I had to take the second one. By the time I got back to my room, Sally was already in bed—all the lights out. I grabbed my phone and went outside.

I couldn't call Julie or Samantha. I'd basically ignored them almost all week and it didn't seem right to lean on them now. And I couldn't stop hearing Caitlin say *You think you're better than us.* The truth of it still hurt.

No one was in the stairwell, so I sat there as I called my parents.

Dad picked up. I was glad it was him—Mom would have just said some Mom-thing that didn't really apply to the situation, like "It will be okay" or "There's always next time." There wasn't going to be a next time.

"I didn't get it," I said. The words didn't sound right. It still hadn't really sunk in.

"Oh, honey, I'm sorry," Dad said.

I could hear him moving around the house—heard the fridge open.

"My pitch was good," I said.

I was starting to sound like a parrot. *Polly want a cracker? My pitch was good. Pretty birdie.* I squeezed the bridge of my nose between my thumb and forefinger. My head hurt.

It wasn't just that I thought my pitch was worthy. It was that I *needed* this opportunity. It was how I could prove to my parents that I knew what I was doing. That they didn't have to worry about me working in animation. That I was good at this.

"I'm sorry, honey, but this happens sometimes," Dad said. "You might think your work is good enough, but you can't always know what others are looking for."

Even though I knew he couldn't see me, I shook my head. I needed him to understand.

"It *was* good enough," I said. "I know it was. The guys that got picked—one of them pitched a fairy tale, and Bryan Beckett hates fairy tales, and the other guy, well, he's Bryan's son, so of course they gave it to him even though he barely prepared at all and I don't even think he wants it. But I wanted it, Dad, I wanted it *so much* and my pitch was good."

My voice cracked on the last word and suddenly the tears were falling, hot and fast. I pressed my lips together—I didn't want Dad to hear it.

"That's really disappointing, sweetie," he said. "But rejection is part of being an artist. If it's this hard for you to accept, then maybe you should reconsider if this is the right industry for you."

I couldn't speak—couldn't form words, so I just managed an "Uh-huh." If he could tell I was crying, Dad didn't comment. He just kept talking.

"And I have to say, Hayley, I'm a little disappointed in you. You should be grateful that you got this opportunity. There are plenty of kids out there who didn't, and this attitude isn't a very nice one."

When Zach got a bad grade, he would sulk in his room for

days, snapping at anyone who tried to reason with him. When Dad got passed over for a promotion, he'd driven to Santa Barbara for the day and didn't tell Mom until he got there.

No one ever told *them* they had to be grateful when they were upset.

I squeezed my eyes closed.

"The last thing you want is to sound like a spoiled brat."

Somehow, I managed a not-too-watery "Okay."

"Why don't we talk again tomorrow when you're not so worked up about this," Dad said. "Sleep on it, and you'll realize that you're making a big deal out of nothing. There's a great wide world out there, kiddo. Maybe this just isn't the right place for you."

He hung up, and I put my head between my knees and cried.

CHAPTER TEN

was grateful I didn't have to tell Sloane. By the time I arrived at her office the next morning, it was clear she'd already been informed about what had happened last night. She herded me inside and closed the door, quickly sweeping me into a hug.

But I had gotten all my tears out last night and done exactly as Dad had suggested. I slept on it, and when I woke, I realized that I had been a real asshole. It wasn't that I thought Bryan had made the right decision—I still thought that he was wrong—but I knew I had handled it poorly.

I apologized to Sally. To Caitlin and the others. And I'd apologized profusely to Emily. They were all still mad at me, though, and no one had saved me a seat on the shuttle. I'd spent the whole ride looking out the window and pretending I wasn't being ignored as the other girls talked about the new plant that Emily had gotten for her room and the song that Caitlin was trying to master on guitar.

"I'm so sorry, Hayley." Sloane pulled out a chair and sat me in it. "Are you okay?"

"I'm fine," I lied. "I was being a sore loser."

She frowned. "These things happen," she said.

I didn't know what to say, so I just shrugged. Sloane sat down in her chair, letting out a loud breath. When she didn't say anything, I looked up to find her staring at the ceiling, shaking her head. She looked angry.

Finally, she scrubbed her hands over her face. "It was a solid pitch," she said.

It should have made me feel better, but it didn't. Solid wasn't the same as good. It made me want to cry all over again and I really didn't want to do that in front of her.

"Can we talk about something else?" I asked.

"Yeah, of course," she said.

We sat there, neither of us saying anything.

"You know what we need?" she asked. "Ice cream."

I looked at the clock. "It's nine thirty."

But she was already standing and gesturing for me to do the same. "Come on," she said.

The only people in the cafeteria were the ones finishing up their breakfast. Sloane marched over to the soft-serve ice cream machine and let out a growl of frustration when she saw that it wasn't turned on.

"Are those Sloane's dulcet tones I hear?" Ron popped up from behind the buffet. He wore a smile, but it dropped away the moment he saw our expressions. "What happened?"

"We need ice cream." Sloane waved a hand toward the soft-serve machine. "But we have been thwarted."

"It's nine forty," Ron said.

I made a gesture to indicate that I had said the same thing. He laughed, but then grew serious. He thought for a moment. "Will cake do?"

• • •

"I've never been back here before," Sloane said as Ron led us past the swinging doors and into the kitchen.

The whole place gleamed. It was all stainless steel and pristine white floors, with bunches of vegetables on counters and boxes of produce stacked on the floor. People were working all around us, focused on the task of chopping onions or beating eggs. Everything smelled incredible—my senses were overwhelmed with the scent of butter and garlic and fresh herbs. Disco music was playing softly.

"Oh, you all think you make magic up in your offices with paper and pencil," Ron said. "But this is where the magic really happens."

"I don't care who has the most magic," Sloane said. "I was promised cake."

"Patience, patience." Ron led us to the back of the kitchen.

The music was louder there and it smelled like chocolate. The source of the scent was immediately apparent as Ron directed us to a counter where there was an enormous sheet cake covered in a thick layer of white frosting.

"Now that's what I'm talking about," Sloane said, and bowed in Ron's direction. "You win. You're the magical one."

"Take a seat, ladies." Ron gestured toward a couple of stools along the wall.

We did as he said, Sloane eagerly rubbing her hands together as Ron cut off two enormous slices of cake, plated them, and handed them to us. I took a bite.

"Mmmmm." Sloane closed her eyes. "This is perfect."

It was good. Really good. Moist chocolate cake with a tangy cream cheese frosting.

"It's not too much frosting?" Ron asked.

"Is there such a thing?" Sloane asked.

Ron laughed and turned to me. "What do you think? Is it good enough?"

Embarrassingly, my eyes began to fill with tears. I had thought I had done all my crying last night, but apparently I still had enough left in me to cry in front of my mentor and Ron, who was very nice but whom I barely knew.

Immediately, Sloane put her cake down and hopped off her stool. She took the plate out of my hands and pulled me into a hug. With her in her heels and me sitting, we were about the same height, so I didn't bother trying to get up, and just accepted her embrace.

Thankfully, after a few unavoidable sobs, I managed to get my tears under control, and leaned back from Sloane with a loud sniff.

"I'm okay," I said.

Ron handed me a napkin. "The cake wasn't that bad, was it?" he asked.

I laughed. It sounded a little watery, but I kept it together.

"They announced the interns directing the short films last night," Sloane said.

"That's that thing you were . . . oh." Ron stopped himself. "I see."

"It's okay," I said. "My pitch wasn't good enough. It happens."

I looked up, just in time to catch Sloane shaking her head at Ron and him sighing. When she realized I'd seen, she pushed the cake back toward me and sat down again.

"Sometimes," she said. "Sometimes, it's not about the pitch."

"It was the wrong project, then." I poked the cake with my fork.

"It's not always about the project, either," Sloan said. "There are some things we don't have any control over. But no matter what, just know that you did the best work you could. Okay?"

I nodded, and we ate the rest of our cake in silence.

We were walking back to Sloane's office when I heard someone calling my name. Nick was speed-walking down the hall toward me with an excited grin. Even though it killed me that he had gotten the director position and I hadn't, I'd already alienated enough people, so I forced myself to smile back at him.

Besides, unlike Bear, I knew that Nick had worked really hard on his pitch. I knew that he cared about this program as much as I did. If anyone else deserved this opportunity, it was him. It still hurt, though.

"Hey!" He was out of breath. "Hey," he said to Sloane, giving her a what's-up head bob.

She all but rolled her eyes. "I'll see you back at my office, okay?" she asked.

I wanted to go with her, but I nodded. When I turned back to Nick, he was staring at my face just like he had last night.

"What?" I put my hand up to my mouth. "Do I have something in my teeth?"

"No, no." He leaned back a little and smiled. "I'm just glad you're back to normal."

I frowned at him.

"I really hate it when girls wear makeup," Nick said. "It's so fake."

I opened my mouth to say something, but he was still talking.

"Question," he said. "First full-length CGI animated film?"

Was he serious? He was giving me the Test? *Now?*

"*Toy Story*," I said. "1995." *That* was the best he could do? Who didn't know that?

"Good one," Nick said. He actually gave me double finger guns. I knew I was being unfair, but the whole thing sucked. I just needed some space, then I could put on a happy face for him.

But before I could escape, he slung his arm around my shoulder—he had to reach a little to do so—and started walking me back in the direction I'd just come from.

"I want to show you something," he said.

"I don't really have a lot of time." It was a lie, of course. I had nothing but time now.

I'd never imagined what the internship would be like if I wasn't directing my own short. Not really. All my plans were based on the assumption that I'd get the chance to direct. That Bryan would choose me.

Where did I even go from here?

I thought I liked Nick—he was usually nice and sort of funny—but he was also sort of annoying. Like now, when he completely ignored what I said and kept walking us to the other end of the story department. I wanted to be supportive, but he was making it really hard.

"Check it out," he said, and led me into one of the conference rooms.

Up on the wall was a big poster that said *Jack and the Beanstalk*. Taped beneath it were sketches and vis-dev art.

"This is going to be our mission control," Nick said.

I stepped away from him to take a closer look at the art—to really examine the pitch that had beat out mine for this coveted position.

It was . . . fine.

Nick was a good artist, there was no denying that, but I struggled to see what was so special about the story he was telling. It was a reimagining of *Jack and the Beanstalk*, with the biggest change being that he'd made it contemporary. According to the sketches, Jack lived in a skyscraper, nicknamed the Stalk. The giant was a Wall Street tycoon named Mr. Bigsworth.

I cringed at the name. The project looked boring and predictable, but I also knew that I wasn't looking at it with clear eyes. I wanted to get out of there. To go back to Sloane's office. Or maybe even back to the dorms. For the first time in my life, I wanted to be anywhere but BB Gun Films.

"What do you think?" Nick asked.

Bryan hates fairy tales, I thought. *My pitch was better.*

"It looks good," I said, swallowing back my bitterness.

"Yeah, I think so too," Nick said. "But I'm really looking forward to hearing your thoughts. You're the only other person here who really gets the BB Gun philosophy."

I realized what he had said when I first walked in. *This is going to be* our *mission control.* "My thoughts?" I asked.

"Yeah," he looked at me, confused. "Didn't you see? You're on my team. You're going to be working for me."

CHAPTER ELEVEN

We'd all gotten emails that morning—they'd arrived when I was in the kitchen with Sloane—that had included who had been chosen as department heads and who was assigned to each short film.

Not only did I have to work on Nick's project, but I wasn't even the head of story. That had gone to his roommate, Karl. I looked at the rest of the projects and saw that none of the girls had been given a department head position on any of the teams. Were none of us good enough?

I thought of asking Sloane about it, but in the end, I didn't see the point. There were only six girls in the program, after all. I didn't know anything about statistics but that probably had something to do with it. Strength in numbers and all that. Besides, it's not like there was anything that could be done.

If I hadn't been such a jerk last night, I probably could have commiserated with the others, but when I waved to Caitlin at lunch, she ignored me. The rest of the girls didn't even look up. If Sloane noticed, she didn't say anything.

Bear was sitting with Josh at the other end of the cafeteria. I made sure to sit with my back to him.

"You know," Sloane said, "I've been assigned to projects I wasn't excited about. We all have to pay our dues when we're starting out."

I moved my salad around on my plate. I'd tried to follow her lead, but while Sloane's meal looked delicious and fancy, mine just looked kind of sad, the whole thing drowning in dressing.

Sloane tried again. "Monica always used to remind me that when Disney was developing *The Lion King*, no one wanted to work on it."

"Really?"

"Everyone thought that *Pocahontas*—which was in production around the same time—was going to be the big hit." She shrugged. "So, you never know."

I was pretty sure that Nick's short film wasn't going to be the next *Lion King*, but she was right. All I'd really seen was Nick's artwork—I hadn't even heard his pitch. Maybe there was something there that had really knocked Bryan's socks off. And Nick's art was good. It had a bold, graphic style that reminded me of *Spider-Man: Into the Spider-Verse*.

"Animation is all about collaboration," Sloane said. "Sometimes, the best thing you can do when you're starting out is to show how good of a team player you can be."

I knew that she was right. I just wished knowing that would make me feel better.

"People don't talk about it, but there's a skill in being able to put aside your own personal tastes and preferences—helping someone else make *their* project the best version of itself." Sloane reached out and patted my hand. "I have faith in you. Animation isn't a sprint—it's a marathon. And this is just your first race," she said. "Don't be discouraged."

Easier said than done, but I wanted to make Sloane proud, so I promised myself I'd try.

When we got up, I noticed that Bear was now sitting alone at the other side of the cafeteria, his head bent over his sketchbook. Even though I was still beyond frustrated and annoyed that nepotism had gotten him the role that I wanted, I couldn't help noticing that the other interns were avoiding him just like Caitlin and the girls were ignoring me.

I didn't want to feel sympathetic toward him, but at the moment, I couldn't help it.

Ron came out of the kitchen with a plate of fresh corn bread, dropping one on Bear's plate as he passed, like a well-rehearsed routine between the two of them. On his way back, he pulled out a chair and sat.

I was too far away to hear what they were saying, but Bear took a bite of corn bread and slid his sketch-book over to Ron, who threw back his head with a laugh at what he saw. Before getting up, he gave Bear a friendly pat on the shoulder. It wasn't until Bear looked up at me that I realized I had been staring. Just standing in the middle of cafeteria, tray in hand, staring at him.

He chewed his corn bread and stared back.

"Ready?" Sloane asked.

"Yeah," I said, even though I didn't feel ready at all.

After leaving Sloane, I headed to the conference room—"mission control," as Nick had dubbed it—for our very first production meeting. My lunch hadn't quite removed the sting of the past several hours, of not just getting denied the chance to direct a short, but also losing out on being head of story, but I was determined to be positive. Last night had made it abundantly clear what happened if I let my ego get the best of me.

Nick was already standing at the front of the room when I entered with the other interns on his team. "Welcome!" He spread his hands wide. "Are you ready to make a movie?"

I couldn't deny that his excitement was infectious. And this was what I had come to BB Gun Films to do—make movies. Make art.

I loved animation. I could make this work. I *had* to make it work.

Already I was recalibrating my plans. I'd just have to make sure to prove myself during the internship. Find a way to get Bryan's attention, to show him that I belonged at the studio. Maybe I wouldn't get to direct a feature before I was thirty, but I could be okay with that. I just had to convince my parents to let me forgo college. I really couldn't waste those four years now.

Nick had us all go around and introduce ourselves. We had also been assigned two PAs.

"I'm Zoe," the first one said. "I'm going to be your story and vis-dev PA during this process. I've been here about four years, so don't hesitate to ask me any questions about how things work on the production side of things."

Our animation PA was a guy named Cole. "I'm Cole," he said.

"The Robot!" Nick said with a big grin on his face.

Cole, or "the Robot," nodded. "I've been here three years," he said.

And that was it. It was clear to see why he'd been given that nickname. He spoke in a monotone and didn't seem particularly friendly. There were twelve of us, but Zoe and I were the only women on Nick's team. She caught my eye and gave me a friendly wink. Once introductions were done, Nick stood, rubbing his hands together. Abruptly, he slammed them on the table. We all jumped.

"All right," he said. "I think the best way to get started is for all of us to get on the same page." He gestured toward Zoe. "Can you set up the art?" he asked.

She gave him a little frown, but did as he requested, putting a stack of eight and a half by eleven foam boards onto an easel behind him.

"I thought I'd show you my pitch," Nick said. "That way you can get an idea of what we'll be working with—and you can see exactly what Bryan saw in me."

Everyone laughed, but I didn't. I was too jealous to even move. I tried to remember what Dad had told me. *You don't want to sound like a spoiled brat.*

Or like a bitch, as Caitlin had put it.

I didn't *want* to be that way. I wanted Nick's project to be the best it could be. I *wanted* him to succeed. He was my friend, after all. He'd worked just as hard as I had to get this opportunity. It wasn't *his* fault that Bryan hadn't chosen me.

"You all know the story of *Jack and the Beanstalk*," Nick said.

"Now imagine what would happen if Jack was a regular guy—just like you and me—and the beanstalk was a skyscraper. The tallest skyscraper in the world."

As I listened, a kind of numbness spread through me. I had hoped that the pitch would be incredible—that I would be surprised, that I would understand why Bryan had chosen Nick over me. Because I was pretty sure I would be able to accept it—to accept all of this—if Nick's idea was truly better than mine. But it wasn't.

It was exactly what it had seemed like when he showed it to me that morning. It was *fine*. It was serviceable. But it wasn't good. It wasn't special. It was *boring*.

I sat there, listening to my fellow interns laugh and clap, and doubt began to creep in. What if I didn't actually know what was good? What if what I thought was a brilliant idea was actually the opposite—and vice versa? Because I didn't understand why Bryan would have chosen Nick when he could have chosen me, unless what he was looking for was completely different from what I had to offer.

"People say that art is subjective," Bryan had said in his CalTED Talk. "But I think that's bull. That's what people say when they want to be nice. It's the equivalent of a participation trophy, and if we're being completely honest, it's unkind. There's good art and there's bad art. We all know it. People creating bad art know it, and it does them—and all of us—a disservice to pretend that what they're creating is of actual value."

Maybe I didn't know the difference. Maybe I didn't know anything after all.

•   •   •

I had promised myself—and Sloane—that I would try. I sat and I listened. Not that Nick allowed us to do anything else. He talked for nearly the entire afternoon and by the time we all had to leave to catch the shuttle, I was drained.

I felt like a bad friend—bitter and angry. And I had to find a way to shake it off.

I ate dinner quickly, alone, and went back to the dorms, alone. I sat at my desk, my sketchbook in front of me, and willed myself to create something. Drawing had always made me feel better. But when I tried to put my pencil to paper, my body rebelled, forcing me up, away from my desk, and out of the room. Out of the dorms.

It wasn't cold but I wrapped my arms around myself as I walked the campus.

I had my car keys in my pocket and thought about going for a drive. Just getting away from everything—clearing my head. I'd never been the type to drive with the windows open, sailing down the freeway, but tonight it was tempting.

"Saffitz."

I turned and saw Bear walking toward me.

For a moment, I thought about taking off—bolting like Wile E. Coyote and leaving behind nothing but a cloud of dust in the shape of my body—but running would have been ridiculous. Instead I didn't move, just waited until Bear had crossed the large expanse of the quad, not bothering to meet him in the middle.

"Hey," he said when he reached me.

His hands were in his pockets, and his gaze was focused down at his shoes. He scuffed them against the walkway. They were expensive. He hadn't had to sacrifice anything to do this internship. He just got whatever he wanted. Whatever *I* wanted.

"Yeah?" I asked when he didn't say anything.

"I just wanted to see if you were okay," he said. "You know, with what happened." He waved a hand—the gesture encompassing everything and nothing.

"Just dandy," I said.

He looked at me. I looked back.

Why had he come over? What did he want? He didn't seem cocky or indifferent. If I didn't know better, I would say that he was concerned. Like he cared that I might be upset.

It was the last thing I wanted. Because I wasn't going to cry. Not in front of him.

"Great," he said. "Good."

Suddenly I wanted to kick him in the shins. Wanted to scream. Wanted to scare the shit out of him. Wanted to punish him. Bear and his dad and Nick and everyone else who had gotten the opportunity that I wanted so desperately.

But no doubt hitting the only son of the studio head would get me booted out of the program. Probably banned from BB Gun Films for life. It might also officially end my career in animation before it even began. For one horrible moment, I thought that I might not even care.

"I'm going to go," I said.

"Yeah," Bear said. "I just—"

I waited.

"Never mind," he said.

"Yeah," I said, and walked away.

CHAPTER TWELVE

Even though the short films were our main focus now, I was still starting my mornings with Sloane. I was eager to soak up as much influence as I could, when I could. She was also the only constant female presence in my life at the moment. Texting with Julie and Samantha was sporadic. I'd told them I hadn't gotten the director position—and they had been sympathetic—but I'd left out the part where I'd effectively alienated myself from the rest of the girls in the internship. Mom texted and called—checking in—but I avoided any details, just telling her that everything was "fine." She didn't mention the conversation I'd had with Dad, but I was pretty sure he'd filled me in on what I'd told him.

That morning Caitlin had shown up to the shuttle with her head completely shaved. It looked amazing. I'd heard giggling and laughing coming from the bathroom the night before but the last time I'd tried to join their gathering, it had just been awkward and stilted. Not exactly a cold shoulder, more like a chilled cheek, but still, it was clear I hadn't been forgiven.

I didn't blame them. I hadn't really forgiven myself, either.

Being able to follow Sloane around was a welcome distraction. The project she was working on—*No One Fears the Woods*—was slated to be released in two years. Parts of the story were assigned to different artists, who storyboarded them—illustrating setting, rough animation, and character interactions. Once they were approved by Josh, they were sent down to editorial, where they were assembled. The editor would add dialogue—usually using scratch vocals.

I got to see that part of the process firsthand when the editor called Sloane and asked her to come provide a temporary voice for a few lines that had been recently added to the script.

"I've done it quite a few times," she said as we took the elevator down to the basement where the editorial team was. "Any time they need a female voice to pick up a couple of lines, and it's between the scheduled recording sessions with the actors, they usually call me." The elevator door slid open. "I like to think it's because I'm good at it, but I also know that it's just because there aren't enough women in the building."

It wasn't the first time that Sloane had referenced the lack of female artists. I saw it too. It seemed like the ratio was pretty similar to the one in the internship.

There were several offices off of a larger common area that had one desk and a familiar face. Zoe, one of the PAs assisting us with Nick's short film, stood up when we arrived. Her vintage style reminded me of Rachel's, with her horn-rimmed glasses and green-checked dress. Even though most of the artists were men, I had noticed that most of the production staff, especially the PAs, were women.

Zoe's desk was clean, but her wall was just as chaotic as Sloane's and she had pinned pictures of herself and a tall, white, dark-haired guy on the wall alongside vis-dev art for *No One Fears the Woods*. Most notably there was a picture of one of the characters—a lumberjack—who had been drawn wearing a very, very tight flannel shirt.

"Sloane did that," Zoe said, noticing where my attention had gone. "Pretty good, huh?"

I blushed. It *was* good, but I felt weird getting caught staring at it.

"You should see the stuff the guys have in their cubicles," Zoe said, reading my mind. "Makes this look beyond tame."

"What am I recording today?" Sloane asked.

She and Zoe exchanged a look, and Sloane rolled her eyes.

"Of course."

Zoe handed her some pages. "They're waiting for you."

We walked into the dark room. There was a tall white guy behind a desk, raised high enough that he could stand while working. He was wearing a colorful button-down shirt and square glasses. His face was blue from the glow of the screen. Along the wall was a wide couch and there were three figures sitting there—but my eyes hadn't yet adjusted to the dark so I couldn't tell who they were.

"Thanks for doing this, Sloane," one of the voices said.

It was Josh. I squinted, trying to figure out if it was Bear sitting next to him on the couch. He seemed tall enough. I frowned.

"Who's this?" the man on the other end of the couch asked.

"This is Hayley." Sloane stepped to the center of the room, where there was a microphone set up. "Hayley, you know Josh."

"Hi." I waved into the darkness.

"Our editor, John Gordon." Sloane gestured to the man behind the desk. "Mike Hanttula, our producer, and you know Bryan, of course."

I stiffened as Bryan came into focus. For the first time I wished that it *had* been Bear. I wondered why he wasn't here—if he was just wandering around the studio free range while Josh was tending to production needs.

Bryan was sitting in the middle, arms crossed, looking at me. And I'd been frowning at him. This was worse than the whole hand-in-the-chip-bag situation.

"Can you close the door?" Josh asked.

"You can sit here." John pulled up a chair next to him.

I sat down quickly and loudly. I wanted to die.

"You have the lines?" John asked Sloane.

"Yep." She held up the paper. "You guys really need to find someone else to be your hag. I'm starting to get a complex."

The men laughed, but Sloane wasn't smiling.

"Let's try the first line," John said. "Give us three different readings, okay? One right after another."

"'Stay *out* of the woods.' 'Stay out of the *woods*.' '*Stay* out of the woods.'"

I could tell why they kept using Sloane for temp dialogue. She was pretty good. Each version she did sounded completely different. They had her read four lines—doing several versions of each.

"Anything else?" she asked.

"Well . . ." John flipped through his script. "I was going to ask Zoe to do some of Hazel's lines, but she always sounds too old." He glanced over at me. "How about you, Hayley? Want to give it a shot?"

I froze. I'd half expected that everyone had forgotten I was there, but now I could sense all attention shift toward me.

"You don't have to—" Sloane said, but was interrupted by Bryan rising off the couch.

He stretched. I could hear his back crack—*pop pop pop*.

"It would be incredibly helpful," he said. "You'd be doing us a favor."

How could I say no to that? Since he hadn't chosen my pitch, I needed to show that I could be useful to Bryan. To the studio.

"Um, okay," I said, and stood.

"Come over here." Sloane gestured for me to join her.

There was a podium by the microphone and the script pages were laid out. There was just enough light for me to be able to read, but my eyes widened when I saw what they were expecting. This wasn't just a line or two. This was a full paragraph. This was acting. And I was *not* an actor.

"Just do your best," Sloane said. "It's only temporary, okay? They'll replace it as soon as they can get the real actress to come and record it."

I knew why they needed it—once storyboards were sent down to editorial, they were given new life with sound and dialogue. It helped the story team, as well as the producer and the director, see what was working and what wasn't. The last thing an animated film wanted to do was waste precious time animating scenes or sequences that didn't work. Sometimes a voice performance was the only thing standing between a sequence being kept or cut.

My palms were sweating and my throat felt tight.

"Relax," Sloane said. "Just read it a few times through. Try it out."

"Okay," John said. "I'm ready when you are."

I wished I had a glass of water.

"We are the trees," I said, each word halting and awkward. "We are the trees and the birds and the grass and the sky, and everything that grows from above and below. Your fire cannot burn us. Your machines cannot destroy us. We were here before you and we will be here when you are gone."

There was silence, and I was pretty sure I was about to be kicked out of the program for butchering some very important dialogue.

"Not bad," Josh said.

"Not great," Bryan said.

My face got hot. I'd failed him. Failed the movie. Just like I'd failed my pitch.

Bryan got up from the couch again, coming over to the podium. The room was dark except for the light from the projector, and he stepped right into it, his outline interrupting the storyboard on the screen.

"Why don't we try it again?" he said.

I nodded.

"Take a deep breath," Bryan said, lifting his hands. "And close your eyes."

I did as he said.

"The forest is all around you." His voice was low, comforting. "The smell of damp earth, the warmth of the sun, the sound of birds and insects. This is your home. This is the only home you've ever known. It's a part of you. You're safe here."

Bryan's words and my imagination conjured a lush canopy of trees, rays of sunlight piercing through the leaves above, the air hot and moist. "But you know that something is coming," he said. "Something that threatens all of this."

My shoulders tensed.

"There are men out there—with machines and tools—whose only purpose is to destroy your home."

I could see it. See them.

"To them, it is expendable. Your world is expendable."

The room was so quiet that I could hear myself breathing. When Bryan spoke once more, it was close to a whisper. "You are the only thing standing in their way," he said. "You are the forest's only hope."

Experiencing Bryan's genius in real time was surreal and powerful. All I wanted to do was please him. To make myself worthy of his attention.

"Try again," he said.

I opened my eyes. The movie was projected on Bryan's palms—most of the forest on one, Hazel in her tree on the other.

"I believe in you," he said.

The praise filled me up like a balloon, and I faced the podium, the script, once more, feeling as if I were invincible. As if I could be exactly what Bryan wanted. Exactly what he needed.

But no matter what I did, no matter how clearly I could see Hazel, no matter how deeply I felt the stakes, I couldn't make my voice reflect that. Each version sounded exactly the same to me—a slow, mumbling monotone. I couldn't even look at the couch. I knew I had disappointed Bryan—*again*—and the thought made me woozy.

"Hayley and I have somewhere to be," Sloane said before John could ask me to do it one more time. I wanted to hug her.

We stepped out of the edit bay, Sloane closing the door behind her. Zoe spotted me and immediately got up from her chair.

"Can you get us some water, please?" Sloane asked.

I wanted to get out of there as soon as possible, but I was

grateful for the cold bottle of water that Zoe pressed into my hand.

"What happened?" Zoe asked, her voice low as we walked over to her desk.

"They had Hayley read Hazel's part." Sloane squeezed my shoulder. "She did great."

It was a lie, but it was a nice one.

"I hate reading for them," Zoe said. "But it's part of the job."

And as it turned out, just another part of the job that I wasn't good enough at.

Josh's office was around the corner from Sloane's, with a desk out front. Usually his assistant, a friendly girl named Steph, was seated there, but today it was Bear, shoulders bent, pencil flying over the page of his sketchbook. I couldn't see what he was drawing, but I could see what he was using.

His art supplies were always top-of-the-line, all the things I could never afford even if I was working this summer. Half of the money I usually earned went into a savings account, while the rest I could spend on sketchbooks and pencils, but my budget was always stretched thin. This year, I'd have to be careful about how quickly I went through my supplies. Especially since the special edition BB Gun sketchbooks had cost way more than my usual ones. I'd stockpiled enough stuff to last for a few months, but after that, things could get dire. Before the internship was announced, I had planned to save for the newest Wacom tablet. That wasn't going to happen now. I bet Bear had the tablet—or could have it if he just asked. I couldn't help wondering what he was drawing. Wondering if it was any good.

There was a watercooler right by Josh's office, so I pretended

I needed a drink, hoping that maybe if I walked slowly enough, I could see what Bear was working on. But when I returned with my water bottle, I found that he was gone.

But not his sketchbook.

It *wasn't* a special edition BB Gun one. That was a little surprising, as everyone at the studio seemed to have them. It was still a nice one, though. Really nice. Unable to help myself, I leaned forward over the little wall around the desk and took a look. He'd drawn a stick figure waving with a word bubble above its head.

Look behind you, it said. I didn't have to.

"You're a terrible spy," Bear said.

I was embarrassed to be caught, but I wasn't going to let him see that. It was the first time we'd spoken since he'd approached me outside the dorms. And I figured he owed me.

"You saw my ducks," I said, reaching for the sketchbook. "Fair is fair."

He slapped his palm down before I could turn the page, trapping my hand between his and the paper. "Nothing's fair in animation," he said.

His skin was warmer than I expected, but the callus on his ring finger matched mine. One I'd earned from hours of drawing. There were other calluses too. Ones I could feel against my knuckles. Heat traveled up my arm. I wiggled my fingers, but he didn't move. He was standing very, very close to me.

I cleared my throat. "The line quality's good," I said. I was joking but not completely. It was a stick figure, but it was a good one.

Bear snorted. He smelled a little like pencil shavings and breath mints.

"Hayley?"

He stepped back at the sound of Sloane's voice coming from the other end of the hall. I lifted my hand from his sketchbook and he slid it away. We stared at each other for a moment.

I was still annoyed at him, still annoyed at the whole situation, but he just seemed wary.

"I didn't want to see it anyway," I said, fooling no one.

"Yeah," he said. "Sure."

"Whatever," I said.

CHAPTER THIRTEEN

I was irritated when I returned to Sloane's office. Bear refusing to show me his sketchbook just confirmed what I knew everyone was thinking: that he'd only gotten the position because of his dad.

Sally had been assigned to work on Bear's team, but I couldn't ask her what it was like working with him. She was still barely talking to me—usually getting up early, going for a run, getting dressed and leaving just as I was coming back from the bathroom.

It didn't seem fair. All I wanted was a chance to prove myself—to show Bryan, to show the studio, to show everyone that I was good at this.

Maybe I wasn't. Maybe I didn't know what good was.

Sloane was sitting at her desk, bent over some storyboards, so I took a look at her shelves, which were full of books. When I reached for one of them, it disturbed something that had been propped up behind it.

"Oh," Sloane said.

I froze, my fingers brushing the side. It was covered in dust. "Sorry," I said.

Sloane came over and took the item from the shelf. It was a framed picture.

"It's okay." Sloane handed it over. "Just some dumb drawing that someone did of me."

The frame was cheap, and it was immediately apparent that it was plastic, not glass, protecting the image.

It was a drawing of Sloane, only it didn't really look like her besides the long hair and funky glasses. Whoever had drawn it had put her in a slinky strapless evening gown that was basically painted to her enormous—and completely inaccurate— boobs. She was holding a whip and there was a word bubble above her head.

I'm not a bitch, I'm just drawn that way, cartoon-Sloane was saying.

"It's a reference to *Who Framed Roger Rabbit*," she said.

It had taken me a moment to place it but now I saw it. The dress, the pose, the body—that was pure Jessica Rabbit. And the quote? A play on her famous line: "I'm not bad, I'm just drawn that way."

I didn't know what to say.

"It's not the first caricature someone's done of me," Sloane said. "And it definitely won't be the last. It's a rite of passage, really."

I couldn't tell if she thought it was funny. The expression on her face—pinched lips, a wrinkle between her brow—indicated that she wasn't very amused by it. But it had still been on her shelf. Framed. Who had drawn it?

Sloane put it back, facedown. "You have to have a sense of humor about these things," she said. "It's part of the gig."

I nodded. There were so many things I wanted to ask her. About the drawing and who had done it, but also about the choices that Bryan had made. The directors he had chosen. Specifically Bear.

"Have you . . ." I tried to choose my words carefully. "Is Bear like his dad?"

I was trying to ask if he was as talented as Bryan, but the shadow that passed over Sloane's face seemed to indicate that she'd taken the question a different way.

"Bear is a good kid," she said. With conviction.

"Okay," I said. I didn't really want to talk about Bear's *personality*, I wanted to talk about his talent—or lack thereof.

"He's a pain in the ass, don't get me wrong," Sloane said. "But he's been through a lot."

"Sure." I was angry and confused. Why was Sloane making excuses for Bear? Didn't she see the obvious nepotism at play?

But I didn't say anything. Sloane was my only advocate right now and maybe my reaction was just further proof that I didn't deserve the director position. That I *couldn't* work collaboratively.

Sloane offered a sympathetic look. "I know this is hard for you," she said. "I know it doesn't feel fair."

That just made me feel guilty. Sloane had told me that there was a skill in helping other people achieve their creative vision and here I was, harping on my own disappointments. It just proved that Caitlin and my dad and even Shelley Cona were right. I was a brat and a bitch.

I promised myself I'd try harder. Because I already felt so alone.

I wondered if Sally was having a better time working on Bear's movie—if *any* of the other girls were having a better time than I was. We were all divided between the four projects and departments— no one working together. I imagined us like little islands. I'd even sketched it out—each of us far away from one another in a big, vast ocean full of sea monsters and stormy waves. Anything to distract myself from the angry, vindictive feelings swirling inside of me. Because despite my best efforts, I still hated Nick's short.

"Okay, let's spitball," Nick said that afternoon.

It quickly became clear that his idea of spitballing was just him and Karl reading aloud the jokes they'd come up with the night before in their dorm room and asking the rest of the story team to find a place for it in the script. Which was a mess.

Nick's pitch had been vague, mostly built around a beautifully drawn world and some visual gags involving the skyscraper, a.k.a. "the Stalk." From a pitch perspective, the story had potential. There were endless ways to make Jack interesting and dynamic—to dig into his motivation. Unfortunately, that motivation—the reason behind Jack's desire to get to the top floor—had yet to be determined.

"The top floor represents the giant's kingdom," Nick said. "It's off-limits, so of course someone like Jack wants to go there."

"But why?" I asked. "Why *specifically* does he want to climb the Stalk?"

That just seemed to annoy Nick.

"Because he's a rebel," he said. "And Mr. Bigsworth is the establishment."

I hated saying the character's name. It made the whole project seem childish.

"Are we sure we can't think of a better name?" I asked.

"Why would we do that?" Nick asked. "It's a perfect name. It hints to the audience who this guy is—I mean, we can't just name him Mr. Giant. That would be too obvious." Karl and Nick shared a laugh and a fist bump. "Now come on, Hayley, give me something I can actually work with."

That's how it went with anything I suggested. Nick would shoot it down immediately, explain why it was a bad idea, and then ask for something better. Not only that, but he ended the day by giving us all homework.

It didn't feel like we were a team at all. I felt especially bad for Zoe, who had to sit at the end of the table taking notes.

"I think you should all watch *The Nightmare Before Christmas* tonight," Nick said. "It's full of inspiration."

Besides the fact that both main characters were named Jack, I couldn't see how they were connected in any way—the style wasn't even the same.

"It does a great job combining the creepy and the funny," Nick said. "I think that's something we should really focus on."

Nick's short wasn't creepy at all. And it definitely wasn't funny. At least not to me.

"Tim Burton is a master of that," Nick said. "Maybe we should have a marathon of all the movies he directed."

"Tim Burton didn't direct *The Nightmare Before Christmas*," I said.

Nick laughed. "Uh, yeah, he did," he said, sharing a *Can you believe this?* look with Karl.

"Henry Selick directed it," I said. "Tim Burton produced it and came up with the idea, but he didn't direct it."

I knew I was right.

"Uh, I think *I* would know if some guy named Henry Selick directed *The Nightmare Before Christmas*," Nick said.

Some guy? I tightened my fingers around my pencil. How many times had I been quizzed on animation trivia by some random dude who thought he knew more than I did?

I thought Nick would be better. I thought we were the same.

"Henry Selick is one of the most well-known stop-motion directors in the world," I said. "He directed *James and the Giant Peach* and *Coraline*."

Nick and Karl stared at me.

"*The Nightmare Before Christmas* is Tim Burton's movie," Nick said, but he sounded less than sure now.

I counted to ten in my head. "Like I said, he produced it. He didn't direct it."

The room was silent, all eyes ping-ponging between me and Nick, waiting for one of us to admit that we were wrong. It sure as hell wasn't going to be me.

"I can look it up," Zoe said, hands poised over her keyboard.

"Whatever," Nick said. "We'll all watch *The Corpse Bride* instead."

I was grateful for the new distraction of our lunchtime lectures.

"What group are you in?" Nick asked on Wednesday. Even though I hadn't seen him that morning, he somehow managed to find me as I headed down to the cafeteria. We were expected to get our lunches and go immediately to the room listed on the schedule.

I was pretty sure Nick had gone back to the dorms the night before, looked up *The Nightmare Before Christmas*, and realized that he was completely wrong and I was completely right. Not that I was expecting an apology or even an acknowledgment of his wrongness.

"Group one," I said.

"That's too bad," he said. "I'm in group two."

I was relieved. Whatever friendship we'd formed based on our mutual love of BB Gun Films and Bryan Beckett seemed to be curdling the longer we worked together. Between that and the silent treatment I was still getting from the other girls, this collaborative animation internship felt incredibly lonely. And I knew it was partially my fault.

Okay, probably entirely my fault.

"You're going to editorial, right?" Nick asked but didn't wait for me to respond. "We're speaking to one of the producers today. Madeline something."

Madeline Bailey. She'd been at BB Gun Films since the beginning and had produced *A Boy Named Bear*. I wasn't surprised that Nick didn't know her name. I was starting to realize he only knew the big, flashy names in the industry—exactly what *I* was usually accused of by guys like him whenever I mentioned my love of animation.

"I've heard she's a real ball-buster," Nick said. "My mentor says she made a story apprentice cry. I can't imagine I'll get much from her talk," he said. "I plan to focus on the creative side of things, not worry about scheduling and money."

I didn't know much about producing, but I imagined it was more than that. I also imagined that BB Gun Films wouldn't have set up these lectures if they didn't think we would learn something important from them. But there was no point in trying to convince Nick of their worth.

He shifted his sketchbook in his arms and a few pieces of paper fell to the floor. I knelt to help him pick them up, but Nick leapt on them so quickly that his head knocked against mine.

"Ouch," I said.

"Sorry." He grabbed at the drawings but one of them was stuck under my shoe.

I lifted my heel and got a good look at what he had been grabbing for.

"Is this me?" I asked.

A rhetorical question. It was very obviously me. A roughly drawn sketch of a girl wearing a button-down shirt and trousers, her hair big, her mouth wide as she shouted, *BUT WHY??* Nick's name was scrawled across the bottom.

"It's a joke," he said. "You know, because you're always asking questions."

I stared at it, my face hot.

"It's funny," Nick said.

It was like the Sloane/ Jessica Rabbit drawing. A "rite of passage," she'd called it. I just hadn't expected to experience it so quickly.

"Yeah," I said. "Funny."

Nick looked relieved. "You can keep it," he said.

I tucked it into my sketchbook. It wasn't a bad drawing, and Nick was right—I *had* spent most of yesterday asking questions— but it still made me feel like my skin was too tight. Like I was being seen, but not in a good way.

"You have to have a sense of humor about these things," Sloane had said.

Nick got his lunch, and I got mine. Today's lecture would be in the same place I'd gone with Sloane to record the lines for *No One Fears the Woods*.

Zoe was sitting at her desk when I walked into the editorial department where a long table and several chairs were set up in the middle of the room. I was the first one to arrive.

"You'll learn a lot from John," she said. She was wearing a pink dress with brown shoes and a red cardigan. It should have clashed, but it didn't. Her hair was pulled back in a ponytail with a little bump at the crown.

"He seems nice." I glanced toward John's office, where I could see him standing behind his desk in the dark, watching something on the screen.

"He is," Zoe said. "Tends to go off on tangents and has some unintentionally hilarious dad jokes, but he's one of the good ones."

I was tempted to ask her to point out some of the "not good" ones, but before I could, other interns began shuffling in. Chris, who was working on Nick's movie, was also in group one. I waved at him, lowering my hand when I saw who walked in behind him.

"Saffitz," Bear said.

I sat down at the table, my lunch in front of me. Ignoring my attempt to ignore him, Bear took the seat next to mine. He put his sketchbook on the table next to my tray. It was closed, but I was deeply tempted to flip it open. No doubt I'd find another stick figure waving at me.

"How's the short going?" Bear asked.

"Fine," I said.

He was being normal. And nice. *Why?*

"*Jack and the Beanstalk*, right?"

"Yep," I said.

I knew I was being rude, but between our brief interaction on the quad and moments like these, I didn't really understand why Bear was attempting to be friendly all of a sudden. Did he feel bad for me? Was this pity-friendliness?

That would be way worse than him continuing to be a jerk.

"John," Zoe called out when all eight of us had arrived. "Are you ready?"

The editor came out of his office, blinking a little at the bright lights. He was wearing a button-down shirt with big green leaves on it and a pair of seventies-style glasses.

"Thanks, Zoe," he said, standing at the end of the table. "So. Editorial. Anyone here know anything about how my department works?"

I raised a tentative hand. I was the only one.

John crossed his arms. "Really, Bear?" he asked. "I'm hurt. Truly hurt."

Bear gave one of his patented *So what?* shrugs.

"This kid used to terrorize my department back in the day,"

John said. "I'm sure I have at least two hours of you screaming directly into my microphone."

"Because you tortured me with lectures on the importance of needle drops," Bear said.

John sighed. "The importance of the *appropriate use* of needle drops," he said. "Jeez, it's like you've learned nothing from my tutelage."

"One can only hope," Bear said. Both of them were grinning.

"Did you work on *A Boy Named Bear*?" Chris asked.

John nodded. "Oh yeah," he said. "I was only an apprentice editor back then. My boss was an absolute perfectionist." He glanced over at Bear and winked. "A real pain."

"She's said the same about you," he said.

"She taught me everything I know," John said.

Were they talking about Bear's mom? They had to be. I'd looked her up at the start of the internship—googling "Reagan Davis" instead of "Reagan Beckett"—but there hadn't been much except a sparse IMDb page listing some projects I hadn't recognized and a few random comments on articles about BB Gun Films. Comments that seemed to suggest that she had worked on *A Boy Named Bear* but had never been credited. Was John implying that she had worked in this department?

On IMDb the only editor was listed as Matt Griffin. Had she edited part of the film?

John seemed to realize that the rest of us were all staring at him with rapt interest. He cleared his throat.

"Editorial," he said. "Even though it's the same basic set of skills, there are a few major differences between the way live-action editors and animation editors work. That difference is most clearly illustrated in how our pipeline functions."

He pulled out a small stack of papers and began passing them around. It was a time line that showed the order and the number of steps between putting a scene into production and getting it finaled.

"Notice anything in particular?" John asked.

I scanned the sheet. "Shots come in and out of editorial a lot," I said.

"Bingo," John said. "In live action, editorial is one of the last departments to work on a scene. It's written, designed, and shot completely independent of this department. Have you ever heard the phrase 'We'll fix it in post'?"

Some of us nodded.

"Editors hate that because most producers think it's true," John said, and laughed. "Unfortunately, as talented as we are, we can't perform magic. In animation, however, the editorial department is one of the first—and last—departments to work on a sequence. We work very closely with the story department to sort out as many problems as we can before anything goes into animation. And even after that, we're working on shots as they cycle through the rest of production. As you'll see in the pipeline, every time something is finaled in a department, it comes back here before moving on." He looked at me. "Good observation. Hayley, right?"

I sat up taller, pleased that he had remembered me.

"Hayley would know a little bit about shots coming in and out of editorial," John said. "Just the other day, she was here while her mentor, Sloane, helped us out with some scratch dialogue." John paused. "You did some voice-over work for us as well, didn't you?" he asked.

Thinking about it gave me a shiver of embarrassment. I'd been terrible. Utterly terrible.

"Is there nothing you can't do, Saffitz?" Bear asked, before turning to John. "Is it still cut in? Can we watch it?"

"No," I said at the same time John pressed his lips together thoughtfully.

"I think it's still in there, actually," he said.

"Only one way to find out," Bear said. He got up from the table and headed into John's office like he owned it.

There was nothing I wanted to do less than relive my horrible voice-over attempt, but everyone was already moving into the edit bay. From her desk, Zoe shot me a sympathetic look as I trailed after John. Guess I'd been wrong about Bear being nicer to me.

John stood behind his desk. His keyboard looked nothing like a regular keyboard.

"Editing shortcuts," he said when he noticed me watching.

"Maybe we could watch something else?" I asked, shooting him a desperate look.

"Don't worry," he said. "I made it sound good."

I had a hard time believing him. I could still remember my performance—shaky and awkward and flat. I hated doing things poorly and I really hated other people witnessing it.

The scene appeared on the screen. Nothing was animated—at this stage, it was only a set of drawings edited together to get a sense of timing and a feel for the dialogue. Dialogue that I had butchered.

Sloane had given me the quick rundown of the story. It was about a boy who lived near a massive forest. His father—who has plans for the land—doesn't believe the old wives' tale about the place being haunted, but when he disappears, the son decides to go into the forest to find him. In it, he encounters the hag—the character Sloane was always being asked to voice—and a mysterious young girl named Hazel.

In the scene I'd recorded, Hazel—who befriends the boy—warns him about following in his father's footsteps to destroy the forest. On the screen, drawings showed her standing up high on a tree branch, hands on her hips.

"We are the trees," my voice came out of the speakers. "We are the trees and the birds and the grass and the sky, and everything that grows from above and below. Your fire cannot burn us. Your machines cannot destroy us. We were here before you and we will be here when you are gone."

My shoulders rose with each word, wanting to escape the sound of my own voice. John was right, though. He'd done something with the audio to make it sound airy and inhuman. It made my toneless delivery creepy and unnerving. And it worked. So much for editors being unable to create magic.

After the lecture, I gathered my tray, preparing to take it back to the cafeteria.

"You have hidden talents, Saffitz." Bear fell into step next to me.

I turned toward him, using my tray to put some space between us, my sketchbook tucked under my arm. I was tired of this. Of Bear's taunting. Of his attempts to get under my skin every time he saw me.

"What do you want, Bear?" I asked. "You got the director role, okay? Congrats. I hope you do something *really* special."

He didn't say anything, looking down at my tray. Then he reached out and wrapped his hands around it—his fingers brushing mine. I was pretty sure the spark I felt was just static electricity.

With a tug, he took the tray from me. It jostled my sketch-book and Nick's drawing fell to the ground for the second time that day. Both Bear and I looked at it. I could see Nick's signature staring up at us.

Bear frowned. "You don't look like that at all," he said.

Then he took my tray and walked away. It wasn't until he was gone that I realized he'd stepped right on the drawing, leaving a big, dark boot print. It was ruined. I threw it out, more than grateful for the excuse.

tried to push Bear's words out of my head, but they kept coming back to me—nudging me every time I tried to wrangle Nick's train wreck of a story. *You have hidden talents, Saffitz*, he'd said.

Talents that were going to waste. By the end of the first week, we barely had a plot, let alone a script. It was bad enough that the short was going nowhere—but I also didn't have anyone to vent to about it. Sally and I were exchanging pleasantries, but we weren't hanging out. The rest of the girls all seemed to get together in the evenings, but I wasn't invited. Samantha and Julie were busy and our schedules barely met up, so the few times I was able to text them, I usually wasn't able to get a response until hours later. It wasn't worth it to try to explain to them what was going on. They cared, but they didn't understand.

I even tried to confide in Zach, but my brother was capable of a single form of sibling support, which was teasing. Anything I told him just resulted in more Willy Wonka GIFs, or the occasional WWVBD text. It stood for "What Would Violet Beauregarde Do?" and he was far too proud of his own perceived cleverness. I didn't bother with my parents. I knew they'd just remind me that I could give up and come home.

"You guys need to create a beat sheet, at least," Zoe told us on Friday. "The rest of your team is waiting and if you don't start getting something into production you're going to run out of time."

The entire short was expected to be ten minutes long, twelve max. Film was usually a page a minute, but with animation it could be longer, so we had been encouraged not to go beyond eight pages. Right now, Nick had thirty pages of mostly unrelated jokes and extended sequences that explained the history of the Stalk—all of which he'd had us storyboard.

"I just don't know what I can cut," he said.

"You'll have to figure it out," Zoe said. "You have too many scenes, for one. A short film needs to be concise. Simplify what you can. Leave only what you absolutely need."

"She doesn't know what she's talking about," Nick said as we headed to the shuttle at the end of the day. "She's in production—she doesn't get what it's like to be creative."

I didn't say anything. Out of all of us, Zoe had the most experience actually making an animated film, and if I were in Nick's shoes, I would be paying close attention to what she said. Then again, if I was in Nick's shoes, we'd already have something in production because not only had I developed a tight, succinct storyline, I'd also had a beat sheet ready to go.

I dreaded every production meeting. Working on Nick's movie was agonizing—it was hours of him and Karl regurgitating the same ideas and jokes and expecting a different response each time. I'd already storyboarded different versions of the same gags multiple times.

Still, I wanted to make the film better. I wanted to be exactly who Sloane thought I could be—a team player. Someone who helped elevate a project.

I tried working in the library that weekend, but it didn't feel right. The space had lost whatever magic it'd had and reminded me of the time when I was still working on my pitch—when I was so sure I'd be chosen. The memory of that girl—so sure, so arrogant—was a little like the lingering soreness I'd felt the last time I'd gotten a flu shot. When I'd have to flex my hand to distract from the pain.

I tried working in my room, but it was tense there, with Sally wearing her headphones or hearing the other girls hanging out in their rooms with the doors open. It was a distraction—that awkwardness—and I needed to focus. It wasn't until Saturday night that I realized that no one seemed to use the central stairwell.

Even though the two sets of stairs—which separated in the middle—linked the boys' and the girls' dormitories, everyone seemed to enter on the opposite ends of the building. I sat on the girls' side, just above where the stairs met, sketching as the ambient noise of feet and doors faded into the background.

I was pretty sure that no one else on Nick's team was spending their evening trying to fix his short. But I couldn't help myself. The thought of just letting it be bad was unfathomable to me.

"*Artist compulsivist,*" Zach told me once. "That's your diagnosis. No known cure."

As if he and I didn't share a perfectionist, ambitious streak. Even before he went to college, he was the all-nighter king, working as long as he had to in order to be prepared. To get things right. All my best tricks had come from him—caffeine, cold water on the face, blasting dissonant music.

Despite everything, I actually enjoyed drawing Nick's characters. His angular, graphic style was completely different from my own, but I liked a challenge. If I could capture Jack, then maybe I could understand him. Maybe I could answer the question I'd been asking—why did he want to get to the top of the Stalk?

I started at his feet and drew upward—legs planted, arms akimbo. His posture was confident—his smile, eager. It was a good drawing, but it didn't accomplish what I wanted it to. It didn't add anything to the story, to the character. It was a basic, boring hero pose.

At the back of the stairwell were two stories of glass that revealed a sunny bank of trees during the day. But now, at night, it acted like an enormous mirror. Extremely useful as I sketched and stared, contorting my features into ridiculous expressions, trying to find the right one.

I was doing something halfway between a smolder and a squint when I realized I wasn't the only reflection in the glass. I shrieked, flinging my pencil out of my hands.

It clacked down the steps before landing between Bear's feet. He bent to pick it up.

"Jesus," I said. I could feel my heart racing beneath my palm.

"Sorry," he said.

He lifted his chin, clearly trying to see what I was working on. I wasn't sure why, but I handed my sketchbook over. He looked down at it. At my drawing.

"It's not done," I said.

"Do you want some help?" he asked.

I nodded before I could think any better of it. He returned the sketchbook to me and took a few steps back. His head was turned away and he was looking out at the darkness—at the mirror of us.

"What does he want?" Bear asked.

He was talking about Jack.

"We don't know," I said. "That's the problem."

"What do *you* think he wants?"

I thought for a moment, trying to imagine what I would do if Nick's story was my own.

"I think he wants to prove himself," I said.

Bear nodded. "What's stopping him?"

Mr. Bigsworth, I thought, though I couldn't bear to say the cheesy name out loud.

"Everyone," I said.

"He doesn't *look* like anyone is stopping him."

He was right. The pose I'd drawn was a confident one, with Jack wearing a cocky smile. And that was the problem. There was no conflict in the drawing—because there was no real conflict in the story. Jack wanted to climb the Stalk; Jack climbed the Stalk.

"Contrasts," Bear said. "Contrasts are interesting."

My pitch had been all about contrasts. Miriam's smallness was juxtaposed against her big feelings, her strength, while the golem was enormous in size, but delicate and childlike in all other ways.

Maybe I needed to find the contrast in Nick's story. In Jack.

We sat there for a while, saying nothing, the stairwell a world of its own. A place where me and Bear were just . . . me and Bear.

"You'll figure it out," he said.

"Thanks," I said.

The whole thing was weird and surreal but also a little nice, too. Sally was ignoring me; Nick waved off all my ideas—Bear was the first person in a while who had just listened to me. Paid attention to what I was trying to say. And responded in kind.

He shoved his hands in his pockets and continued up the

stairs away from me. I waited until the door swung closed before I turned back to my sketchbook. I tried again.

This time, I made Jack's expression confident, but his pose was more reserved. His hands tightened into fists at his side, his foot scuffing the ground. Whatever he wanted, he wasn't sure he could get it. Or he wasn't sure he deserved it.

The drawing wasn't perfect, but now it had something it hadn't had before.

By Monday morning, I had some sketches and ten pages of a trim, fairly strong script. Even though the drawing itself still wasn't right, I'd discovered how to fix the story. I felt better about myself. It had been like solving a puzzle, and once I figured out the right pieces, the whole thing had come together in a way that thrilled me. It made me feel creative and useful again. This was proof that I could put my own ego aside and help other people. That I could be an asset to a project.

Bear had helped, though I had a feeling I couldn't just go up to him and tell him that. That moment in the stairwell had seemed like an anomaly. Something that we'd both be better off pretending didn't happen.

"Good weekend?" Nick dropped into the seat next to me.

The shuttle was practically empty.

"Yeah," I said. "You?"

"It was okay," he said. "Karl and I watched a bunch of Tarantino films. You know, for inspiration."

I had no idea how Quentin Tarantino movies related to Nick's version of *Jack and the Beanstalk*, but I'd given up trying to decipher his creative process. Instead, I tried to focus on my feeling of accomplishment and usefulness—my hand resting on my bag where the treatment was.

Bear got on the shuttle. He looked at Nick and then at me, lifting his chin slightly in acknowledgment. I returned the gesture, watching as he took a seat toward the front.

Then, all of a sudden, I felt Nick's arm coming up and around, his fingers brushing my shoulder. It was weird. Bear turned away.

"I'm glad you're on my team," Nick said. His voice was just a little louder than usual.

"Uh, thanks," I said.

"You're good at keeping all of us on track," Nick said. "Taking care of the team, you know? Motivating us."

He made me sound like I was their mom rather than someone contributing in any creative way. Still, it was nice to hear that I was an asset.

"It's very inspiring," he said. He patted my shoulder awkwardly.

"I actually came up with some ideas this weekend," I said.

"Yeah?" He shifted in his seat, turning to face me completely, and thankfully removing his hand. "Lay them on me."

"I thought I'd just pitch them to the team," I said. "Get everyone's feedback at once."

"Come on," Nick said. "I'm the director. I should get to hear it first. That way we can iron out any issues before we present them."

I didn't like the way he said "we," but animation *was* all about collaboration. Still.

"I'd rather wait," I said.

"Don't be like that." Nick made a face. "I thought you were a team player, Hayley."

I kicked myself for saying anything. There was no way Nick

was going to shut up about this and we hadn't even left the parking lot. Did I want to listen to him plead with me for the ten-minute ride to the studio?

Reluctantly, I pulled the treatment out of my bag and handed it over. I didn't give him the sketches, though. Nick didn't need them for the pitch to make sense and I was feeling strangely protective. I wanted to keep them to myself.

Up ahead, Bear was staring out the window.

Somehow, he noticed me and turned back. Like before his gaze shifted from me to Nick and then back to me. Specifically, to my shoulder where Nick's hand had been. As if it was still there, I shrugged it backward. Bear's smile was small and brief.

The girls got on the shuttle and headed to the back, where they usually sat. I kept my gaze down as they passed—it felt worse being ignored when I attempted to get their attention, so I had just started pretending I didn't notice them or didn't care. It sucked.

"No more plants," Jeannette was saying to Emily. "We have too many."

"No such thing as too many plants," she said.

"You can't make me choose," Rachel said to Caitlin and Sally. "I can like both Lin-Manuel Miranda's lyrics *and* Howard Ashman's."

"Hmm." Nick made a noise, and I looked over at him.

He was scanning the script, his eyebrows tilted downward as he read. By the time he was done, his whole face was contorted in a frown. The excitement I'd felt in putting the treatment together faded.

"What is this?" he asked.

"It's just some suggestions," I said. "I thought we could simplify the story—focus on Jack instead of on Mr. Bigsworth, and that would give the short more energy."

"This is a totally different film," Nick said. "You completely rewrote my idea."

"Not completely." I pointed to the script. "I kept the jokes you and Karl liked."

"Yeah, and you cut a bunch of great ones. All the good stuff is gone."

I didn't say anything. Nick's tone—his whole posture—had gone from interested and eager to annoyed and petulant. I started second-guessing the work I'd done. Was it really that bad?

"I don't think you should show this to anyone," he said. "It looks like you're undermining my authority."

His authority? I thought it was the final product that mattered—not who came up with each idea. That's what Bryan had said. Disheartened, I reached for the script I had written, but Nick held on to it.

"I'm sure you have another copy," he said.

I thought about snatching the paper away from him, but the whole thing just made me tired. Leaning back against the seat, I stared out the window as the shuttle pulled away from the campus.

Zoe was already in the conference room when we arrived. "Did you figure something out this weekend?" she asked Nick. "Something we can share with the rest of the team?"

He crossed his arms defensively. "Karl and I did some brainstorming."

Zoe let out a slow breath before speaking again. "Okay, but do you have something concrete? Gena told me that Bryan is going to be stopping by each production today to see how things are going."

"What?" Nick went pale. "When?"

"I don't know," Zoe said. "Could be this morning, could be this afternoon."

Nick looked like he was going to be sick. I didn't blame him— the production was a mess. We didn't have anything to show Bryan.

"Where's Karl?" He looked around, clearly hoping for Karl to magically appear. He hadn't been on the first shuttle with us that morning.

"Maybe in the cafeteria," I said.

The three other story interns—Germain, Daniel and Chris— had just arrived.

"Can you go find him?" Nick asked me. "We need him. Like, now."

I didn't move. Was he really telling me to go track down Karl? Like I was his assistant or something?

"Hayley!" he barked, making me jump. "Be helpful, okay? This is an emergency."

If the door had been closed, I would have shoved it open. Instead, I had to settle for walking very, very loudly out of the room.

Karl wasn't in the cafeteria. He wasn't at his mentor's desk. I did a sweep of the story department, but he was nowhere to be seen. Annoyed that I had just wasted fifteen minutes looking for him, I stormed back into the conference room.

"I couldn't find him," I said, before I was even fully in the door.

I stopped short. Nick was standing at the end of the table, his drawings displayed on an easel. His eyes, and the eyes of everyone else in the room were turned toward me. Karl was there, but so was Bryan. *Fuck*.

"Sorry," I said.

"We were wondering where you were." Nick gave Bryan a nervous grin. "Bathroom break, you know." He made some sort of motion that seemed to imply that maybe I had gotten my period, his hands gesturing down below his hips.

My face grew hot. Nick had known exactly where I had gone. For a moment, I thought about taking one of the pencils that was stuck in my hair and lobbing it at him. There was a fifty-fifty chance I could get him in the eye. Maybe forty-sixty, because I was so angry. Instead, I sat down at the back of the room where Zoe was taking notes. She patted my leg.

It calmed me down, but just a little. And only for a minute.

"Can I continue?" Nick asked, and it was a beat before I realized he was talking to me.

I glared at him, my fingers itching to grab that pencil.

"As I was saying," he said, directing his attention toward Bryan. "We've been working hard as a team trying to come up with a way to streamline the story." He gestured toward Karl. "My head of story and I spent most of the weekend brainstorming. As you said, creativity never takes a break."

Bryan *had* said that. He'd also said that true creativity existed independent of outside influences. If Nick was smart, he wouldn't mention that he was spending his free time being inspired by Tim Burton and Quentin Tarantino.

"How exactly will you be streamlining the story?" Bryan asked.

"Uh, well . . ." Nick's eyes scanned the room, though I wasn't exactly sure what he was looking for. "I thought, well, if we focused more on Jack than on Mr. Bigsworth, that would help."

His gaze skipped over me. My mouth fell open. Was he serious? Was he actually about to present the ideas I'd come up with this weekend and pass them off as his own? In front of Bryan?

"Interesting," Bryan said. "Go on."

"Uh, yeah. So . . . um." Nick groped outward and I watched as he reached into his bag and pulled out the treatment I had given him on the shuttle. The treatment he claimed had completely ruined his story.

"There are some ideas here," he said, looking down at what I had written. "We managed to keep the best jokes, of course, but it's a more streamlined version of what we originally had."

"Let me see." Bryan reached out, and Nick passed the document over.

I hadn't put my name on it. I hadn't seen the point—after all, I had planned to present it to the story team. I hadn't expected Nick to literally take it from me and pass it off as his own.

"This is very good work," Bryan said.

I waited, staring daggers at Nick, waiting for him to admit that he hadn't written it. We'd been butting heads lately, but I couldn't believe he would do something so blatantly dishonest. But he didn't say anything. In fact, he completely avoided looking at me.

"I really like where you're going with this." Bryan stood. "Keep it up."

"Are you kidding me?" I blurted out. "Are you fucking kidding me?"

"Hayley!" Zoe said. She grabbed at my arm, but I was already on my feet, pointing an accusing finger at Nick.

"That was my idea," I said. "You stole my idea."

"Hayley"—Nick's gaze darted around wildly—"you're making a scene."

"You stole my idea!"

"We're a team," Nick said to the floor. "You're being hysterical."

"And you're being a fucking liar!" My voice cracked under the strain of my shouting.

"Excuse me, young lady," Bryan said. "You need to calm down. Right now."

I shut my mouth, my skin hot, my lungs bellowing like I'd been running.

Everything was silent and tense. All eyes were focused on me, except for Nick, who was too much of a coward to look up.

"Oh, Hayley," Zoe said.

Bryan faced me. He looked disappointed. Angry.

"Hayley, is it?" he asked. "I think you'd better come with me to my office. Now."

At least this time he'd gotten my name right.

CHAPTER FIFTEEN

When I fantasized about being called into Bryan Beckett's office, it was always because he was going tell me that I was the most talented young person he'd ever met and would I please, please, please consider taking a job at BB Gun Films after I graduated high school?

I never imagined that I would be brought there by the man himself, after yelling at another intern for stealing my idea.

I was still furious, but by the time we got to his office and he gestured for me to sit, fear had begun to kick in as well. Was I about to be booted from the internship? I had only skimmed the document on employee conduct, but I was pretty sure that calling someone a "fucking liar" was frowned upon.

Bryan's assistant closed the door. It was just me and him.

I'd always wanted to see the inside of his office. Besides the blink-and-you'd-miss-it shot of him behind his desk from our welcome video, none of the interns had been here before. Except for Bear, but that was different. Everything was different for Bear.

It was exactly as clean as I had imagined. Bryan's desk was an enormous black piece of marble that seemed to spill over one side. The floor was white. The walls were white. There wasn't a piece of paper or a pencil or a knickknack anywhere. My chair was round—almost like a ball sawed in two—balancing on a plastic stand. It was white. The leather inside of it was also white and it squeaked when I sat. It was like being inside of a spaceship.

I didn't know what to do with my hands, so I folded them in my lap, crossing my legs at the ankle. The chair wasn't comfortable.

Bryan himself was sitting behind his desk. His chair was enormous—a big, black leather thing that loamed up and around him. The top curved downward, the back itself like a menacing bouncer or bodyguard. It was so quiet the air almost seemed to buzz with the absence of sound.

"Hayley." Bryan's hands were flat on his desk.

"I'm sorry," I said, but he shook his head. I pressed my lips tightly together, hoping I could keep my mouth shut. Minutes ticked by. I didn't move—I was pretty sure any movement I made would be audible thanks to the leather in the chair. My butt began to hurt.

"I understand where you're coming from," Bryan said.

Out of all the things I'd expected him to say, that hadn't been one of them.

"When I started out in animation, all I wanted was to make the projects I was working on better. I had a vision, and most of the time, I found that people I worked for didn't understand that vision," Bryan said.

The pressure in my chest began to loosen.

He leaned back in his chair, smiling slightly. "I was fired from quite a few of those earlier jobs. From companies that cared more about making movies that would sell toys than making something that was good," he said. "They didn't like what I had to say. It was easier to fire me than question the quality of the work they were doing."

We were the same—Bryan and me. He understood. He understood where I was coming from.

"When it comes to situations like that—where you're willing to risk your career to make a stand—you have to have a certain level of arrogance."

It was similar to what he'd said in his CalTED Talk. Part of me couldn't believe that he was saying all this to me. Just to me. Like my own private pep talk.

"All artists need to be arrogant. You need to believe that you're the best."

I nodded.

"But you also have to have the goods to back up your arrogance," Bryan said. "You have to be as talented as you think you are." He looked at me. "Unfortunately, you aren't."

It would have hurt less if he had just kicked me in the stomach.

"Look." Bryan stood. "You're clearly a passionate young lady. And sometimes it's easy to mistake passion for talent. I blame myself, to an extent."

He came around the desk, resting one hip on the edge of the massive black marble. "With all this attention on diversity these days, there was a lot of pressure to make space for applicants like you. We're all being asked to consider an artist's background before we even look at your work. And that's not really fair to you, is it?"

Applicants like me?

"The problem with your work—with your pitch—is that it just isn't universal," he said. "The audience wants to *relate* to the characters on the screen. They can't do that if they don't even know what you're referencing. I mean, how many people have even heard of a goldum, or whatever they're called."

Was he saying that audiences couldn't relate to a grieving girl if she was Jewish? That the golem made it unrelatable?

"An audience can only suspend their disbelief so far," he said.

He'd made a movie with a talking bird as a narrator.

"I've always believed in honesty at all costs, but some people disagree with me. They think we should treat everyone equally, regardless of skill. Build them up, even if they'll never have a chance of succeeding."

I thought I was going to be sick. If I threw up, how hard would it be for someone to clean my projectile vomit off of Bryan's clean white walls?

"You have some talent, I'll give you that, but you're just not cut out to be a director. You have to have that something special in order to lead a production. You don't have it." Bryan crossed his arms. "But it's clear that you're frustrated working on the project you've been assigned to, so I'll make you a deal."

I looked down at my hands and saw that my knuckles were pale.

"Bear is *extremely* talented," Bryan said.

I literally did not think this conversation could get any worse, but apparently it could.

"He just struggles with motivation," Bryan said. "With focus."

So Bear's abilities were something that could be developed. Cultivated. Unlike me, who was already a failure at seventeen. I'd been judged and found lacking.

"He needs guidance," Bryan said. "He's so gifted and yet . . ."

He wasn't thinking about me anymore.

"I'll put you on Bear's team," he said. Magnanimously. "It will give you another chance to be a team player. That's what animation's about, after all. Collaboration."

It was exactly what Sloane had said. I slumped in the uncomfortable chair, hating that she would probably be upset at my behavior. The thought of that—of her disappointment—was almost as painful as Bryan's words. I wanted to leave, but he wasn't done.

"There's power in that. In guiding others. Inspiring them," he said. "All great artists need a muse."

My feet looked very small and very far away. There was a long pause. I glanced up and found Bryan looking at me. Was he expecting a response? If so, what did he want me to say? *Thank you, sir, I'd be honored to inspire* your *son to excel in the industry that I want to succeed in?*

I didn't say anything. Bryan let out a small laugh.

"He talks about you, you know. Bear does," he said. He looked at me expectantly. "I think he's got a bit of a crush," he said. "And he's never been great with the girls at his school. . . ."

I stared, not sure what he wanted me to do with that information. Despite how devastating this was for my professional life, I couldn't help thinking that Bear would probably rather impale himself on his pencil than know his dad was attempting to help him out in the dating department by saying that he was romantically challenged.

It was so awkward and so dad-like that for a brief moment I forgot that I was talking to Bryan Beckett, four-time Academy Award–winning director, and felt like I was talking to a friend's socially inept father. I was surprised, but at the moment, that revelation was pretty low on the list of things I needed to process.

Bryan frowned. "I've made my point," he said. "I'll have you switched to Bear's team tomorrow." He waved a hand. "You can go."

I'd never been so grateful to be dismissed.

I walked out of his office, down the staircase, and out to the lobby. I barely registered any of it. My notebook and all the rest of my stuff was still in the conference room. I didn't care. I didn't care about any of it.

"Can you the call the shuttle?" I asked one of the guys at the front desk. "I'm not feeling well."

got back to the dorm, went to my room, got my keys and my phone and headed to the garage. The inside of my car was silent as I pulled away from the CalAn campus. I didn't want to listen to the radio or a podcast or music. I rolled down the windows and filled my ears with the sound of Los Angeles—honking cars, everyone else's blasting tunes, dogs barking, people yelling. I wanted to get lost in all of it. Wanted to be overwhelmed with everyone else's problems. Everyone else's lives.

It was hot and the air hitting my face was hot and I still had on the cardigan I'd been wearing inside the studio, which was always kept at an icy 60 degrees.

How could I go back to the dorms? How could I go back to the studio? I thought about calling my parents—telling them I was quitting the program. Telling them I was done.

You have to be as talented as you think you are.

And I wasn't. According to Bryan Beckett, all I was good for was inspiring other people. Inspiring *his* son, apparently.

Did I believe him? I'd lived the last year of my life by his rules—following the guidelines he'd laid out. I wore what he said I should wear. I worked the way he said I should work. I had collected his wisdom, treated his words like good-luck charms—as if knowing everything I could about him and his movies and his studio would make me the best artist I could be. As if it would make me worthy.

He'd stood in front of me and told me, in no uncertain terms, that I wasn't.

It was late when I drove back to the dorms. I couldn't even remember how I'd spent the time—where I'd been. The dining hall was dark when I walked across campus, and most of the dorm windows were too. I should have gone to my room, but the thought of being ignored by Sally on top of everything else that had happened today made my heart ache. Taking out my phone, I pulled up the intern directory.

He was on the third floor at the end of the hallway.

I knocked before I could second-guess myself. Beneath the door, I saw the light flicker on and then I heard footsteps. He didn't have a roommate, I knew that, so I was prepared when he opened the door. Except I wasn't.

"Saffitz?" Bear asked.

His hair was sticking straight up, his eyes at half-mast. He wasn't wearing a shirt.

For a moment, I just stared. I'd been so focused on my annoyance at Bear—at his disinterest in the internship, the nepotism that had gotten him the position I wanted—that I'd mostly been able to ignore how extremely attractive he was. Mostly.

But I wasn't ignoring it now.

Looking at him—shirtless and slightly confused—made my palms all sweaty and my knees wobbly. I felt very, very warm inside. Whoever had drawn the grown-up version of Bear online had done a really, really good job. He did have chest hair. Not as much as the drawing, but enough.

I'd come here not thinking. Not really.

I'd wanted to get away from Bryan's words, but I couldn't. They kept circulating in my head, a whirling vortex that had decimated all my hopes and dreams. There was only one thing that Bryan had said to me that didn't make me feel completely terrible.

One thing that I could actually do something about. That I had control over. For the first time in months—maybe in years—I found that I was interested in something other than animation. Very, *very* interested.

And if Bryan was right, then maybe that explained some things. Maybe it explained Bear's reaction to the caricature. The moment in the stairwell. All those times he had been nice to me. Maybe . . .

"You have a crush on me," I said.

Bear's eyes widened, the sleepiness immediately gone. "I—"

Not waiting for a full response, I pushed past him into his room. Losing everything I thought I'd wanted had made me brave. He closed the door behind him, leaning on it and regarding me with suspicion.

"You like me," I said.

"What are you doing here?" he asked.

I pulled off my cardigan and let it drop to the floor.

"I'm here to inspire you," I said.

It was a lie. I was there for myself. I crossed the room, curled my hand around the back of his neck, and pulled his mouth down to mine.

CHAPTER SEVENTEEN

Bear didn't move.

His lips were soft and warm, but his entire body had gone stiff. Doubt froze me from the inside. Thinking I'd totally misread everything, I dropped my hand and drew my head back. But before I could step away, Bear's hands wrapped around my waist, around my back, as he pulled me against him. His mouth came down hard on mine.

Yes. Pushing up on my toes, I kissed him back, pressing him against the door. My hands got lost in his hair, his palms hot between my shoulder blades. My shirt was open just enough that I could feel his skin against my chest—it was warm. He smelled like deodorant and pencil shavings. I leaned hard against him—my whole body—and I felt him brace himself, his hips hitting the door, his knees bent.

His tongue was in my mouth, or maybe mine was in his, but it felt good, really good, and I never wanted to stop.

It wasn't my first kiss, but it felt like the first kiss that mattered. The first kiss that took me out of myself—that shut my brain off. The first kiss where I wasn't thinking about storyboards or stories or all the ideas that I had that I was terrified I'd never get to finish.

All I was thinking about was how good I *felt*.

It was exactly what I wanted.

Then Bear was pushing away from the door, and the two of us were stumbling deeper into his room. He guided me backward, and I tripped over something—his shoes?—before falling back onto his bed. I pulled him down with me, my hands sliding over his back—my fingers finding muscle and smooth skin.

He was a good kisser, and pressed his mouth—his hot, open mouth—against my throat. I closed my eyes and leaned my head back, my brain processing nothing but how good everything felt—his lips, his hands, his body.

Giving him a push, we rolled awkwardly on his twin bed until I was above him, my knees on either side of his hips. My hair had come out of its bun and was falling into my face, but he reached up and pushed it aside, bringing my head down so he could keep kissing me.

I wanted more. I wanted to feel everything and think nothing.

I reached for my shirt, fumbling with the buttons, bothering with just enough for me to pull the whole thing up and over my head. Bear's hands found my stomach, his fingers hot against my ribs.

"Wait," he said. He sat up, displacing me back onto his knees.

No.

"Hayley." His hands reached through my mass of hair, smoothing it back.

I didn't want to look at him. Not when he looked so concerned. I just wanted him to kiss me. To make everything go away. To make my brain stop racing.

"What's going on?" he asked.

I crossed my arms over my chest, feeling extremely naked in

my boring cotton bra. Rolling off of his lap, I stood and reached for my shirt. He grabbed my pants by the waistband and pulled me back onto the bed next to him.

"Hayley."

I yanked my shirt over my head. It was inside out. And backward. Now that my hormones were cooling off and my thoughts kicking back into high gear, I remembered why I didn't usually do things like this. I was not very good at them.

"What happened?" he asked.

"Does it matter? I thought most guys would be happy if a girl just showed up their door and took her shirt off," I said to his floor.

Bear touched my elbow. "You don't like me," he said.

"I thought that *you* didn't like *me*," I said. "But you do."

"Yeah," he said, rubbing the back of his neck. "You said that."

My face was hot. "It's true, isn't it?" I asked.

"Obviously." He gestured between us. "You think I do *this* with just any girl who shows up at my door?"

"Are other girls showing up at your door?" I asked.

"Hayley," he said.

I put my head in my hands, my hair providing a much-needed curtain between us. I didn't want to talk. I didn't want to think. I just wanted to feel.

"What happened?"

"Your dad," I said, but it was muffled by my hands and my hair. Saying that felt more intimate than what we'd just been doing. Made me feel even more naked. I wrapped my arms tightly around myself.

"What?"

I leaned back, my head against the wall. "Your dad," I said again.

I didn't have to look at him to know that Bear's entire body tensed.

"My dad," he said.

"We had a long talk today." I stared up at the ceiling. My words were flat. Halting.

It was like being on the staircase again. A place—a moment—outside of reality, where I didn't know why I was saying what I was saying.

Bear blew out a breath. "Inspiring and informational, I imagine," he said.

"He thinks you have a crush on me," I said. "Also, I'm not 'as talented as I think I am.'" I made my finger quotes extra sarcastic. "And the only reason I got into the internship program is because I'm a girl."

I didn't repeat the whole dumb thing about inspiring others. It had been hard to enough to say everything else. Even now, even here, there were limits to what I could share.

Bear's head made a loud *thunk* as it hit the wall.

"I hate him," he said.

"He's a genius."

"He's an asshole."

We sat there quietly. I could hear Bear breathing. I could hear myself breathing.

There was an uncovered mattress on the other side of the room, but Bear had pictures up on the wall above it. Most of them were of large groups, with Bear grinning from somewhere in the middle or toward the back. There was a photo of his soccer team, all of them lined up and in uniform. There were a few with him and two of the same guys, and some Polaroids of a yellow dog and black cat. There was one photo of him in the snow, standing next to someone wearing matching goggles that covered most of their face. I assumed it was a woman because of her long hair, which was escaping her knit beanie. It was probably his mom. They had the same nose.

Bear had nailed all of them to the wall, which I knew was against the rules. He reached out a hand and entwined his fingers with mine. I could feel his callus. The same one that I had.

"My dad was right about one thing," Bear said. "I do have a crush on you."

I felt warm and wobbly inside. It was much better than just feeling wobbly.

"He also thinks you need some help with girls," I said.

There was a long silence, and when I looked over at Bear, he had his eyes closed as if he was praying for guidance. The tips of his ears were very red.

"I am going to kill him," he said, and then opened one eye. "Is that why you're here? Because you feel sorry for me?"

"What? No," I said. "Look at you. I don't feel sorry for that at all." I gestured at his chest.

His ears got redder, and he gave me a grin that was half embarrassed, half pleased.

"I don't need help," he said.

I shook my head. "Nope."

"I just . . ." He looked at me. "You're just intimidating, okay?"

"Me?"

He shifted on the bed until he was facing me, his fingers still laced with mine.

"I made Josh tell me about your pitch," he said. "He said it was incredible."

I turned toward him. "It was," I said, even though I wasn't sure I believed it anymore.

Bear laughed. "See," he said. "You're probably the most intense person I've ever met. In a good way."

I squirmed a little, uncertain how to react. Bear's compliments made me feel vulnerable.

"You just know exactly what you want," he said.

Maybe that had been true a few hours ago. Now, I wasn't sure.

"And you're really talented." Bear gave my hand a squeeze.

This time, I was the one blushing. "Your dad doesn't agree," I said.

"You know why this internship exists?" he asked.

I shook my head.

"Because my dad wants me to come work at BB Gun Films," he said.

Our very first day here, Nick had accused Bear of asking his dad to include him in the internship. But even though Bear had confirmed it, everything he'd done since then illustrated nothing but a complete lack of interest in the program.

I shifted, tucking my legs up underneath me. "And you don't want to."

"I don't know," Bear said. "My dad and I, uh, we don't have a very good relationship. I'm sure you know that my mom got custody after they got divorced."

I nodded, shooting a quick glance toward the photo of him in snow goggles.

"My dad had visitation rights but he's a workaholic, so I barely saw him when I was a kid. All my memories of him when I was little were of this guy who cared more about getting all the credit for his movie than paying attention to his family." Bear shook his head. "He only started to show interest in me when I got older—and when he found out I could draw."

I was intensely curious about Bear's artistic skills. Besides the stick figure, I'd never seen anything that he'd done. He didn't have any drawings at all on the walls. But I knew it wasn't the time or the place to ask him to show me his sketchbook.

"Ever since then, he's been trying to get me to commit to working at BB Gun Films once I graduate. 'Think of the publicity.'" Bear did a passable imitation of his father's voice. "'The investors will go crazy for it!'"

I hated that I felt a twinge of jealousy. Even after everything Bryan had said to me, I knew that if he offered me a job at BB Gun Films, I would probably take it. I still wanted it. You couldn't erase a lifelong dream just like that.

"He basically created this internship as a way to test the waters," Bear said. "He doesn't care about the other short films—he just cares about mine."

I let all of this sink in. Even if what Bear was saying was true—Bryan had still chosen the other short films for a reason. He'd still *not* chosen me. But I didn't want to think about it anymore.

"What do *you* want?" I asked.

Bear shrugged. "I don't know. To be left alone long enough to figure out if I even want to work in animation."

"At all?"

"I know that no one in the program thinks I deserve this," he said. "And that's what it would be like if I took a job here—or even at another studio. I'll never be anyone other than Bryan Beckett's kid."

I didn't say anything, because it was true.

"I know I shouldn't complain," he said. "There are people, like, dying and I'm bitching about being an intern in my dad's billion-dollar company. The internship is bullshit," he said. "It means nothing."

"That's not true," I said. "Even if your father did this just to give you a chance, that doesn't mean it isn't an opportunity for the rest of us. That doesn't mean I want it any less."

We sat in silence. The conversation had gotten heavy, and it wasn't what I'd come here for. I wanted to escape. To forget.

"I was pretty sure I was going to hate everything about this internship," Bear said. "I knew someone would figure out who I was, I knew everyone would be weird about it, and I knew my dad would do something totally embarrassing."

I didn't bother to point out that he was right on all three counts.

"But I didn't know I'd meet you," he said.

My heart did a somersault. "You like me," I said.

He grinned. "I do."

"Cool," I said.

I kissed him. He kissed me. And I didn't have to think about anything else for a long time.

CHAPTER EIGHTEEN

I stayed in Bear's room the rest of the night. We kissed and talked. Not about the internship, not about animation, but about other things. We mostly kissed. And I developed a grudging respect for Shelley Cona, because distracting myself with a cute boy turned out to be exactly what I needed.

At least I wasn't going to have to work on Nick's project anymore. This time I would try—*really* try—to be a team player. Even if I never managed to impress Bryan, I wanted Sloane to be proud of me.

I took off my shoes before I got to my room—I didn't want to wake Sally. But when I opened the door, I found her sitting on her bed, wide awake, chewing furiously at her fingernails. She looked tired and scared and a little bit manic, which for Sally was saying a lot.

"Hayley, omigod!" She leapt off the bed and pinned my arms to my sides with her hug. "Are you okay? Where were you? Are you okay? I heard what happened yesterday—everyone's been talking, and then you didn't come back last night and you weren't answering my texts and I was going to call Gena, but I didn't want to get you in trouble but I was really scared. Are you okay?"

She released me, hands on my shoulders, peering at my face like she was reading tea leaves or something.

I felt horribly guilty. It hadn't even crossed my mind that she would notice I wasn't there, let alone that she would have worried this much. Pulling out my phone, I realized that I had a dozen text messages from her, each getting more and more frantic.

"Are you okay?" she asked again.

"I'm okay," I said.

She nodded and then hit me in the arm.

"Ow," I said.

She hit me once more and then wrapped her arms around me.

"I was so worried," she said, her voice slightly muffled by my shirt.

"I'm really sorry," I said. "I didn't even think. But I am okay."

We stood there for a while, her hugging me and me awkwardly patting her sides because she'd pinned my arms again and I could just barely move them.

When she finally pulled back she gave me a bracing nod. "You can't do that again, okay? You have to tell me where you are. You're my roommate. We're responsible for each other."

This was more than we'd said to each other since I'd blown up the only decent friendships I'd had in this internship.

"I'm sorry," I said. "I didn't think you wanted . . . I mean, we haven't really been speaking." I swallowed. "Which I know is my fault. I know I messed up. I'm *really* sorry."

It wasn't the first time I had apologized, but I hoped that this one would stick.

"You told me something in confidence and I just . . . I just totally betrayed you," I said.

Sally nodded. "It was pretty messed up," she said. "But *betrayed* is kind of over-the-top, don't you think? It makes this whole thing sound like some Real Housewives fight. I mean, I know I kind of let it get that way because I was mad and didn't want to talk to you, but by the time I stopped being mad, we weren't speaking at all and it was just awkward and weird and I didn't know how to stop it."

She squared her shoulders and looked at me. "You did a crummy thing," she said.

"I did," I said.

"And it won't happen again."

"It won't," I promised.

"Okay," she said.

We just stood there for a moment, looking at each other. I wasn't sure what I should do next. "Are . . . we friends again?" I asked tentatively.

Sally threw her arms around me once more. "Yes!" she said. "I hated not being friends. It was the worst."

A part of me—the part that had been tense ever since our fight—relaxed. I didn't want to be on my own anymore. It was too lonely and too hard. I'd missed Sally. I'd missed the other girls, too. Even though I was still texting and talking with Julie and Samantha, this was different. This was what I had lost out on by not being a team player, I reminded myself. I didn't want to make that mistake again.

"Were you up all night?" I asked.

Sally nodded. "I heard about what happened yesterday. Between you and Nick."

I sat down on my bed. I'd forgotten about that. For a few blissful hours, I had completely forgotten the whole reason I'd been called to Bryan's office in the first place. Everything good that had happened last night seemed to shift backward. My emotions felt layered like a multiplane image—one on top of the other—with the embarrassment of the Nick stuff returning to the forefront.

"Did you really throw his drawings at him and start screaming about how you were a genius, and everyone should listen to you?"

I looked at her, feeling a little queasy. "What?"

Sally frowned. "That's what Nick has been saying."

I could only imagine the kind of drawings he'd be doing of me now. With a bigger mouth and bigger hair. "You're kidding."

She shook her head.

"Ugh," I ran my hands over my face. "That is *not* what happened."

But everyone in the internship had probably heard Nick's version by now—mentors included. My stomach clenched. And who knew what *Bryan* had said about the whole thing? What he might have told the brain trust.

"I didn't believe it for a second," Sally said. "You didn't even yell, you know, *that* night. You were just kind of quiet and intense."

"I did yell at him, though," I said. "I might have even called him a fucking liar."

Sally's eyes were wide. "You didn't! You did!? Was he? Of course, he was. You're such a badass."

"No, I'm not." I buried my head in my palms. "I did it in front of Bryan."

Saying it out loud made the whole thing feel surreal. Like it had happened to someone else. I felt the bed shift as Sally sat down next to me.

"Holy. Shit."

"Exactly," I said, my voice muffled.

I could practically hear all the questions circulating in Sally's head, but thankfully she didn't ask any of them, rubbing my back gently instead.

"What . . . what's going to happen to you?"

"I didn't get kicked out of the program," I said, leaning back. "But I did get reassigned."

"Reassigned?"

"I'm on Bear's team now. With you." I hadn't planned to say anything else, but when I said his name, my face got hot and I had a feeling I was flushed from my hairline to my chin.

"You are? That's great! It's going to be so much fun to work together. . . ." Sally's excitement slowly tapered off. "You're really red. Omigod, are you blushing?"

"No," I said. Too quickly.

"Hayley," Sally said. I was looking everywhere but at her.

"I should probably get dressed," I said.

"Where were you last night?" Sally asked.

There was a knowing tone in her voice, and I was a terrible liar.

"Maybe I was with Bear," I said as quickly as possible, making it sound like "MayzebemumbleImumblebear."

There was a long silence, and when I dared to look over at Sally, I found that she was staring at me, her mouth wide open.

"*No*," she said.

"Yes," I said, feeling so, so embarrassed. I was extremely glad that I'd put my shirt on right side out before I left Bear's room. After I had taken it off again.

"No!" Sally said.

"Yes," I said.

"With Bear?"

I nodded.

She let out a shriek that probably woke everyone in the dorms. "Hayley Saffitz!" Sally grabbed my hands. "You tell me *everything*."

I did, and by the time I was done, I was blushing so hard I was sweating and Sally had tucked her hands under her chin and was looking at me like she was the human version of the heart-eyes emoji.

"Oh. My. God," Sally said, and I could practically see those hearts floating up into the air around her and popping in a sparkly, fireworks fashion. "How was it? Was it great? Was *he* great? I bet he's a great kisser. Is he?"

"Yes," I said. "Yes, he is."

Sally squealed, hands clasped to her chest. "He's definitely the cutest guy in the program," she said. "He smells nice and doesn't say much."

"I thought he hated me," I said.

Sally hit me on the arm again. "You did not," she said.

"Ow," I said. "Yes, I did."

She shook her head, looking at me in an endearing way, like I was really dumb but couldn't help it.

"He's been into you since the beginning," Sally said. "It's so obvious. Everyone knows. I mean, everyone who's paying attention. So, probably just me and the other girls. But like, so obvious. You didn't know?"

I shook my head.

"Wait. If you didn't know, then how did last night happen?" Sally asked.

I wasn't sure if I wanted to get into the whole post-Nick, getting-sent-to-Bryan's-office, slow-and-meticulous-destructionof-my-dreams part of the story. The Bear-kissing stuff was much more fun.

Thankfully Sally's alarm went off. "Shit!" she said. "We have to get dressed. You're going to have to tell me everything else later. This is the most exciting thing to happen all summer. Well, besides you yelling at Nick."

She yawned, and then I yawned. When I did, Sally gave me a knowing look that had me blushing again.

"Stop it," I said.

She skipped off to the bathroom, leaving me alone and thinking that while the last twenty-four hours had begun in a spectacularly awful way, it had redeemed itself in the end.

That feeling changed the minute Sally and I left the dorms. It was clear that the story Nick had been telling people had spread rapidly. Everyone on the shuttle kept eyeing me with caution and suspicion like I might start screaming and throwing things.

"Ignore them," Sally said, shooting death glares at anyone that was staring openly. "The only people who would actually believe what Nick said are either dumb or jealous. Or both. Totally not worth your time."

Unfortunately, it seemed like a large majority of the intern group wasn't going to be worth my time.

When we arrived at the studio, there was a large crowd in the lobby. I spotted Nick, but he did his best to avoid my gaze. I wasn't that surprised, but I was disappointed. When this whole program started, I'd thought of him as a friend. A kindred spirit. It still hurt to know that he was anything but.

The group gathered was mostly interns, but I saw a few mentors standing there as well.

"Hayley!" Sloane appeared, looking concerned. "What happened?"

She had my bag. The one I'd left in the conference room yesterday.

"Zoe brought it to me," Sloane said. "Are you all right?"

Shame gathered in the pit of my stomach. I hadn't told her what had happened either—I'd just left the studio without a word. She must have been as worried as Sally had been.

"I'm okay," I said, feeling selfish and guilty. I pressed my bag to my chest.

"Bryan's called a meeting," Sloane said.

"What?"

She nodded. "We all got an e-mail this morning telling everyone involved in the program—interns and mentors—to gather in the lobby."

Oh no. Oh *no*. I felt dizzy. Maybe I hadn't been appreciative or contrite enough during my meeting with Bryan. Maybe he wasn't going to switch me to Bear's team. Maybe he was just going to toss me out of the program—and make an example of me in front of everyone.

"Come on." Gena appeared at the front of the crowd. "We're in the theater today."

"I heard about what happened with you and Nick," Sloane said, pulling me aside as everyone began heading out of the lobby.

"From who?" I could only imagine how many versions of the story were floating around.

"From Zoe," Sloane said.

I relaxed a little. At least Zoe had actually witnessed what had happened, even if she didn't know all the details.

"She said you were very upset. That you yelled at Nick in front of Bryan and that you were called to his office."

I hung my head. "Yeah."

"We should talk about it," Sloane said. "After the meeting, okay?"

I didn't want to. Sloane had told me that animation was all about collaboration. It wasn't about screaming at your director, even if he had stolen your ideas. I could have handled myself better, and I didn't.

As we headed to the theater, I heard whispers all around me.

"What do you think this meeting is about?"

"I don't know, but I bet it has to do with what happened yesterday."

"Did you hear that she broke an easel?"

"I heard that she tried to rip up Nick's drawings."

I curled my shoulders forward, wishing that I wasn't so tall, wishing I wasn't so easy to spot in a crowd. It felt like everyone's eyes were focused on me. I just wanted all this to be over.

"Hey." Bear appeared out of nowhere. I was beyond relieved to see him, and a part of me wished we were back in his room, where the only thing I had cared about was touching his chest and kissing him.

"Hey." I kept my head down.

"Heard that you're being switched to my team," he said. He seemed completely oblivious to all the chatter around us.

"Is that all you've heard?" I asked.

He gave me a puzzled look. "I mean, I also heard that you punched Nick in the face, but I'm pretty sure he deserved it."

Despite myself, I laughed. Bear grinned.

"It's going to be fine." He patted me on the shoulder before disappearing back into the crowd.

Sloane caught my gaze, one eyebrow lifted. "Hmm," she said, but didn't pry any further.

We moved into the theater, and the general warmth and butterflies that I'd gotten being near Bear shifted back to my previous stomach-clench of shame and embarrassment. The abrupt changes in mood were giving me a headache. This was the most emotionally complicated twenty-four hours of my life.

I sat with Sloane on one side of me, Sally on the other. It was so similar to our first day. All of us sitting there, unsure what to expect, not knowing who would emerge from behind the curtain. This time, instead of Josh, it *was* Bryan.

"Good morning," he said.

People shifted in their seats as they echoed his greeting. I didn't say anything.

"I'm sure most of you are wondering why I called this impromptu meeting," he said. He had his hands in his pockets and was wearing a pair of gleaming white sneakers. "I just wanted to take a chance to commend all of you. This program was a brainchild of mine, but I wasn't quite sure how it was going to work until it actually began. I want you all to give yourself a round of applause for exceeding my expectations on how smoothly this internship is going so far."

We all obliged. When it was silent again, Bryan rubbed his chin thoughtfully.

"Of course, with every new venture, there are the inevitable wrinkles."

I was certain that Bryan was referring to me. I also knew that most people in the audience were aware that he was referring to me. I imagined myself as a literal wrinkle in Bryan's big book of expectations, just lying there, crinkling the smooth paper around me.

"I thought it would behoove all of us to take a moment to discuss the purpose of this internship—and the heart of animation in general. Because believe it or not, they are one and the same."

I saw a few people around me taking out their notebooks, pencils poised above blank pages. A week ago, I would have done the same.

"Here at BB Gun Films, we're a family," Bryan said. "Even though we aren't working on the same movies at the same time, we're all working toward a shared goal. We're here to make art. We're here to make something special—something that will inspire an entire generation of thinkers and dreamers." He gestured out toward the audience. "Just as our previous films have inspired you."

I glanced over at Sloane, who was staring straight ahead. Her face was impassive.

"It's important to remember that," Bryan said. "It's important to remember that we're all part of a larger process—that no matter our role in it—each of us are valuable to the development of everything we make."

He looked out into the crowd, and I stared at my feet. For once in my life, I didn't want Bryan to notice me. Didn't want him to see me.

"We're a team," he said. "We have to work together. Animation isn't a place for self-importance. It isn't about the individual. It's about the group. If you're worried about getting credit, you're worrying about the wrong thing. Worry about what you're creating—what you're putting out into the world. Worry about the collective accomplishment."

If yesterday's lecture hadn't made it clear enough, Bryan was telling me—telling everyone—that all that mattered was the final product.

"Real artists make art for art's sake," he said. "They don't do it to satisfy their wallets or their egos. They do it to satisfy this." He put his fist against his heart. "Because that's where real art comes from."

CHAPTER NINETEEN

Stick around for a minute," Sloane said, as the lights came back on in the theater.

I did, sinking down even lower in my seat as Nick and his buddies came up the aisle. He noticed me but pretended not to.

"I'm glad Bryan cleared that up," he said loudly as he passed. "I wouldn't want to be on a team where people couldn't collaborate."

I curled my fingers around the arms of my chair.

"I feel like my job as director is to make sure the best movie gets made, not cater to individual egos," he said. "No one likes a diva."

The other guys laughed. I stared down at the floor.

Finally, the theater emptied out and it was just me and Sloane.

"Do you want to talk about what happened yesterday?" she asked.

I shook my head.

"Hayley, you know you can talk to me, right?"

I released my grip on the armrests. "It's fine," I said. "I overreacted, and I wasn't being a team player. I'll do better."

Sloane opened her mouth, and then closed it again. I felt terrible. My behavior was a reflection on her. The last thing I wanted was for Bryan—or anyone at BB Gun Films—to think that Sloane was a bad mentor. I needed to do better. If not for myself, then for her.

"They told me you'd be working with Bear now," Sloane said.

"Yeah," I said.

"Maybe that will be a better fit," Sloane said.

"I think so." I turned toward her. "This won't happen again, Sloane. I promise."

She patted my arm. "I know it won't," she said.

Even though I was disappointed that I wouldn't be working with Zoe anymore, everyone else on Bear's team seemed nice. We did some introductions and I finally got to see exactly what Bear had pitched to his father.

It wasn't nearly as boring as Nick's *Jack and the Beanstalk* story was, but it was almost as chaotic in terms of plot and concept. Still, there was potential. This time, I did my best to swallow my concerns—knowing that if I wasn't careful, my jealousy would get the better of me again.

At least I got to see Bear's artwork for the first time.

"Wow," I said.

We were huddled around his sketchbook, the rest of the story team working on individual sequences. Bear's project had enough of a through line that they could assign out sections, even though they still needed help tying them together. Already my brain had started spinning, thinking of ways to make the jumble of ideas work.

"Yeah?" He was sitting close to me, his knee pressed against mine. I was a little self-conscious that people would notice, but Bear didn't seem to mind. Or care.

"These are really good," I said.

They *were* good. He might not have put together the most comprehensive pitch, but his work was incredible. I looked at it and *felt* something. Felt a sense of wonder at what could be accomplished with paper and pencil. It was a good feeling.

His work was simple, but effective. He didn't use a lot of color, or go over his final drawings with smoother line, but it didn't matter. It was still evocative. They were rough sketches, most drawn in charcoal. There were often smudges on the edge of the page. With just a few lines he was able to capture an emotion—a feeling. There was a tactical quality to them that I really loved.

"I'm glad you like them," Bear said.

I noticed there were quite a lot of drawings of fish and anemones and seals and other marine life.

"I like going to the Long Beach Aquarium," Bear said when I lingered on a page full of sleek, twisting otters. "Plenty of inspiration there."

There were also lots of sketches of mountain faces—craggy peaks and jagged walls. There were people in some of them, climbing those rocks with bare hands, their flexing, tensing back muscles captured in Bear's quick-and-dirty style.

Between this and soccer, it was clear where he had gotten *his* muscles from. Bear was wearing his usual snug T-shirt today, and I couldn't resist glancing over to check out his biceps. His very, very nice biceps.

He flexed. I blushed.

"You should come with me sometime," he said. "It's fun."

"I don't think I'd describe a possible plummet to my death as *fun*."

"It's totally safe." His fingertips traced my knuckles. "You really clear your head when you're up there. All you can focus on are the rocks and your path upward." He looked at me. "And I'd never let you fall."

I got goose bumps, but the nice, tingly kind.

"These are great." I turned my attention back to the drawings. "Very visceral."

"That's the word my mom used too."

I thought of the photo of the two of them in ski goggles. It seemed like his mom was just as outdoorsy and athletic as Bear was. I tried to imagine Bryan hitting the slopes or climbing a rock face, but I couldn't picture him anywhere that wasn't BB Gun Films.

"Well, your mom has a good eye," I said. "And vocabulary."

"I think she'd agree."

I flipped to the beginning of his sketchbook and began to look through his drawings again. He really hadn't done much preparation for his pitch, and it was clear why it had been untitled when it was announced. It was more a collection of feelings than a specific story.

"What if we didn't have a plot?" I asked, an idea coming to me.

"What do you mean?"

"What if it's more of an emotional piece, rather than an intellectual one."

I turned to where he'd drawn a girl looking out the window. It was mostly dark lines and smeared swaths of charcoal, but because of that it was the negative space that stood out. The pale line of her neck, the curve of her ear.

"You could do something like *Fantasia*," I said. "Pick some music—three or four songs that fit the ideas you already have—and have your animators work to that."

Bear looked at me. "That's brilliant," he said.

"Is it? It's just an idea."

"A great one," he said. "I would have never thought of it. You're—you're very inspiring."

My smile faltered.

That's what Bryan had told me my strength was. Maybe he was right. Maybe what I was good at was encouraging *other* people to do their best work. I felt slightly nauseous at the thought.

"What is it?" Bear asked.

"Nothing." I turned back to his sketches. "Why don't you make a list of songs, and we can go from there."

"Why don't you come over tonight, and we can make a list together?" he asked.

Thankfully he did it quietly enough that no one heard. And gave me a grin that made my heart do a little flip.

"I'll think about it," I said.

I didn't need to think about it all. I definitely planned on going to his room tonight.

"Oh, I see," he said, and poked me with the eraser end of his pencil. "Playing hard-to-get."

"Shut up," I said, doing a bad job hiding my smile. "We have work to do."

"This could work for the second sequence," I told Bear as we lay on his bed hours later.

We were on our backs, barely fitting side by side. His leg was dangling off the edge of the mattress, while my hip was pressed up against the wall.

"You know, I wasn't actually thinking we'd listen to music when I asked you to come to my room," he said.

"I know," I said. "But this is a good song option."

I'd fully intended to go to Bear's room to make out with him, but during dinner, I'd come up with several ideas for songs, and I wanted to play them for him before I forgot.

I looked up at the pictures he had above his bed. There were a few more of friends, but it was mostly photos of his pets—a yellow mutt with a round ruff of a neck and a small black cat that seemed to enjoy sleeping near or on top of the dog. I'd always wanted a pet, but my parents said the house was too small.

"What are their names?" I pointed up at a photo of the two of them sleeping with their heads pressed together.

"Howl and Calcifer."

I turned my head toward him. "You really do love *Howl's Moving Castle*," I said.

He shrugged. "I said it was my favorite movie."

"*Spirited Away* is better," I said.

He lifted an eyebrow.

"I'm just saying."

"Uh-huh," he said, before shifting up onto his side. "Hey."

I looked up at him. He was extremely cute. "Hey."

He lowered his lips to mine, his hand on my hip. I reached up, threading my hands through his hair. Even though I'd been eager to share my music ideas with Bear, I was definitely more interested in doing other things now.

I liked kissing him. Liked touching him.

It made everything else fade away. I could focus on the little things—the way his thumb was stroking my stomach, the way his tongue felt against that spot behind my ear, the way his feet tangled up with mine at the foot of the bed.

His hand moved upward, where he dragged his fingers along the line of my chin. It felt really good. Covering his hand with mine, I directed him downward to the buttons of my shirt. He didn't need much more encouragement, undoing one at a time. So. Very. Slowly.

By the time my shirt was completely unbuttoned and pulled free of my pants, I was eager to go further. It would be my first time going this far, but I wanted this. And I trusted Bear.

How could I not? He'd named his dog *Howl*.

"Hayley." His voice was hot in my ear. "Can I ask you something?"

"Uh-huh," I said, hoping that he was going to ask if he could take off my bra.

The answer was definitely yes.

He leaned back, his eyes meeting mine. "Would you do your pitch for me?" he asked.

I stared at him. "What?"

He propped himself up on his elbow. "Your pitch," he said. "The one you did for my dad and the brain trust. Would you do it for me?"

I sat up. "You want me to do that *now*?" I gestured toward my completely open shirt. "Really?"

His ears got red. "I'm not in any rush when it comes to—" He mimicked my gesture. "That."

It was both sweet and a little disappointing.

But my disappointment faded quickly, because there was a part of me that kind of *wanted* to do my pitch for him. To hear what he thought of it. I knew he wasn't his father—not even close—but maybe there was some Beckett gene in there that would give me insight into why Bryan hadn't liked my project. Because I had a hard time believing that a company that made movies with talking animals and forest hags couldn't suspend their disbelief long enough to accept a story with a golem in it. Among other things.

"You really want to hear my pitch?" I asked.

"Do you remember it?"

"Of course I remember it," I said.

He smiled.

Maybe he could give me his honest opinion. Tell me if I was crazy for thinking it was as good as it was. Tell me that yeah, his dad was right, I just didn't have the kind of talent required for directors. I didn't want to hear that, but I felt like I needed to.

"I'll do my pitch under one condition," I said.

"Okay."

"You have to take your shirt off," I said.

Bear didn't even hesitate, sitting up, reaching back, and pulling it over his head in one smooth movement. He tossed it at me. Climbing over him, I held his shirt hostage as I buttoned up my own.

"Hey," Bear said.

I held up a hand. "I'm a professional, okay?"

He faced me, hands on his knees. He had such a good chest.

But I wasn't going to let it distract me.

I tucked in my shirt and closed my eyes. The pitch was there—I'd done it so many times that I knew once I got started, it would all flow out of me. I just had to remember the first sentence. I opened my eyes.

"This is a story about a girl. And a golem." It wasn't quite the same without my drawings there, but I pretended that they were, gesturing toward an imaginary easel, pretending the foam board was actually sitting there.

"And when Miriam reaches out her hand to the golem, she discovers that he has returned to his original form—his journey over, just as hers is beginning," I said.

I was still holding Bear's shirt in my hand. And just because the whole thing was already a little ridiculous, I bowed. When I lifted my head, I found that Bear was just sitting there, staring at me.

Immediately my silly mood vanished. He hadn't liked it. He'd hated it. He'd seen exactly why his father hadn't given me the director position and now he was second-guessing even wanting to be with me right now. I threw his shirt at him. It hit him in the face.

"Say something."

"Shit, Saffitz." Bear wadded his shirt into a ball. "That was amazing."

"What?"

He reached out a hand and pulled me toward him until I was standing between his legs. He looked up at me, palms on my hips.

"That was amazing," he said.

I put my hands in his hair. It was soft.

"You're just saying that."

I felt—and saw—him shake his head.

"That—" He put his head against my stomach before lifting it again. "That puts my pitch to shame. I mean, I'm actually super embarrassed by what *I* did."

"Do I want to know?" I asked.

"I don't think so," he said. "If I were you, it would really piss me off."

I moved out of his grasp and sat back on the bed next to him. He was staring at the other side of the room.

"My dad is such an idiot," he said.

"He just has different standards, I guess."

He snorted, putting his head down. "He's an idiot. Or an asshole. No, he's both."

I didn't know how to feel. I was relieved that Bear had liked my pitch—it made me feel less crazy, less alone. But it still didn't make a difference. If anything, it made what I was doing—what Bryan had told me to do, what he told me I was good for—even more painful.

I was torn between anger at not getting something I felt I deserved and guilt for feeling like I *deserved* anything. I didn't know what to do with any of it.

"I should just make my own short," I said.

Bear's head jerked upward. "Yeah, yeah, you should," he said.

"I was joking," I said.

But maybe I wasn't?

Was it even possible? Bryan had effectively taken away my only chance to distinguish myself from the rest of the interns, but what if I made my own opportunity? The thought was selfish, arrogant, and deeply, deeply tempting.

Bear was looking at me. I could tell he wanted to talk more about this—I got the sense that he would be on board with anything that might piss his dad off—but my brain hurt. My heart did, too. Just that little bit of hope felt like pressing on a healing bruise. It ached. I didn't want to talk about it. I didn't want to think about it. I didn't want to think about anything.

"You know," I said, "I came here to listen to music."

I didn't want to listen to music.

"Yeah?"

"Yeah." I reached back to pull my hair out of its bun.

"You want to listen to some music?" Bear asked.

His lips were against mine.

"I liked that song that you were playing before," I said.

"Mmm?" His hands were in my hair. "Which one?"

"The slow one," I said.

I felt him smile. "The slow one. With the drums?" He kissed me between words.

"Uh-huh." I curled my fingers around his shoulders. "I think they went 'bom, bom, bom.'"

He leaned back on the bed, pulling me with him.

"Bom, bom, bom," he said.

CHAPTER TWENTY

Our next lunch lecture was with the head of animation—a guy named Hal Whitley. I knew his work—most people did. He was a thirty-year animation veteran who'd surprised everyone in the industry by joining BB Gun Films when it was just getting started. Hiring him had been a huge coup for Bryan. He greeted Bear emphatically with a loud slap on the back.

"My man," he said once we'd all settled at the conference table.

Hal was short with a ring of gray, fluffy hair circling his crown. Like a lot of the men in the building, he wore cargo shorts and a T-shirt. I could see the hole that was fraying under his armpit. He sat with his feet up, arms crossed, shaking his head at Bear as if he couldn't believe he was there.

"I can't believe you're here."

Bear rubbed the back of his neck. He seemed to do that when he was embarrassed. I imagined all of this was a lot for him—most of the people at the studio had known him since he was a little kid. They all had memories and knowledge of him from various different times in his life. Some probably not very flattering.

"I did the scene where Bear goes through the window," Hal said. "You know the one."

Of course, we all knew it. In it, a terrified Bear is trying to escape the government agent's facility where he's being experimented on. He has to maneuver himself onto a filing cabinet and out a tiny window, all while clad in a flimsy hospital gown completely open in the back.

"Bet you're glad we didn't rotoscope it." Hal smacked Bear's hand as he laughed.

Bear pulled his arm away.

Rotoscoping was a controversial animation technique used to save time and money when most companies still made handdrawn films. Instead of animating from scratch, artists were given live-action footage which they then traced. Bryan Beckett had decried the form as "lazy man's animation."

Under the table, I gave Bear's knee a squeeze. He didn't look at me, but he smiled down at his notebook and put his hand over mine, the gesture hidden from view.

"Animation." Hal stood. "Or as I like to call it, the true heart of any animated feature." He laughed. "The other departments hate it when I say that."

"My mom calls them the jocks of the industry," Bear said.

I was the only one who heard. Hal was still talking.

"Now, I'm a little old-school, so you'll have to forgive me if I say something that's not too 'PC,'" he emphasized with finger quotes. "After all, I can still remember when animation focused more on the work instead of *who* did the work."

He looked at me.

"We had a pretty good system back in the day," he said. "When most things were drawn by hand, everyone got to play to their strengths."

A Boy Named Bear and BB Gun Films's second movie, *The*

Grand Adventures of the Frog King, were the only ones that had been done primarily by hand. Though they still occasionally did hand-drawn sequences, most everything was CG now.

Our shorts, however, didn't have the time or the budget to build CG models, so we were doing everything the old-school way. The expectation, of course, was that our final product wouldn't have the same polish as a BB Gun film, but they were expected to look finished. In the case of Bear's film, that meant rough-style animation.

Hal was still talking. "It worked out well that way—the guys would be in charge of really shaping how a character moved—how they interacted with the world. Then the ladies would come and do the kind of work they're good at—finalizing lines and cleaning everything up."

It was true that most of the best clean-up artists in the business had been women.

"You can tell by looking at a drawing whether a guy or a gal drew it," Hal said. "Men and women just have different styles, no matter what the PC police wants to tell you."

I stared at Hal, not taking notes. I knew how the work had usually been divided up in the "good old days," but I'd thought that things had changed. Apparently, here in Hal's world, he seemed to be doing his best to keep those old-fashioned dreams alive.

Maybe he wasn't the only one.

Was that part of the reason that none of the other girls in the internship had gotten to be the heads of any departments? Between Hal's soliloquy and Bryan's comment about me being a "diversity hire," it didn't seem like a coincidence. I also knew Sally had been doing the bulk of clean-up for our short, as assigned by our head of animation, even though she had a better grasp of movement and timing than he did. But there wasn't anything I could do about it.

Could I?

The thought of doing my own short film returned, like a little boat bobbing on the surface of water. Maybe if I recruited the other girls in the program . . .

Unfortunately, only Sally was speaking to me at the moment. I wondered if the rest had heard the story about me and Nick and accepted it as true. I couldn't really blame them, given how I'd lashed out at Emily.

"Things change," Hal said. "Now that most everything is done with computers, newer artists don't have to rely on the same skill set—anyone can learn how to animate a puppet." He shrugged, clearly missing the times when women were relegated to a different department, officially or not.

"And I'm not saying that the girls here can't pull their weight. When it comes to those emotional moments—those real tear-jerkers—well, the ladies in our department do a great job with them." He put his hand on his chest. "They just have a knack for the sappy stuff."

This time it was Bear squeezing *my* knee.

"Instead of just talking about the process of animation," Hal said, "why don't I show you? The real way. Follow me."

His office was at the other end of the hall. Leaving the remainder of our lunches in the conference room, we obediently followed. I saw Cole—the PA who was working on the back-end part of Nick's film—sitting at his desk nearby.

"Hey, Cole." I waved at him. He ignored me.

It seemed like his nickname—the "Robot"—was even more fitting than I had previously assumed. Or I was persona non grata with him and Nick's entire team after what had happened in front of Bryan.

"Come in, come in," Hal said.

But I stayed in the doorway. His office—which was twice the size of Sloane's—was intense. There was a giant ram's head directly above his desk, as well as several sets of antlers on the walls and a literal bearskin rug on the floor.

The other interns didn't seem to mind, crowding behind Hal as he took a seat at an old-school animation desk. It was massive, with an illuminated circle in the middle where Hal could lay several sheets of animation paper on top of each other, flipping back and forth between them as he drew. They were held in place by pegs, and the whole thing could be rotated and adjusted.

Bear stood with me in the doorway. "The rug's fake," he said.

"The rest?" I asked.

He shook his head. "If you can believe it, it used to be worse." I couldn't.

"The whole wall used to be covered with all sorts of animal heads," Bear said. "There were PAs who refused to come in."

"I don't blame them," I said.

Hal, who had pulled several sheets of paper out of the shelves lining either side of the desk, seemed to notice that we were lingering in the doorway.

"Oh, come on," he said. "Don't be a coward. Nothing in here will bite you."

Now that I knew the rug was fake, I tentatively moved farther into the room. I also didn't like being called a coward.

Bear stayed in the doorway, arms crossed. "What happened to the rest of the menagerie?"

Hal waved a hand. "You know what happened, Bear," he said. "Word came down from on high—the queen herself told me there needed to be a limit to my artistic expression."

The queen? I wondered if Hal was talking about Madeline Bailey, the producer we'd be meeting with in a few weeks.

"How PC of her," Bear said.

"Too true," Hal said, completely missing the irony in Bear's voice. "All right, gather round, everyone, and I'll show you how to make a character come alive."

Even though I wasn't directing Bear's short, even though I wasn't even the head of story for it, I found that I enjoyed working on his team. Working with him. He was interested in what his story crew had to say, though most of them seemed too intimidated to do anything other than agree with him.

I didn't do that. He asked for suggestions and I gave them. And he listened. He didn't always agree with me, but he listened. The whole thing actually felt collaborative, unlike my brief experience with Nick. Now that we'd settled on a clear vision for the short—four songs, thematically connected—all of us were working hard.

But not hard enough to keep thoughts of directing my own short out of my head. Ever since I'd said it out loud, the idea had wedged itself into my brain like a splinter I couldn't stop prodding.

"What if each sequence had a different style?" I asked.

We were all sitting outside of the cafeteria, our work spread out across three tables we'd pushed together. Whenever possible, Bear preferred to work outside.

At first, I found it distracting, but I was starting to appreciate it. There was a lot of inspiration to be found beyond the walls of the studio. Even if I still hadn't seen the ducks.

We'd reunited with the rest of the team after the illuminating lecture with Hal. Despite his penchant for rhapsodizing about the golden, gender-segregated days of animation, he was still extremely talented and had shown us, step-by-step, how he approached new scenes. Annoyingly, I'd learned a lot from his lecture.

"Every moment with a character is an opportunity to reveal something new about them," he'd said. "It can be as simple as the way they hold a pencil—or as complicated as the way they process anger."

"A different style?" Bear had his sketchbook open. He liked to draw while we brainstormed.

"The songs are all thematic, right?" I asked. "There's a happy song, a sad song, an angry song, and an inspiring song."

Bear was making a cross hatch of lines. I'd discovered that, with his work, you'd never know what he was drawing until he was done. It all seemed to unfold the moment he lifted his pencil from the paper.

It was completely different from how I worked—I liked to imagine what I wanted, crystallizing it in my brain before I even put my pencil to the page. I wondered what it would be like to work the way Bear did.

"I hadn't really thought of them like that," he said. "But yeah, that makes sense."

"What if the songs are reflections of one person?" I said. "All these things that they're feeling—that's the connection between them; this one person experiencing them."

Bear nodded, his pencil creating large half-circles in the corner of the page. My brain was spinning—like a spider, building a vast web from a single thread.

"And each of the sequences will have a style that reflects that emotion," I said. "Not only will they feel different, they'll look different, too."

"I like it." Bear drew what looked like a swooping *M* in the middle of the page. "Except, won't that undo some of the work the animators have already been doing?"

I bit the inside of my cheek. "It would," I said. "Not too much, though. A few days."

Bear lifted an eyebrow. We both knew that even a few days were a substantial amount of time, especially given the short time line of the project itself.

"We could hold a meeting and ask what they think," I said. "We could vote on it. Present them with the option to do their sequence in the style of their choosing, or let them continue to do it in the same style we've been working in."

"Animation by democracy." Bear let out a whistle. "My father would hate that."

"Does that mean you love it?" I asked.

He grinned. "Absolutely."

The sketch was now starting to take shape. I could see that the *M* was the top of a mouth, now that Bear had drawn a smudgy eye.

"Can I ask you a question?"

"Shoot," he said, adding an arched eyebrow to the page.

"How did you decide who would be your department heads?" I asked.

It had been something I'd wondered about, especially after seeing the quality of work demonstrated by the animators in our short. Not only was Sally the best artist among them, but she also was extremely good at taking direction—easily adapting her style to fit the project. Bear could tell her exactly what he wanted, and she'd deliver. Our current head of animation seemed to only half listen to Bear's comments, coming back with sloppy, unfinished, incorrect work that usually needed another round of notes.

Bear sketched out another eye.

"I didn't," he said.

"Really?"

When Karl had been chosen as Nick's head of story, I had assumed that the director of each project had assigned the other roles as well.

"My dad and the brain trust chose all that," Bear said. "I had nothing to do with it."

A girl was taking shape on Bear's page. She was lying on her back, hair spread out around her in big, stylistic curls. It reminded me a little bit of Ariel after she'd sunk down to the ocean floor at the end of "Part of Your World."

"Huh," I said.

That all but confirmed my suspicion that Bryan's claim that "talent was the only thing that mattered" was at best insincere, and at worst, a complete lie. I'd thought that the gender bias in animation had existed in the past—that we had moved beyond it. Apparently, I'd been naive. Eagerly accepting Bryan's word as gospel.

I rubbed my forehead. I didn't know what to believe anymore. *Who* to believe.

"Here." Bear turned and pushed the sketchbook over to me. "What do you think?"

I looked at it and saw . . . myself.

He'd captured the round curve of my cheek, the bump on the bridge of my nose, the freckle on the side of it. I looked focused. Determined. It was nothing like the drawing Nick had done of me.

"She looks like trouble," I told him.

He grinned. "Oh, she definitely is," he said.

CHAPTER TWENTY-ONE

H ow do you feel about the decision?" I asked Sally over dinner on Friday.

Bear's entire team had met up yesterday to discuss
changing the design of some of the sequences. We'd voted,
and I'd been pleased, but surprised, when everyone agreed to scrap
the work we'd been doing so we could lean harder into a more
conceptual piece. Each animator had pitched their own ideas for
the sequences and Bear had picked the final four that afternoon.
I'd helped him choose, but he'd made the final decision. He was
still the director, after all.

I wasn't completely free of jealous feelings, but they were different from the ones I'd had around Nick. They weren't as jagged
or painful. More like a dull ache that I could mostly ignore. That
I had to ignore.

"I like it a lot," Sally said. "It's really different—a little unusual
but I think it's good. Really good. Such a cool concept—totally
unique."

Sally was now going to be leading one of the sequences. Her
ideas had been the best of the group, and she was going to do
extremely graphic, minimalistic animation for the "sad" song.

"I think it's going to be good," I said.

"Definitely," she said. "I already have tons of ideas that I can't wait to try out. It's going to be a lot of fun to animate."

"Speaking of, we met with Hal Whitley," I said.

She made a face, and I laughed. Her group had met with him last week.

"Did he tell you how nice it is to have women around so they can animate all the touchy-feely stuff?" she asked. "All those emotions are just, like, too much for someone as tough and masculine and manly for him to handle. He might actually have to *feel* things if he drew them, you know? He might develop empathy."

"You must have felt really good knowing that as long as movies have feelings in them, you'll have career stability," I said.

"I was truly relieved," Sally said. "You know I just live to animate the stuff men don't want to. It's my dream, really."

"You don't think he can actually tell from a drawing who drew it, right?" I asked.

It seemed ridiculous, but Hal had said it with such confidence.

"I don't know," Sally said. "I mean, I have had people tell me that I draw like a guy. I think it was supposed to be a compliment."

No one had ever assigned a gender to my drawing style. At least, not out loud.

Sally shivered. "His office is so creepy."

"The rug is fake," I said. "And apparently it used to be way worse."

"Ugh," she said. "I can't even imagine. How did you know that the rug was fake?"

"Bear told me," I said.

Sally lit up. "Oh, *Bear* told you," she teased.

I smacked her hand.

"Things are good with you guys?" Sally asked. "You know I

want to ask all the questions, but I will respect your privacy. Unless you want to tell me everything, and in that case, I am definitely interested in listening."

"Things are good," I said. "Though, he keeps threatening to take me rock climbing. Or snowboarding."

Sally laughed as I wrinkled my nose. "Oh no, outdoor things."

"I like being outdoors," I said.

Sally gave me a look.

"It's outdoor *athletic* things that I don't like."

"Mm-hmm."

I tossed my napkin at her, glad to be spending time together. Since I spent a lot of my evenings with Bear, I didn't see Sally as often.

We were taking the shuttle together again but talking about Bear wasn't something I wanted to do when we were surrounded by prying eyes and ears. She was the only one who knew about us. I hadn't even told Samantha or Julie. I knew they'd be excited to know, but telling them felt like it would result in a much bigger conversation that none of us seemed to have time for.

And there was no way I was going to tell my parents or Zach. My parents would want to know everything about him, and Zach would threaten to send him embarrassing bare-butt pictures from when we were kids. He'd also probably send him the list of obscure, random—possibly made-up—disorders that Zach was certain I had.

I was 99 percent sure there was no such thing as reverse brain spatial syndrome.

And I really didn't want any of the other interns to know. Gossip traveled fast, like with the incident between me and Nick. But the truth was usually mixed up with a lot of falsehoods, and I didn't care to contribute to either. I had the sense that some people suspected there was something going on between me and Bear, but we'd done our best to avoid confirming it.

"They're going to figure it out," Bear had said the other night. "We barely spoke to each other for the first few weeks and now we're always together."

"That's not true," I'd said. "Besides, we're working on a team. We spend the appropriate amount of time together."

I knew he was right—I just didn't want to deal with it. Not yet. Until then, though, it was nice to have Sally to talk to.

"The short is looking a lot better," Sally said. "It feels like it has momentum, you know? There's a real purpose to what we're doing now. Even though it's all different things, all these different styles, it feels more cohesive."

"I'm really looking forward to seeing your stuff," I said. "You deserve this opportunity."

"Thanks," she said. "It's nice that we're getting free rein."

"Do you like the idea?" I asked.

"About having four unique sequences?" She speared her penne. "Yeah, it's really cool. Definitely better than what we originally started with. No offense."

"It wasn't my idea."

Sally laughed. "Bear definitely seems more focused now. More inspired."

"He just wasn't very motivated before."

I knew he was still conflicted about his place in the internship—in the world of animation in general. We had that in common. And now that we were spending more time together,

I saw firsthand how he was treated. He was right about no one thinking he deserved to be there. I'd been guilty of that, but seeing his work, I knew he had talent. But he'd definitely been given opportunities that he didn't want and hadn't worked for. I should have felt jealous, and I did, but mostly I felt sad about it.

It was complicated.

"Lucky we have you to motivate him," Sally said. "He seems a lot happier to be working on the project, too."

I knew she was being playful, but her words just reminded me of what Bryan had said. Every day it seemed like I returned to this internal battle—did I believe what Bryan said about me, or did I think I was capable of something more? And if I did—what was I going to do about it?

I imagined myself being tugged in two different directions— by the screaming version of myself that Nick had drawn, and a mini-size Bryan. Would I be giving up and giving in if I listened to Bryan? Or was it arrogant and self-centered to believe that I deserved more?

The internship was speeding by. Pretty soon, I wouldn't have to make a decision—the clock would make it for me.

"Ugh." Sally looked behind me. "Your least favorite person. Twelve o'clock."

I didn't need to turn around to know who she was talking about.

"Sally," Nick said, walking up to our table. "Hayley."

"What do you want?" I asked.

We hadn't really spoken since I'd been taken off his team, but I didn't think he was coming over here to apologize for stealing my ideas. The thought that we had been friends before—that I'd believed we were the same—made me clench my teeth.

"Oh, nothing." Nick picked up our saltshaker. "Just wanted to see how you were doing with your new director. Have you accused him of being a liar yet?"

"He hasn't given me a reason to," I said.

Nick pursed his lips. "No, I guess he wouldn't," he said. "But I've heard he's been giving you other things."

I looked at Sally, who was glaring at Nick.

"Go away, Nick," I said.

"Get it?" He made a dumb, lewd gesture with his hips and his hand. "Giving it to you?"

I wasn't going to allow myself to be surprised, or hurt, by anything he said to me.

"Fuck *off*, Nick," I said.

"Where is he tonight?" Nick looked around. "What does he do without his creative-support animal?"

When I was a kid, I'd hated the scene in *Pinocchio* where Lampwick and the other boys were turned into donkeys. It had always terrified me a little. But right now, I imagined Nick getting turned into a donkey—braying and crying—and I didn't feel sad at all. Instead I had to bite back a smile. The "ass" jokes would write themselves.

"What I don't get"—Nick put his hands on our table, leaning down close to me—"is why you wouldn't give me the same kind of *inspiration* you're giving Bear."

I looked up at him, not finding this funny anymore.

"Because you're a shitty director," I said.

Red spots appeared on his cheeks. "At least I'm not sleeping my way through the program," he said.

Before I could say anything, Nick's head jerked forward.

"What the fuck?" He put his hand to the back of his neck.

When his fingers came away, they were covered in mashed potatoes.

He turned, revealing Caitlin, Rachel, Emily, and Jeannette. They each had spoons and Emily was holding a giant bowl of mashed potatoes.

"Goodbye, Nick," Caitlin said.

With her shaved head and ripped black shirt, she looked a bit like Furiosa, with her Mad Max–style army behind her. I wouldn't want to mess with her, but Nick didn't seem to realize the danger he was in.

"You're all fucking crazy," he said.

"Good*bye*, Nick," she repeated, digging her spoon into the mashed potatoes and brandishing it like a miniature catapult.

Everyone in the dining hall was staring at us now.

Nick glanced around, realizing that he had an audience. He raised his hands, making a face at the room as if to say *Can you believe these bitches?* and backed away from the table. Still, he couldn't resist one last glance at me.

"You know, the closest you're ever going to get to the director's chair is if you're on your knees in front of it," he said. "Slut."

Sally was on her feet before he could even close his teeth on the *t*. Picking up her plate of pasta, she dumped it down the front of his white shirt. He yelped in surprise, the sound muffled by the bowl of mashed potatoes that Emily pushed into his face.

The entire dining hall erupted in laughter as Nick sputtered through mashed potatoes, slipping on the spilled pasta as he scrambled to get away from us.

"Fuck you," he managed before running away.

"Fuck *you*," I said.

CHAPTER TWENTY-TWO

Gena quickly learned about the incident, and Sally and the other girls were sentenced to clean up the mess they'd made in the dining hall. I offered to help, since the only reason the whole thing had gotten chaotic was because of what had happened between me and Nick.

"I still think that Nick should be punished as well." Caitlin mopped the floor.

"It's probably better this way," Sally said, picking noodles off the table. "At least we don't have to spend another hour with him."

"That's true," Jeannette said. "His punishment would have been *our* punishment."

"I still hate that he's getting away with saying what he did," Caitlin said. "He's such a shithead."

I was wiping off the table. "It's fine," I said.

As crappy as the whole incident had been, I was glad that it had ended the long, tense standoff between me and the other girls. In that way, Nick's bullshit, ineffectual attempt at slut-shaming had been worth it. Also worth it had been watching him run into Gena *and* his mentor on the way out of the cafeteria—mashed potatoes and pesto dripping from his face and shirt.

"It's *not* fine." Caitlin leaned on the handle of the mop. "He's the fucking worst."

"And he stole Hayley's idea," Sally said. "That's what actually happened. Everything else that Nick said was totally a lie."

I was grateful for Sally. Trying to change the existing narrative seemed like a fool's errand, but I cared what the girls thought. Especially since they'd already seen me at my worst. I hated the idea that Nick's story might have reinforced my already bad reputation.

"I mean, I *assumed* you didn't try to attack him with his own pencil, but I kind of wished you did," Emily said.

"I'd heard that you broke the easel over your knee and threw it across the room," Rachel said. "And then stomped on his drawings. But I didn't believe it."

Suddenly all of them were looking at me hopefully.

"*Should* I have believed it?" Rachel asked, looking very bloodthirsty for someone wearing a skirt with a petticoat and bow-tie blouse.

"Sorry to disappoint," I said. "I didn't throw or break anything."

"She *did* call him a fucking liar, though," Sally said.

Four pairs of eyes widened.

I nodded. "I *did* do that."

Caitlin held out a hand and I gave it a high five.

It didn't take us long to finish cleaning up, but we were all little grubbier and sweatier than we'd been when we headed to dinner.

"Look," Caitlin said as we left the dining hall. "I'm sorry I called you a bitch."

"I deserved it," I said. "I'm sorry. For acting like a bitch." That part I directed to Emily.

"You're forgiven," she said.

"Now that we're all friends again," Jeannette said, "I've got all the Miyazaki films on Blu-ray." At some point, she'd dyed the tips of her blue hair pink, making her braids look like thick, dipped paintbrushes.

"I've got popcorn," Rachel said. "The extra-buttery kind."

"I've got sheet masks," Caitlin said. "Last one back to the dorms has to say something nice about Nick."

We all broke into a run. Unsurprisingly, it turned into a full-on race between Sally and Jeannette, with the latter winning by a hair. Emily was the last in the door.

"I'm not going to do it," she said. "He's a right wanker."

"I need a shower." Sally flapped the hem of her shirt. "Meet in our room in thirty?"

I went back to the room to send Bear a quick text. **Girls' night. See you tomorrow?**

His response was a thumbs-up emoji. I couldn't help wondering what he did on the nights we didn't hang out. He'd always been alone when I saw him before or having lunch with Josh or other BB Gun employees.

Bear in real life had friends and a daily existence that was completely separate from animation. It made sense that he hadn't wanted to be part of the internship. That he might not want to work in animation. Ever.

Our room smelled like popcorn and aloe vera as we piled onto my bed or the floor while Caitlin passed around sheet masks. They had animal faces printed on them, so when we smoothed them into position, we all looked like extremely creepy human-animal hybrids.

"My dad hates it when I wear these," Caitlin said. "Sometimes I put one on just to freak him out."

"It is pretty terrifying." Rachel was looking at herself in the full-length mirror, stretching her mouth wide and making a variety of contorted expressions. "Good inspiration, though."

"Someone should do a short film about sheet masks that transform the wearer into a wild animal," Jeannette said. "A herd of well-moisturized girls roaming the streets of Los Angeles."

I looked around the room, that splinter of an idea poking at me again. If I enlisted everyone here, we *could* make a short-*short*

film of our own. We'd have to work crazy hours to get it done, especially since we'd still be working on projects for the internship, but it wasn't impossible.

"How are your shorts going?" I pushed the boat out tentatively.

Even with masks on, everyone's expression of displeasure was obvious.

"I've heard Nick's film is a train wreck." Emily was sitting cross-legged on the floor.

The most disappointing part was that Nick had the makings of a good project, he was just unable to put it together in a cohesive way.

"The one Rachel and I are working on is okay." Caitlin ran a hand over her prickly haired head. "It's just not really challenging."

Rachel peeled off her mask, tossing it in the trash. "I feel like it has jokes I've seen a billion times before."

"That's the opposite of ours," Jeannette said. "Jeff wants everything to be completely new, even if it doesn't make sense with the story."

"He's also really bad at explaining what he wants," Emily said. "Whenever we share scenes with him, he just tells us he hates them and that we need to do better—but never gives us any indication of what he thinks 'better' *is*."

"Bear's has gotten a lot stronger." Sally shot me a look. "But he was totally hands-off at the beginning. Our head of story had no idea what he was doing—I think he was so starstruck that he just said yes to everything Bear suggested and wouldn't listen to anyone else."

She was talking about Alec, who despite still being the head of story, seemed perfectly happy to step back and let me take over.

Unofficially, at least. He'd still get the credit on the final film.

"I mean, none of them have experience directing anything, so it could just be really stressful," Jeanette said. "Maybe I'd do the same if I was in their position."

"Maybe," Emily said.

"I don't think so," Sally said.

"Do you guys think it's weird, you know, that none of us were chosen to direct?" I asked. "And that none of us got to be the head of any department?"

"I'm sure the directors just picked the people they knew to be department heads." Emily twisted her long blond hair into a topknot.

It's what I'd assumed as well, until I'd learned the truth.

It was also true that BB Gun Films had never once had a woman direct any of their features. They also didn't have any women heading up a single department. Even the production staff, which was mostly women, still had a guy in charge. If anything, the internship just reflected what was already happening at the studio.

And they weren't an anomaly. I could count on one hand— *maybe* two—the number of animated films that had been directed by women.

It wasn't as if I hadn't *known* the numbers, I'd just never really stopped to think about them. About what they meant. I'd been so focused on myself and *my* goals, that I hadn't seen the bigger picture. Or the problems behind it.

"Bear said that the directors didn't actually pick their department heads—the brain trust and Bryan made the assignments," I said.

"Oh, did *Bear* say that?" Caitlin asked.

The question was casually asked, but pointed. Everyone looked at me.

"We're friends now," I said, even though I could tell I'd convinced no one.

"That makes sense, I guess. About the brain trust picking assignments," Sally said, changing the subject. "They saw all our portfolios and applications."

"I thought it was because we all hung out together," Jeannette said. "And I assumed some of the guys might have been jealous."

"They're not jealous." Caitlin frowned. "They don't like that girls are in the program. We're invading what they think is *their* space."

I thought about what Hal had said. Clearly he wasn't the only one at the studio—or in the industry—who felt that way. And I'd definitely met enough guys who'd had the need to test my animation knowledge before they would even deign to speak to me about *my* favorite movies.

"Not all blokes are like that," Emily said.

"No," Caitlin said. "But enough."

"That's always the way it is, though," Rachel said. "I don't know how many times I've been accused of liking animated movies because I wanted to impress boys." She rolled her eyes. "They also didn't believe me when I told them that I had literally no interest in *boys*."

"My brothers thought the only reason I liked animated movies was because there were cute guys in them," Jeannette said.

"I've heard that one before," Caitlin said. "As if I couldn't possibly just like it because it was, you know, amazing. For lots of reasons."

"At least you didn't have to listen to Nick and his mentor talk about the new Star Wars movies," Rachel said. "My mentor sits next to them, and they used to spend hours talking about how the new ones are a desecration of the originals."

"Let me guess, it's not because he's sexist," Sally said.

"Oh no, of course not," Rachel said. "How dare you even say that."

"A 'desecration.'" Emily snorted. "You should have heard the guys at school bitch and moan about Rey and Rose Tico and how they're both such Mary Sues."

Caitlin practically growled. "I *hate* that term."

"Let's not even get started on how upset all those dudes were that Harley Quinn wasn't half naked in *Birds of Prey*," I said.

"Yet *we're* the emotional ones," Sally said.

"I know so many guys like that at my school." Rachel leaned back against my bed. "They're 'just trying to have an opinion.'"

"The guys in my drawing class like to quiz me on my favorite animated movies," Emily said, before lowering her voice. "I bet she doesn't even know that the same guy who directed *Iron Giant* directed *Ratatouille*."

I thought about how Nick hadn't known that Henry Selick had directed *A Nightmare Before Christmas*.

"Like you have to be an animation nerd to love animated movies," Rachel said.

"But I *am* an animation nerd!" Emily said.

She looked so indignant that we all laughed.

"That's probably why there's only six of us in the program," Rachel said.

"Maurene said it was because BB Gun Films didn't have

enough female employees to mentor any other girls," Sally said.

Was this all some big, unending cycle? Where the lack of support was considered disinterest, which then created even less opportunity? Were there more of us out there—a "render" of girls who loved animation as much as we did—only they'd been shut out?

Or shut themselves out.

I imagined it like a snake, trapped in a cage with no food, eating its own tail.

"Why do women have to be mentored by other women?" Jeannette asked. "That's kind of strange, right?"

"I don't mind it too much," Emily said. "I like having a female mentor."

"But it doesn't feel like they were thoughtful about it at all," Caitlin said. "Like they just randomly paired the female artists with female interns, and artists of color with interns of color."

"While Caitlin and I got designated by gender over ethnicity," Rachel said. "Because, you know, I can't be both a woman *and* Asian."

Both Rachel's and Caitlin's mentors were white women. And I hadn't really stopped to think about how much harder navigating all of this would be for them. How much harder it had probably been for Sloane when she started out—how hard it probably *still* was. The directing and department head ratio was just as disappointing if you were a guy of color. And a thousand times more dismal if you were a woman of color.

"I bet they were more thoughtful about who they paired the white dudes with," Caitlin said. "They probably matched them based on style and interest, rather than gender or skin color.

Because you know they think that gender and race count as personality traits."

Rachel nodded. "And since there are, like, a dozen people of color at the studio, I bet you anything it allowed them to put a cap on how many of us they were going to accept in the first place."

We all sat there, absorbing this information. Some of it new, most of it previously unexamined. I didn't think that Bryan had lied to me—at least, not intentionally. I was pretty sure that he believed exactly what he had told me. Believed that I wasn't good enough, believed that I didn't deserve to direct one of their short films. But I was also starting to think that he was wrong.

About me. About all of us.

I had a hard time imagining that the only reason *all* of us were here was because the program needed more diversity. Everyone in the room was extremely talented, and it sounded like each one of us felt we could do a better job than those who'd gotten more opportunities.

Unfortunately, if Bryan—and the brain trust—believed that we weren't worth taking a risk on, there wasn't much we could do within the program to get them to change their minds. If we wanted opportunity we'd have to create it for ourselves.

"What if we made our own short?" I asked.

There was silence.

"They'd hate that," Caitlin said. "Bad enough that we individually want to work in animation—all six of us collectively doing something? Heads would"—she mimed an explosion, much like Bryan had done at the banquet—"explode."

"So?" I asked. "So what if their heads explode? So what if they don't like it? At least we'd be doing what we came to this program to do—create something. Create something that *we* own. Something that's *ours*."

Everyone looked at one another as it became clear that I wasn't joking.

"The internship's almost halfway over," Sally said.

"And?" I leaned forward. "We basically just restarted, didn't we?"

"Sort of," she said. "But we had a story. And a pipeline."

"I have a story. Rachel has a story. Emily has a story," I said. "And I bet they're better than any of the things we're working on."

"I don't know." Emily chewed at her lip. "My pitch was okay."

"It was good," I said.

"You never even saw it."

"Okay," I said, standing up. "Then pitch it now. You, me, and Rachel will pitch our projects. We'll decide—together—which is the strongest. And then we'll make it into a really short film. Maybe it won't be better than what the guys are doing, but at least we'll be working on something that we're proud of. And it will be collaborative. Truly collaborative. The way we wish the shorts were being made."

I could sense the hesitation in the room shift to excitement.

"The other animators never listen to me when I suggest things," Jeannette said. "They pretend like I'm not even there."

"I'm stuck doing the in-between drawings for Patrick," Caitlin said. "And he still gets all the credit." She looked at me and the others. "I'd like to see the pitches," she said. "Your idea is ridiculous, but I think it's important to consider all options—even the ridiculous ones."

We didn't watch a movie. I pulled my drawings out of the closet, while Rachel and Emily went to their rooms to get theirs. We didn't have an easel, so we ended up using one of the chairs. Emily went first, and then Rachel. We were a good audience. We laughed and cheered, and we heckled—in a good-natured way. Everyone applauded once Emily and Rachel were done.

"Well, that was a way better reaction than the one I got from the brain trust and Bryan," Rachel said as she sat down.

Caitlin turned to me. "You're up next," she said.

Their pitches were good, but I was sure mine was the strongest. Still, I knew that if we did this—and the girls voted to pick Emily's or Rachel's pitch—I couldn't be an asshole about it. This was my idea, but I had to be willing to listen to the group if this was going to work. I really had to be a team player.

No one said a word during my pitch, and I went through it like it was second nature, which it was. I wouldn't have been surprised if I'd done it more than twenty times by this point. The muscle memory was deep.

There wasn't a cheer when I was done. Instead there was a long, tense silence.

"What. The. Fuck," Caitlin said.

"I—" I started to apologize but she got to her feet and gave me a hug. "Uh."

Suddenly everyone was on their feet, surrounding me, embracing me.

"That was *aces*," Emily said. "No wonder you were so upset that night."

"I would have punched Bryan Beckett in the face if I'd written something like that and it didn't get picked," Caitlin said. "This is ridiculous. All three of those pitches were way better than the projects we're currently working on."

"I would settle for punching Nick in the face," Sally said.

"Don't even get me started on what he named his villain," I said.

They all looked at me.

"Mr. Bigsworth."

"Blech!"

"You're kidding!"

"I'm embarrassed for him."

"What an absolute nob."

I grinned. The whole Nick experience might have been worth it just to have all of them confirm how dumb that name was.

"It has to be your pitch," Rachel said. "It was really good, plus it's the most polished."

I looked around the room at the nodding faces, my heart speeding up with excitement. We were doing this.

"It won't be easy," I said. "We'll all be working on two projects at the same time."

Jeannette waved her hand. "They're wasting my efforts on our short—I'd happily work extra on something that I actually cared about. And that would let me do some real animation."

"Do you have any ideas for how you'd want to animate it?" Sally asked. "Because I think there are some really cool opportunities for some interesting, unique drawings. To really lean into the mysticism of the whole project."

"I might have a few ideas." I pulled out my notebook.

"Of course you do." Caitlin rubbed her hands together eagerly.

"And don't forget about music. Because I can do a lot with my guitar and the music app on my phone."

We all gathered around my desk as I flipped through my sketchbook, showing them some of the drawings I'd done. As I did, though, my brain was already beginning to make adjustments based on what I knew about everyone's strengths and skills. Even though Bear wasn't as motivated as I was, I had learned a lot from watching him. He was really good at listening to others, at absorbing their suggestions, and making space for new ideas. I wanted to do the same.

"What if we did two different types of animation?" I asked. "The whole thing could be really simple and sparse—very little background, not a lot of color—but I think it would really be interesting if we did something like what Sally did in her animation test."

I pointed to the wall where her cut-out drawings were currently posed doing jumping jacks. "Maybe everything is handdrawn, except the golem. He can be more like a shadow puppet," I said. "It would make him stand out even more and really separate him from Miriam and her world."

"That's a really cool idea," Jeannette said.

"How do you imagine the rest of the animation?" Caitlin asked.

I'd noticed that everyone had taken out their notebooks and was either drawing or writing things down.

"It should feel really tactile," I said. "Miriam is grieving, so she's much more disjointed than the golem, who's solid and graphic. I don't imagine any clean lines on her—more like she's radiating out into the world—like she might disappear herself if she's not careful."

"I like that," Sally said. "The contrast will look really cool and interesting. It will be really effective if we pull it off. What if we tried something like this for the golem?"

She held up a quick sketch that showed the golem—a big Frankenstein-looking figure with hulking shoulders and giant hands. It was extremely simplistic, so there were no facial details indicating what the golem might be thinking or feeling, just two dark circles for eyes. It was way more minimal than what I'd done in my initial pitch, but I loved it.

"That's incredible," I said.

"And this for Miriam?" Emily passed over her notebook.

She'd drawn a very sketchy image of a young girl walking forward, her head bent down. Emily had captured the same general essence of Miriam from my sketches—dark hair and eyebrows, with a tense jaw and tightly clenched hands. Her hair was loose, blowing in the wind, the lines of it extending outward to meet the line of the horizon. Emily had done the same with her shoes, so that she looked like she was part of the ground she was stepping on. Like she was dissolving into the breeze.

"Perfect," I said. "That's absolutely perfect."

We brainstormed and sketched for almost two hours, taking my beat sheet and building out our sequences—compressing others. We couldn't do the full project; we didn't have time. Instead of a ten-minute short, it would have to be five minutes. A taste of what the project could be instead of the whole thing. Just the essentials.

This was something that would prove to my parents that this was a worthwhile use of my time. I'd been avoiding their calls and their texts. Even Zach's. I didn't want to consider that Dad could be right—that I didn't belong here. I didn't want to admit defeat to them. I didn't want to be defeated.

This was my chance to change the story.

A few hours in, and it was already way more fun than I'd ever had on Nick's film, and even though I enjoyed working on Bear's project, there was something special about making *my* idea come to life. Taking something that had been mine for so long and watching other people experiment, explore, and make it better.

"Here's the real question." Caitlin leaned back against the bed.

We'd eaten all the popcorn, and the wrappers from the face masks were crumpled up alongside sheets of sketchbook paper, overflowing the trash can.

"Even if we managed to get this made—how are we going to get it into the final lineup?" Caitlin asked.

I hadn't thought about that.

"They all have to go through the editorial department," Rachel said. "We had our lunch lecture with John in editorial this week and he said that he's going to be in charge of running the actual screening."

"Also, we probably need a PA to help us out," Jeannette said. "There's no way we can figure out the schedule all by ourselves—plus, our PA helps with a ton of things I wouldn't even think to remember."

"I might know someone who could help on the PA side of things." I thought of Zoe, currently trapped in a Nick-made hell. "She might even be able to help us talk to John in editorial."

"Won't she have to tell Gena or Bryan what we're doing?" Emily asked. "We could all get kicked out of the program."

I didn't want Zoe to risk too much to help us, but I thought of someone else who knew John personally. Someone who usually got whatever he wanted when it came to the world of BB Gun Films. Someone who was damn near untouchable. Someone who had been completely on board the first time I'd thought of doing a short film of my own.

I took out my phone. "I think I know who can help us."

You up? I texted Bear. **Come over if you are.**

Rachel held up a quick sketch of an idea for the background. It was exactly what I'd imagined, but better—the lines were smudged and blurry—like we were staring into a sandstorm. There wasn't much on the horizon but a few scraggly trees and some tumbleweeds.

"The whole background could be a variation on this," she said. "You can only tell that they're making progress by the movement of the trees and other landmarks."

"That's perfect," I said.

There was a knock. Everyone looked up.

"Are you expecting someone?" Caitlin asked.

"Reinforcements," I said.

I opened the door to find Bear leaning against the wall—his casual stance offset by the way he was breathing, as if he was out of breath.

"Did you run here?" I asked.

"Nice pajamas," Bear said.

He hooked his finger into the neckline of my top and gave me a tug, his mouth coming down to meet mine as I was pulled forward. He kissed me deeply, his hands reaching around my back, one palm coming to rest on my butt.

There was a round of applause from inside the room.

Bear froze. Slowly, he lifted his head and pulled back.

"Hey, Bear," Sally said.

All five of the girls were gathered in the doorway. Bear's hand was still on my butt.

"Ladies," he said.

"Just friends, huh?" Caitlin asked.

CHAPTER TWENTY-THREE

'm going to talk to Zoe this afternoon," I told Sally on the shuttle Monday morning.

Thankfully, Bear hadn't been too embarrassed on Friday night, and once he'd heard what we were doing, had been more than happy to help. The seven of us spent the whole weekend working on the short and by Sunday night we were pretty much neck-and-neck with where Bear's was after our quick animation reboot.

"My dad is going to be so pissed," he said. "I can't wait."

I wasn't super excited about making Bryan Beckett mad, but I also understood that if we wanted to do this, it was probably inevitable that he'd be upset. At least the program would be over by that point. He couldn't retroactively kick us out.

"Do you think Zoe will be willing to help us?" Sally asked.

I shrugged. "I hope so. I can't imagine she's having fun working with Nick."

"Did you tell Bear what Nick said to you?" Sally shot a quick look to where Bear and Nick were sitting. Far away from each other.

I shook my head, though I wondered if I should.

"If he's your boyfriend, then I definitely think he should know," Sally said.

I didn't say anything.

"I mean, it seems like you guys are keeping it pretty casual, but he's helping us with the short, so maybe it's a little more serious than that," Sally said, mostly to herself. "He did also, like, run to our room after he got your text message, so clearly he's really into you. Then again, the internship will be over in a few weeks, and you guys don't go to the same school. But you *do* live in the same city."

In spite of all the time we spent together, Bear and I had never really gotten around to talking about *what* we were. I knew there wasn't another girl, and I knew that I would occasionally catch him looking at me with this really intense stare. Like he was trying to figure something out about me. I caught myself staring at him sometimes, too. He was nice to look at. I just didn't know what that meant when the summer ended. And I didn't know what I wanted it to mean. Right now, all I wanted to focus on was the work.

"I just hate that Nick keeps getting away with things," Sally said.

"Nailing him with pasta was a good punishment," I said.

"You know what I mean," she said. "It's not enough."

I agreed, but I also didn't think there was anything that could be done about it. Right now, the short film was the priority. Revenge against Nick would have to wait.

After lunch, I went down to editorial to talk to Zoe.

"She should be back soon," John said. "I think she had a meeting or something."

After twenty minutes, she still hadn't returned to her desk. I had to get back to working on Bear's short and I also had to pee. I waved goodbye to John and headed to the bathroom at the end of the hall.

I spotted a pair of shoes in the stall and heard the sound of sniffling. For a moment, I thought about leaving and going upstairs to use the bathroom in the story department, but before I could go, the toilet flushed, and Zoe came out.

She was wearing a blue vintage dress with embroidered flowers down the front and a pair of gray flats. Her glasses were in her hands and her eyes were red.

"Hayley," she said, looking surprised to see me, and a little embarrassed.

"What's wrong?" I asked. "Is everything okay?"

Zoe shook her head. "Just a bad day," she said, moving toward the sink.

"I'm sorry," I said.

Zoe pulled a wad of paper towels out of the dispenser and wet them. Dabbing gently at her eyes, she checked herself in the mirror before looking at me.

"What are you doing down here?" She slid her glasses back on. "Did they need you to record more of Hazel's lines?"

"Ha," I said. "Doubtful. Pretty sure Bryan doesn't want me to come within ten feet of that movie ever again."

Zoe turned and leaned against the sink. "You know, after John did all his editorial magic to your voice-over, we played it for Bryan, and he loved it. Wants the actress to record all of Hazel's lines with that same monotone style."

"It's not a style," I said. "It's just my voice."

Zoe laughed. "I know. It's just that when John reminded Bryan who had done the voice-over, Bryan said that he had known immediately that you would be perfect."

"He said that?" I asked. *Not great*, I could still remember Bryan saying.

Zoe nodded. "He's a man that likes to rewrite history when it suits him."

She glanced back at the mirror, peering at her red eyes.

"It looks like I've been crying, doesn't it?" she asked.

"A little," I said.

"Dammit." She pushed her glasses up onto her forehead and pressed her palms against her face, shoulders slumped.

"Did something happen?" I asked.

She sighed. "I just had a meeting with one of the production managers," she said. "Apparently, someone made a complaint about my conduct."

My eyes widened. "What?"

Zoe was one of the nicest, friendliest PAs in the building.

"I know exactly where the complaint came from," she said. "I was helping out in animation last week—prepping scenes. And one of the lead animators walked by the desk I was working at. I was wearing headphones, trying to meet a deadline—I was a little distracted, so I didn't stop and say hi to him."

I thought of Cole—the animation PA—and how I'd greeted him last week and he hadn't even bothered to acknowledge I was there.

"There was a PA meeting a few days later where management talked about how we were expected to act, especially when walking around the building. We're supposed to set the tone for productions—cheerful, upbeat, and positive. Then this morning, I was called into my supervisor's office, where she told me that they'd had that meeting because of *my* behavior. Because I'd been rude."

I stared at her. "Do you know who made the complaint?" I asked.

She snorted. "Of course. It was Hal. He thinks of all the female PAs as his personal secretaries. Like, old-school secretaries. The ones that were expected to be pretty and accommodating." Zoe pressed the wet paper against her eyes.

"But what about Cole?" I asked. "He's super rude."

"You noticed that?"

I nodded. "I mean, everyone calls him the Robot."

"Hilarious, isn't it?" Zoe adjusted her glasses. "It's kind of his schtick that he's such a sullen asshole. We've been working here about the same amount of time, but I've heard that he's up for a promotion." She shook her head. "This is probably all the excuse they need to withhold mine for another movie. Another year and a half stuck at minimum wage."

I felt terrible for her.

"The worst part is that my supervisor is a woman," Zoe said. "She thinks that because *she* had to deal with this same kind of stuff when she was starting out, that the rest of us should as well. 'Rites of passage' and all that bullshit."

I was silent, thinking about how unfair it all was. Not just for the female interns, not just for the female artists, but even the production staff was apparently dealing with this kind of crap on a regular basis.

"But enough about me. What are you doing down here?" Zoe asked.

"I actually came to see you," I said.

"Yeah?" She looked a little more cheerful.

I hesitated, though. After everything that had happened, could I really ask her for a favor?

"Please tell me Bear wants me to work on his project," she said.

"Between helping out Cole last week, Hal's power trip, and having to sit through Nick's train wreck of a short, I need a break from arrogant assholes."

"It's not that. . . ." I said. "Not exactly."

Zoe raised her eyebrows. "Go on," she said.

"It's probably a terrible idea," I said. "But me and the other girls in the program, we're thinking of doing our own short."

Ten minutes later, Zoe was all in. "This sounds amazing," she said. "Right now, I have to go home after work and listen to Bikini Kill to cleanse myself of the all the sexist shit I have to deal with all day. This sounds like a much better use of my time."

I gave her the lowdown on the project, and she promised she'd give us a schedule by the middle of the week. I practically ran back upstairs to tell Bear the news.

We had a solid story, a strong beat sheet, and soon, we'd have a schedule and an extremely capable PA guiding us through the process. This short was going to happen—and it was going to change everything.

The seven of us interns started spending whatever free time we had together. We sat together on the shuttles, met in the evenings at the library, and ate in the dining hall at the one long table by the window.

"Who did you hang out with before?" I asked Bear as we walked back to the dorms after dinner Tuesday night.

"I have friends," he said, a little defensively. "At my school, I have lots of them."

"I know you do," I said. I gave him a gentle push on the arm to show I was teasing. I'd seen the pictures.

And when he sat with us, with the girls, he fit right in. He made everyone laugh, but didn't try to be the center of attention. The other day, he and Jeannette had spent at least thirty minutes discussing the US women's soccer team. She stanned Megan Rapinoe, while he was an Alex Morgan fan. He sometimes joined her and Sally for runs in the morning. He and Caitlin had started making each other Spotify playlists. He told Rachel all the behind-the-scenes stories he'd learned when his dad had gotten a private Disney World tour a couple of years ago, and shared pictures from his trip to London last year with Emily. He asked questions. He listened. They liked him.

"You're friendly and nice," I said.

"I *know*," he said.

We went into his room and he pulled me down onto the bed, into his lap. I let him, looping my arms around his neck, my knees on either side of his hips.

"What would you be doing if you weren't here?" I asked.

Bear thought for a moment. "I was going to learn how to surf," he said.

"You were not," I said, even though I could picture it clearly.

He grinned. "I probably would have spent the summer rock climbing with my friends. Hiking with Howl. Trying to train Calcifer to walk on a leash so she and Howl could go on adventures and become Internet famous."

"I'm sorry you didn't get to do those things," I said.

"It's not so bad."

At least he didn't have to spend all his time alone anymore. He had our little group now.

"Do your friends—people at school—do they know who you are?" I asked.

"Sure," he said. "But you know where I go to school. I'm like, the least famous kid there. Some of my classmates have paparazzi waiting for them at the end of the day. I'm pretty invisible."

"Not here, though."

He sighed. "I knew it would be a big deal. Like that time I went to Comic-Con with my dad when I was a kid."

I'd seen some of those pictures. Bear had been so much younger, and not very good at hiding his feelings. He'd been visibly overwhelmed and terrified, both he and his dad mobbed by fans.

"At my school, no one cares. Animation people, though," he said, "it's just different."

"They think you're special."

"I *am* special," he said. He was joking. "Fans have expectations. No one knows how to treat me—they either want to be my best friend or ignore me completely. Like they're scared of me. Of what I might tell my dad. Or they're hoping I'll introduce them to him. It's just easier to avoid all that, if I can." Bear looked up at me. "I was worried you'd be like them," he said. "At first."

I could see why. I'd basically been a walking, talking Bryan Beckett fan club. I would have been exactly the kind of person he would want to avoid. "And now?"

"Hmm." Bear put his lips to the curve of my jaw. "Still not sure."

"Oh?"

He kissed my neck. "You *are* pretty awkward," he said.

I shoved him, and he fell back on the bed, bringing me with him. "Oof."

"Pretty awkward?"

"Did I say that?" he asked. "I think I meant pretty."

I rolled my eyes. "Sure you did," I said. "You're pretty too, I guess."

"Why, Hayley Saffitz." He turned so we faced each other. "You say the nicest things."

I pulled him close and showed him exactly how nice I could be.

"Which department are you going to today?" Zoe asked when I met her Wednesday morning for breakfast.

"Layout," I said.

She made a face. "That's Charles," she said as we sat down at a table. "Check out the right side of his desk when you're in his office."

"Uh, why?"

She gave me a cryptic grin. "Oh, you'll know why when you see it."

Reaching down, she pulled a colorful spreadsheet out of her bag.

"I can't decide if you guys are geniuses or lunatics. Probably both," she said. "But I had a lot of fun putting this together."

I gave her a look.

"What?" she asked. "You guys are nerdy about animation, I'm nerdy about production schedules. Why do you think I'd put up with all the other crap if I didn't love the work? Besides, I never get to run point on projects like this." She gestured to the page. "It's a very aggressive schedule, but if you want to get your short done by the end of the internship, this is the only way to do it."

I examined what she'd given us. We were all about to become very, very busy.

"Making it half the length of the other shorts is really smart," Zoe said. "It's still going to be a crunch, but you'll be able to focus on quality over quantity."

With a schedule and deadlines laid out neatly in front of me, the whole thing suddenly felt very real. Very ambitious. And extremely risky.

"Maybe this is a bad idea," I said.

Zoe shook her head. "Most of the guys here—most guys in general—think they're twice as talented as they actually are," she said. "What *you're* making—it's good. Trust me."

I wanted to. I wanted to trust my own instincts that said that the story—that the short—*was* strong. That there was something there. But I couldn't stop thinking about Bryan's assessment of me. Of my abilities. No matter what, would I ever be able to get his voice out of my head? Would I ever be able to stop hearing him tell me that I wasn't good enough?

"Did you get the schedule from Zoe?" Bear asked as we headed to layout.

I patted my bag. "I saw her in the cafeteria at breakfast," I said. "Where were you?"

He'd been absent this morning—our production PA had told us to work without him.

Bear frowned. "My dad," he said. "He wants to meet with all of the directors this Friday, but of course, he had to give me the heads-up first. Can't spell 'nepotism' without Bryan Beckett."

The head of layout was a surprisingly well-dressed man in black slacks, a white short-sleeve button-down shirt, and dark-rimmed glasses.

"I'm Charles Osbourne. Welcome to layout." He nodded in Bear's direction. "Bear."

"*Mr.* Osbourne," Bear intoned formally.

Charles shook his head, less than amused. "How many of you are familiar with what our department does?"

We'd all been in the internship—and working on our shorts—long enough that everyone lifted a hand, albeit tentatively.

"A good way to think about our department is if we were a live-action film, we'd be the DPs—the directors of photography," Charles said. "We'd also be the ones building the sets and providing all the props."

Even though I was interested in what Charles was saying, I was distracted. What had Zoe been talking about when she said to check out the right side of his desk?

"Why don't we go into my office and I'll show you the layout we've been working on for *No One Fears the Woods*," Charles said. "You'd be amazed how complicated a 'simple forest' can be. Then again, everything is complicated if you're building it from scratch."

We followed him into his office, but I got stuck in the back so I couldn't see anything but his enormous screen.

"What are you doing?" Bear asked as I stood on my tiptoes, trying to see around the other interns. "Since when are you so curious about layout?"

"Zoe told me to look at something on the right side of Charles's desk," I said.

He frowned. "I don't think that's a good idea," he said.

Now I was even more curious. "Why? What is it?"

"Trust me," he said. "You don't want to see it."

I narrowed my eyes. "You know that's just going to make me want to see it more."

"Yeah, I realized that as soon as I said it." He sighed. "Fine. You're going to regret it, but come on."

Taking my arm, he gently moved forward. All the other interns immediately got out of his way, scooting back until we were at the front of the group. Right behind Charles's desk. Charles was still moving us through the forest layout for *No One Fears the Woods*, but I wasn't paying attention anymore.

Taped on the right side of his desk was a drawing of Jennifer Pride, a character from the second BB Gun film, *The Grand Adventures of the Frog King*. In the movie, she'd been the shy best friend/romantic interest of teen hero Thaddeus.

In the drawing she was grown up and topless, her mouth in a surprised O. She was wearing the same outfit that she had been wearing in the movie, but with her shirt wide open. Her nipples were drawn with plenty of detail.

In my shock, I backed up, stepping on another intern's foot.

"Ow," he said.

That caused Charles to turn around, see me, and see exactly where I was looking.

"Watch your step," he said.

CHAPTER TWENTY-FOUR

Mom called that night. I thought about not picking up, but I knew that if I kept avoiding my parents' calls, they'd get worried, and when they were worried, they had a tendency to just show up places.

Zach had texted me the other day to warn me that Mom kept mentioning that she might just casually "drive by" the dorms to check on me. I was a little surprised he hadn't encouraged it. Then again, I'd done the same for him when he wasn't responding to their calls during his first year away.

"Your father told me what happened," Mom said.

It was funny how that seemed so long ago. How everything had changed since then.

"I'm fine," I said.

"It's okay if you're not," she said.

I wondered how much Dad had told her. I didn't think I could take it if Mom started lecturing me on sounding spoiled and ungrateful. I really didn't want to talk about it.

"I'm over it," I said.

"Okay," she said. "How is the rest of the internship going?"

Mom and Dad didn't know about Bear. And they definitely didn't know that I was basically doing a whole "alternative" internship on the side. I knew that they thought this whole summer was a waste of time and resources, useful only insomuch as it could be used for college applications. It made me even more determined to complete the short. So I'd have something to show them. Something tangible.

Especially since I was no longer sure what I wanted to do after the summer. I still loved animation, but instead of feeling like a place where I belonged, BB Gun Films had become a place where I had to fight tooth-and-nail just to be seen. And it was starting to feel like the whole industry might be that way.

"Are you learning things?" Mom asked.

"Yeah," I said. I *was* learning things. Just probably not the kind of things she wanted me to be learning.

I thought about that afternoon, about Charles Osbourne's drawing. I'd hated it. Hated that Bear had been totally right—that I wished I hadn't seen it at all.

But I understood exactly why Zoe had told me it was there. It made it clear that a lot of people in this studio—in this business—didn't think that I was supposed to be here. Not as an artist, at least. Support staff, maybe. Or as cleanup artists, or in-betweeners. Inspiration.

Girls like me, we were expected to inspire. We weren't supposed to *be* inspired.

"Are you getting enough sleep?" Mom asked.

"Yeah," I said.

"I worry about you and Zach," she said. "About how hard you both work."

"I'm fine," I said.

We lapsed into silence for a bit. What else was there to say?

"Did you know that your dad applied to art school?" Mom

asked. "When we were in undergrad, he wanted to go to graduate school to study sculpture."

That surprised me. He always talked about his sculptures as a hobby.

"That's cool," I said, not sure what I was expected to do with this information.

I could hear Mom nodding, her earrings jangling. "I think that, maybe, your dad is trying to protect you," she said.

From what? I thought. *From myself?*

"You've always been so determined and motivated," Mom said. "I just wish . . ."

I knew what she wished. What both my parents wished. That I could take that determination and motivation and do something like Zach was doing. Something they understood. The pressure of that, plus the work that had to be done, felt like a scarf wrapped too tightly around me. I didn't have time for it.

"I have to go," I said. "Lots of work to do."

I told the other girls about Charles Osbourne's drawing. None of them were surprised.

"You should see some of the stuff the guys hang up in their cubicles near me," Rachel said. "I've seen more nipples and butt cracks in the past few weeks than I've seen in my entire life."

There was something especially funny about her saying "nipples" and "butt cracks" while delicately dabbing the corner of her mouth with the monogrammed handkerchief she carried in her Mary Poppins–esque bag.

"What is it with guys and nipples?" Sally asked.

I shrugged.

We were working late—it seemed like the whole studio was. Deadlines of all sorts were approaching, so the cafeteria was open almost all night. Ron kept bringing us cups of tea and coffee, and plates of doughnuts, fresh out of the oven.

"Tell me what you think of these," he'd say.

No one around us seemed to notice that we were working on something of our own.

"I knew a guy in my drawing class who always gave his girls square, puffy nipples," Caitlin said, her big black boots up on a chair. "I couldn't tell if it was ignorance or just wishful thinking."

"I mean, I've drawn my share of naked men," Emily said. "Nipples and butt cracks included."

"We've all gone to figure drawing classes before," Sally said. "You *have* to draw naked people to get an idea of shape and form. It's not the nudity that's the problem."

"I bet we're the first teen girls that have ever really spent time in the building." Jeannette folded a piece of paper into a tiny, taut triangle. "Let alone gone to hang out in the head of layout's office."

"That's it, though," Caitlin said. "The feeling that we don't belong here."

"They want us on the walls," Rachel said. "Not working with them."

We were all silent.

I noticed Bear enter the cafeteria. He'd been at the directors' meeting in his dad's office, so I wasn't surprised when I saw Nick trailing behind him, talking up a storm. For all of Nick's bluster about Bear not belonging in the program, I knew that he would twist himself in knots if he thought they could be friends. If he thought it would get him closer to Bryan. Bear's attention, however, was focused on our table.

"Hey, doughnuts," he said, and grabbed one from my plate.

Caitlin lifted her feet off the chair and pushed it toward him so he could sit.

"We should definitely get together sometime this weekend," Nick was saying. "You know, all us directors. Finalize what we're going to say. Oh, hey, girls," he said, faux-noticing us. "Bear and I are just talking about what we have to do for our final presentation. You know, when we show the films that *we* directed to the entire studio."

He said that last part to me. I thought about what he would do if I dumped my scalding hot tea down the front of his pants.

"Pretty sweet setup you've got here," Nick said. "Your dad loves your film and you've got a whole harem of ladies waiting for you with doughnuts."

Bear didn't look at him.

"He liked everything you came up with," Nick said.

Bear's hand was on my knee.

"I'm going to have a little reception the night before the final screening," Nick said. "In my room. We'll have beer. For directors only."

Bear turned slowly. "I'm not going to hang out in your room," he said.

Nick turned red. "Whatever," he said. "Don't be all gay about it."

"Is that supposed to be an insult?" Bear asked.

"I dunno . . ." Nick tried a mocking tone. "Is it?"

He just sounded like an idiot.

"You're annoying me," Bear said. "And who even says 'harem' anymore?"

Nick clenched his jaw, his bottom lip curling outward. I'd seen that look before—it was the one he'd given me when he'd read the treatment I'd done for him.

"Your film isn't even that good," Nick said. "Everyone knows the only reason you're directing is because your daddy owns the studio."

I mentally face-palmed. Nick was burning bridges left and right.

Bear stood. He towered over Nick.

"Do you want to know why *you're* directing?"

Nick puffed out his chest. "Because I'm good at it."

Bear smiled and shook his head slowly. "Because my *daddy* didn't want me to have any competition."

I watched as the implication sunk in. It wasn't true, not really, but I could see it plant a seed of doubt in Nick's mind.

"Your dad said it was good." Nick sounded like a whiny little kid.

"My dad's a liar," Bear said. "We both know you suck."

Everyone at the table was watching the exchange with wide eyes and barely concealed amusement, our gazes bouncing back and forth between the two of them like we were at a tennis match.

"You're just jealous," Nick said.

Bear laughed. "You're right," he said. "I'll just sit here, being 'gay' with my 'harem' and all these doughnuts, wishing I was more like you." He leaned down toward Nick. "Go away, or I'll tell my dad what you've been saying about me and some of the other people in the program."

Nick hurried off, shooting a few angry looks over his shoulder as he departed.

I wiggled my fingers in his direction.

"Sorry about that." Bear sat down at the table. "What are you guys talking about?"

"Nipples," I said.

Bear didn't even blink. "You told them about Osbourne's picture?" he asked.

"How has he not gotten in trouble with HR for having that there?" Caitlin asked.

Bear shrugged. "He's been here a while. Most people ignore it. It's not even his sketch."

He placed his elbows on the table, using his hands to make a goal for Jeannette's paper football. She gave it a flick with her fingers and it sailed through. They high-fived.

"Let me guess," I said. "The drawing is Hal's handiwork."

Bear pointed at me. "Bingo."

I wondered if Hal was responsible for that drawing of Sloane. It seemed like his style.

Bear ate a doughnut. "Osbourne's surprisingly straight-laced. If anything, people find it funny that he keeps it up."

"Somehow that just makes it worse," I said.

"Yeah," he said.

"How was the directors' meeting?" I asked.

"Fine," he said. "My dad really did like your stuff. He just doesn't know it's yours."

We'd decided that it would be easier to just finish the short before Bear told his dad how involved I'd been in making it better.

"Did you watch all the shorts?" I asked.

Bear ate another doughnut. "They're okay. Serviceable, I guess. But this one's better," he said, pointing at my notebook. "Way better."

Everyone at the table grinned. We worked for a few more hours, all seven of us with our heads bowed around the table, until Sally let out a loud yawn.

"I need some sleep," she said.

It set off a chain reaction and pretty soon the rest of the girls were packing up their things. I'd just had another cup of Earl Grey so I knew I would be good to work for a while longer.

"I'll stick around," Bear said.

"See you back at the dorm," Sally said.

Bear and I were among the only ones left in the cafeteria. There were a few people working together at a table across from us, but mostly it was a steady flow of one or two employees wandering in, grabbing some doughnuts and coffee, and wandering back out. Most of them would nod or wave to Bear.

"Your group seems to have shrunk," Ron observed when he came out to replenish the doughnuts. "Hey, Bear."

"Hey, Ron," he said. "Good doughnuts."

"These still your favorite?" He held out a plate of cinnamon-and-sugar ones.

"Hell yeah." Bear grabbed two.

Ron pulled out a chair. "I hate crunch time," he groaned as he sat.

"Part of the process," Bear said.

I didn't know how he could keep eating doughnuts without getting sick.

"This happens every movie?" I asked.

"It wasn't as bad on the first film," Ron said. "But it seems to get worse with every production."

"Is it a problem with the schedule?" I asked.

"Just the nature of the business," Ron said. "The never-ending struggle between the creative side and the production side."

"Dad calls it 'art versus money,'" Bear said.

Ron laughed. "Madeline calls it 'ego versus reality.'"

Madeline. The producer. The ball-buster. The queen on high. I'd be meeting her in two weeks, during our last lunchtime lecture.

"Who's right?" I asked.

Ron shrugged. "Both. Neither. You can't make a movie without creative vision, but you can't finish a movie without a schedule. Or money. Both sides need each other." He stood and stretched. "That's enough of a break for me." He turned to Bear. "I like her," he said, pointing at me.

"I do too," Bear said.

"Don't work too hard, you crazy kids." Ron headed back into the kitchen.

Bear reached for my hand and threaded our fingers together.

"Does Ron comment on your love life a lot?" I asked.

"What love life?" Bear asked.

I looked at our hands. We still hadn't had *that* conversation, but I didn't have the time or the bandwidth to focus on it. Not when we were working so hard.

I watched a few more people wander into the cafeteria. They all had sort of a zombie gait, their eyes blurry and unfocused. I'd see it on people in the hallways sometimes—in the middle of the day—if you paid attention, you could tell who was on deadline.

"What's it like?" I asked. "Being here?"

Bear shrugged. "I basically grew up here, so it's sort of like my second home."

We were sitting at my favorite table in the cafeteria. It was right by the doors, so you were close to the food, but also had a really nice view of the campus—especially the stream. The path across the bridge was illuminated with little mushroom-shaped lights. Sometimes you could see the shadow on the ground of a bug scurrying across the bulb.

"Was it cool?" I asked. "Being around to see all these amazing films getting made?"

"Not really." Bear looked down. "I mean, yeah, there were cool things about it, but it all gets kind of old after a while. Most people probably think it would be fun to live at Disneyland, unless, you know, you actually live at Disneyland. There's fun stuff, but you're also seeing behind the scenes, and I think you've realized that things look different from the inside. It's a lot dirtier and messier."

I didn't say anything, but I didn't have to. He was right. I'd thought the studio was going to be heaven for me. That it would be a place where I belonged.

Most of the office lights in the main building were out, but I watched some of them come on as the cleaning crew made their nightly rounds. Through the windows I could watch the work that mostly went unseen—trash cans getting emptied, floors being vacuumed.

"I came to the studio because I wanted to spend time with my dad," Bear said. "But he always passed me off to PAs or his assistant. I was never more important than whatever film he was working on at the time. I just kind of wandered around the studio when I visited, trying to entertain myself. That's why I know everyone here."

"It's like your family," I said.

Bear leaned back. "Yeah. I think a lot of people here feel like they had some hand in raising me. And they did. But they also still see me as a kid. As *that* kid. The one that used to run through the halls, interrupting meetings and causing trouble."

"I'm pretty sure you're still causing trouble," I said.

"You know what I mean," he said. "It's like, I changed my last name when I was seven, but most people still think of me as Bear Beckett. And I'll always be that to them." He shrugged. "But it could be worse. They still think of me as a kid—but at least I'm real to them, you know?"

I'd thought a lot about that. About what it was like be part of something as well-known and well-loved as *A Boy Named Bear*. What it was like to be *the* symbol for a generation of creative kids.

I heard the sound of Ron puttering around in the kitchen. I knew it was him because he was listening to disco music. He'd told me that it was the best music to clean up to. Kept it from being too boring.

"It must be weird," I said. "Being famous. Being famous here."

"I used to think about it a lot—like, what it would be like if no one knew who I was," Bear said. "Or if people didn't meet me and immediately assume I was just like my character in the movie." He stroked my hand with his thumb. "It's not so bad, though. I've gotten better at figuring out when people want to get to know *me*, or when they want to know me because of the film or because of my dad."

He looked across the cafeteria. "Sometimes I think there are people here who know me better than my dad does. *He* sees me as Bryan Beckett's kid, you know? Like I'm an extension of him."

He said it casually, but there was a tightness in his voice. I thought about the conversation I'd had with Mom the other night. How she'd said that Dad was trying to protect me.

"I kind of know what you mean," I said.

I didn't want to be protected—I wanted to be seen.

Bear wanted his dad to notice him. Wanted him to see who he actually was instead of who his dad wanted him to be. I felt a little bad for Bryan—that he was unable to see the real Bear. Because I really liked the real Bear.

"What about your mom?" I asked.

I was curious about her—wondering if any of the online rumors were true. *Had* she been involved in *A Boy Named Bear*? And if she had, why hadn't she gotten credit for it?

"Mom's pretty great," Bear said. "She's always given me a choice, and whatever I decide, she's totally behind it. My dad likes to pretend he's doing the same, but he just expects me to give him the answer he wants, and if I don't, he'll do everything he can to convince me that I'm wrong."

"Is that what happened with the internship?" I asked.

Bear rubbed the back of his neck. "He put the whole thing together without asking me, and then made it impossible for me to say no. It would look really bad for the studio, you know? Didn't I care about the company? About all the people who worked at BB Gun Films? We're a family here. Except, we're only a family when it suits him."

I looked out toward the water running under the bridge—in the quieter moments, I could hear it. I still hadn't seen any ducks, though. I was starting to think that they didn't actually exist.

"Is the studio in trouble?" I asked.

"Yes, and no," he said. "The movies aren't breaking the same records they used to, but they're still doing well at the box office. That's not enough for my dad. He's always worried about his 'legacy,' whatever that means. Nothing is ever enough for him. My mom told me I didn't have to do the internship. She said she'd talk to my dad, but—" Bear shook his head. "The two of them have barely spoken since the divorce. I know my mom is glad she walked away from all of this, and the last thing I want to do is drag her back into the middle of it."

I wanted to ask him more questions about his mom, but I knew that I couldn't really ask him what I wanted to know. When he said she walked away from *all this*, he had to mean animation. BB Gun Films.

"I'm kind of tired," Bear said. "Want to go back to the dorms?"

I started gathering up my things. I probably could have worked for another hour, but I could sleep, too.

"Maybe we could go to your room," I said as we walked out of the cafeteria.

"Listen to some music?" Bear's arm was around my waist.

We were alone, so I leaned into him. "I'd like that," I said.

never thought that working on two shorts at once would be easy, but I didn't expect it to be as hard as it was. It wasn't just the actual work that was starting to wear on me—it was the difficulty I had in switching between the two projects, going from working on *Golem Goes West* in the evenings and weekends, to spending the day at the studio focusing on Bear's short, which still didn't have a title.

"Can't I just call it *Bear's Fantasia?*" he asked on our way to the story department.

I gave him a look.

"*Hayley's Fantasia?*"

"We can do better than that," I said.

"We need to do it fast," he said. "I have to make the credits and the title card this weekend."

"Have you talked to John yet?" I asked.

He shook his head.

"*Bear.*"

"I'll get around to it," he said. "I've been busy."

The other night, I'd caught him watching the Long Beach Aquarium otter cam while both of us were supposed to be working.

"We've all been busy," I said. "And all that hard work is going to feel like a waste if we can't get our short into the lineup."

He didn't say anything.

Annoyed, I sped up, walking ahead of him. It was our second-to-last lunch lecture, and we'd be speaking to Isaac today. Even though I really liked Isaac and was interested in what he would have to say, I felt like I had a pretty good idea of how the story department worked, and right now I needed as much time as I could get in order to finish the two projects I was working on.

Isaac waved when I entered the conference room.

"I thought Josh was the head of story," one of the other interns said under his breath.

The room was quiet, though, and everyone heard him.

"Josh is the executive head of story," Isaac said. "His attention is focused on *No One Fears the Woods*. We still have a lot of other projects in development, so I often step in to take on some of his responsibilities."

We sat, and I could immediately tell that this wasn't going to be like the other lectures.

"I'm not going to talk to you about story," Isaac said. "You're all here because you know something about story. I'm going to talk to you about being an artist. About being a *working* artist."

I looked over at Bear. He was watching Isaac but there was something in his expression that told me that he knew something was going on.

"This is a hard life," Isaac said. "It's not easy making your living off of something you love. Or something you used to love."

I was confused. Was Isaac saying he didn't love animation anymore? That it was something he could live without? That you could choose something different?

I heard people outside the conference room—the increase and

decrease of sound as people walked by. The studio was rarely quiet—even at night—but right now, it all seemed kind of hushed.

"Sometimes you end up making sacrifices that you regret," Isaac said. "We all have to put our own visions—our own ideas—aside once in a while, but if you're not careful, you'll become too accustomed to that. You'll spend years building someone else's dreams at the expense of your own. And you might forget that this—all this—used to be something you did for fun."

I didn't understand what he was trying to say, and it seemed like I wasn't the only one.

"What was that about?" one of the interns asked as we left the conference room afterward. "All that cryptic shit about sacrifices? What was he trying to say?"

I glanced back at the empty room. Isaac had already left.

"What's going on?" I asked Bear.

He slowed his step, separating us from the rest of the interns.

"Isaac's leaving BB Gun Films," he said. "He quit."

"What? Why?"

Despite everything, I couldn't imagine that anyone would willingly stop working here. It wasn't the perfect environment, but they made amazing films. I still felt it was worth the trade-off.

"He's been here forever," I said.

"Yeah," Bear said. "And my dad was super pissed. I guess there was some yelling and name-calling. My dad said he was being ungrateful."

It had been hard enough listening to Bryan tell me I had no talent—I don't know what I would have done if he yelled and called me ungrateful, too.

"Don't worry about him," Bear said.

Selfishly, I was worried about myself. The thought that anyone could choose to walk away from BB Gun Films, maybe even from animation completely, was terrifying.

Because animation had never felt like a choice, and I didn't like thinking that it was. Despite everything, despite my doubts about BB Gun Films and my place at the studio, I'd never really questioned my love of animation. My ultimate goal was still to make and direct my own films. Even if the industry still had one foot in the past, I was determined to make a place for myself. Animation was a part of me. It made me who I was.

I never thought there'd be a point where I'd be able to give it up. And if I did, what would be left? Who would I be without it?

That fear must have shown on my face, because Bear looked at me and stopped.

"Hey, it's okay," he said. "Everything is going to be fine."

CHAPTER TWENTY-SIX

By the time we reached the end of the week, I didn't feel fine. I felt tired and overcaffeinated and stressed and very, very annoyed. We were behind on our schedule, because everyone kept missing deadlines.

"I meant to finish the final golem last night," Sally said as we headed back to the dorms on Friday. "But I just fell asleep."

"I guess we need to get more coffee," I said, trying to figure out how I could motivate the others to get their work done.

I didn't need any motivation, of course. I was planning to work all weekend.

"I'm getting jittery." Sally held up her hand, which was trembling slightly. "I don't want to use an X-Acto knife if I can't hold it still. I'm going to rest and get a fresh start on Sunday."

I bit my lip, holding in my frustration. All the other girls were taking Saturday off as well. No one had asked—they just told me they were doing it. They even had plans to watch movies together tonight. I was the only one in our group who was getting things done when they were supposed to be done. I was also sleeping the least. It would all be worth it, though, if we pulled it off.

When we pulled it off. There wasn't any other option.

Sally slept in the next morning. I didn't. I'd worked until two, but I was still up at seven. And I planned to do the same thing today.

"We've been cooped up in here for hours," Bear said. "Let's go for a walk."

I'd moved to his room in order to keep from yelling at Sally, who still hadn't finished the paper cut of the last golem. We were running out of time, and it seemed like I was the only one who cared.

This was my last chance to impress Bryan—to prove to him that he was wrong about me. To prove to myself that he was wrong.

"I don't have time to go for a walk," I said.

I'd taken over Bear's desk—not that he seemed to mind. He was sprawled out on his bed, sketching something that I was pretty sure had nothing to do with our film or his. The aquarium otter cam was playing on his computer, and the fuzzy little bastards were annoying me with their freewheeling ways, squeaking and diving and playing with one another.

"Did you think of a title?" I asked, even though I already knew the answer.

"Not yet," he said.

"Did you talk to John?"

"Not yet," he said.

I put down my pencil and glared at him. I hated this. I hated pushing and nagging and trying to get other people to do the work they had already agreed to do. I hated being the only one who cared.

"The screening is coming up soon," I said.

He shrugged. I balled up a piece of paper and threw it at him. He caught it easily.

"You need to take a break," he said. "You have murder in your eyes."

"I wonder why," I said.

The otters squeaked. I definitely wanted to murder *them*.

"Come on." Bear pushed up off the bed. "You can't just keep working nonstop. You need to do something else for a little bit. Let's go outside. Five minutes. Maybe ten. You remember what outside looks like, don't you? Big blue ceiling, brown tall things with green tops. All that stuff you draw in your notebook? Outside—it's real."

He was always trying to get me to take a break. Sometimes it was cute. Right now, I was about as amused by him as I was by the otters who were currently floating together holding hands. A few minutes ago their chaotic playing had bothered me; now it was their inactivity that was getting on my nerves. Didn't they have better things to do?

Bear gave my chair—his chair—a spin, forcing me to face him, his hands on the backrest, bracketing my shoulders. He *definitely* had better things to do. Like finish our project.

"We could go for a drive," he said, and nodded at his computer screen. "Go to the aquarium. Sketch some fish. Or sketch nothing at all. Leave our sketchbooks in the car, even."

"I have to work." I tried to spin away.

He held tight. "You're burning yourself out," he said. He wasn't teasing anymore. He actually looked a little worried.

"I'm fine," I said. "All I need is some more tea and some more time."

"This isn't sustainable," he said.

"I know," I snapped. "I just have to get through the next few weeks. And it would be great if everyone else would help me out instead of slacking off."

"They're exhausted," Bear said. "We're all exhausted."

I threw up my hands. "What do you want me to do about

that? We all knew this would be hard. We knew we'd have to make sacrifices."

Bear knelt down, taking my hands. He held them in my lap. I wanted to pull away.

"I have an idea," he said. "Instead of trying to kill yourself to get two shorts done, why don't I give you a director's credit on my project?"

I stared at him. He wasn't serious, was he?

Bear didn't seem to notice the way I'd gone completely still. In fact, he was smiling as if this was a brilliant solution. "This way you only have to focus on one movie. You can finish your short film another time," he said.

"You're kidding." My voice was flat.

He finally registered that I wasn't pleased.

"Hayley," he said, but I tugged my hands from his and stood.

"Do you really think that a codirector credit on your movie is the same as presenting something that *I* created—something that *I* made—to your father and the brain trust?"

Bear had stumbled back a little when I released him, but he pulled himself to his feet.

"I think that you're exhausting yourself over something that doesn't matter," he said.

My eyes nearly bugged out of my head. "What the hell?" I asked. "When I first brought it up you were *all* on board. *You* encouraged *me*."

"I know," he said. "But I also know you're doing this to impress my dad, who is never going to give you what you want."

I was so angry. This wasn't just about the short film anymore. It had become so much more. It was bigger. Bigger than me, bigger than the internship—hell, it felt like it was bigger than the entire animation industry.

"I get it," I said. "Now that my project is taking me away from *your* movie, suddenly it's not important. Suddenly it doesn't matter."

"That's not what I'm saying."

"You don't like it that I don't have time for your project anymore. For you."

"It's just a movie, Hayley."

But if I failed, I wouldn't just fail myself. I'd fail everyone. And it would prove them right. Bryan and Hal and Nick and every other guy who had made me feel like I wasn't good enough to be a part of something I desperately loved.

If I couldn't do this, what *could* I do? What good was all this ambition and drive and talent? Was it all a waste?

"Of course you'd feel that way," I said. "Because it *is* just a movie to you. And no matter what you do—no matter what half-baked, bullshit short film you present at the end of the showcase, your father—the whole fucking studio—is going to applaud you and tell you what a genius you are."

"Yes," Bear said.

"It's not fair," I said. "I try *so* hard. All I want is a chance. That's all. Just a stupid fucking chance to prove myself."

My face was hot. Hot and prickly and not in a good way. Bear didn't say anything. What could he say?

"And you don't even care." My voice cracked. "You have *all* this opportunity and you don't even care enough to do something with it."

"I care," Bear said. "I just don't care about getting credit for a fucking movie when it comes at the expense of the people I love."

"That's not the point," I said. "You don't get it!"

There was a long pause.

"I'm not the only one who doesn't get it," Bear said. "Didn't you hear what I said? I think I'm in love with you."

I *had* heard him. But I couldn't deal with this. Not now.

"No, you aren't," I said.

My pulse was racing. I was sweating. It was like I was standing outside my body, watching as I tore Bear's heart to shreds.

"If you loved me, you would understand exactly why this is important to me," I said. "You'd understand that what you're asking me to do is impossible." I put my hand to my chest, my palm sticky and hot. "This is who I am, Bear. And it's not about the credit. It's about recognition. I want to be able to stand in front of your father—in front of the whole studio—and say, 'I made this. This is mine.'"

We stared at each other. I waited. Waited for him to understand.

But it didn't happen.

"It's never going to make you happy," Bear said. "There's more to life than this. Than chasing credit. Chasing approval. I saw my mom do it. Saw how miserable it made her."

His mom *had* deserved credit on *A Boy Named Bear*. Suddenly I hated Bryan Beckett so much I couldn't see.

"She had a choice," Bear said. "She could fight my dad in court, or she could get custody of me. Walking away was the best thing she could have done," he said. "It saved us. Saved her."

Maybe Reagan Davis didn't regret what she'd done—the decision she'd made—but it didn't matter. I wasn't like that. I couldn't just give up. I wasn't going to be erased from my own story.

"What about us?" Bear asked. "Doesn't that count for something?"

Isaac had said that sometimes you had to put yourself first.

"I have to do this, Bear," I said. "I really thought you would understand."

I desperately wanted him to, but it was clear he didn't.

"I'm going to go," I said.

Part of me thought he'd try to stop me. But he just lifted his hands and stepped away. It was only a foot or two, but it felt like an entire ocean had opened up between us.

He'd never fully comprehended what this short—what this whole internship—meant to me, and it was clear now that he never would.

We were done.

I gathered up my things, praying that I could hold back my tears until I was out of his room. I felt numb, my chest, my heart, my everything, encased in ice.

"Your movie will be great, Hayley," Bear said. "But it won't be enough."

CHAPTER TWENTY-SEVEN

I was still working on Bear's short film so avoiding him was nearly impossible, but we did our best. We sat on opposite sides of the table in the conference room and managed to keep from speaking directly to each other whenever possible.

It hurt to look at him.

I'd never fully understood why Shelley Cona had fallen apart so completely when she'd broken up with her boyfriend, but I got it now. Because I felt totally and utterly adrift in my own life. I didn't want to do anything. I didn't even want to draw. Didn't even want to pick up my pencil.

I wanted to lie on my dorm room bed, staring up at the ceiling and willing each day to end so I'd be one step closer to being done with this internship and with Bear. Having to see him every day was torture, and every time I did, every time I felt that horrible twinge in my chest, I sent out a silent apology to Shelley.

I didn't know anything besides animation could make me feel such big things.

I was exhausted and heartsick. And it wasn't just Bear. I was tired of fighting what felt like an endless battle. Against Bryan's words. Against the studio's indifference. Against my own self-doubt.

I knew that Bear was right about one thing—that no matter

what I did, no matter what I put in front of Bryan, he would never—*ever*—say that he had been wrong about me.

And even though I'd told Bear that I had to finish the project, after our fight, I couldn't find the strength to work on it anymore. I wanted to put my pencil down, push away the sketchbook, and say, *Enough*. To just be done with it all. For good.

Isaac had said that this was a hard life. Maybe I wasn't up for it. Maybe I wasn't as strong as I thought I was. As strong as I needed to be. Maybe I was exactly the person I was afraid of being. The person who *could* give it all up.

When I told everyone that the project was done, I'd put a happy spin on it.

We don't have to finish to be proud of it, I'd texted Sunday after leaving Bear's room. **Everyone did a great job. That should be enough.**

I wished I believed it. Instead I just felt like a failure.

I'd ignored the flurry of texts that followed—the questions, the confusion. I avoided the dining hall—going out for long drives during dinnertime and not coming back to the dorms until late. Whenever one of the girls caught me in the hallway, I forced a smile and said that the short had run its course. I didn't tell them about Bear, but it was clear that things had changed between us. I came back to the dorms every night on the first shuttle. I spent my evenings texting Julie and Samantha, telling them nothing, just responding with as many emojis and GIFs as I could muster.

"You can talk to me," Sally had said the morning after I'd shut everything down.

She'd just gotten back from her run. I hadn't asked if Bear had joined her.

"If you want to talk," she'd said.

"There's nothing to talk about. It was too much to take on and we all knew it," I'd said. "The whole thing was a Hail Mary."

"A sports reference?" She'd jokingly put her hand on my forehead. "Hayley, if you've been possessed by a less-ambitious boy, blink three times."

I hadn't blinked. Her smile had faded.

"It's just a movie," I'd said.

"Hayley," she'd said, but I'd gotten up and out of bed before she could pry further.

"It's fine," I'd said. "I'm fine."

I wasn't. I didn't know who I was anymore. Didn't know what to do without this intense, unrelenting drive that used to push me forward. I didn't feel anything except failure, which was like a huge, gaping wound—a black hole of ambition.

I felt like nothing.

On Wednesday, I got an e-mail from Sloane. She wanted to see me after our last lunchtime lecture. With everything moving at full speed with the short films, and the studio focused on *No One Fears the Woods* deadlines, we'd all stopped meeting regularly with our mentors. I missed Sloane but didn't know why she wanted to see me.

I nearly walked right into Zoe when I entered the cafeteria that morning.

"Your shirt's untucked," she said.

I didn't even look down.

"Sorry the short didn't work out," she said. "I thought you guys were making good progress, but it was a pretty ambitious project."

I shrugged.

"Everything okay?" she asked.

"Yep," I said.

"Last lunchtime lecture?"

"Yep."

She paused. "Who's your final speaker?"

"Madeline Bailey," I said.

Zoe's face lit up. "Madeline is the best," she said.

It was one of the few times I'd heard anyone say anything nice about the producer. Despite everything that had happened, I felt a precious spark of curiosity.

"You like her?" I asked.

"I love her," Zoe said. "She's smart, she's focused, and she's probably the one person in this studio who doesn't take any shit from Bryan. I wish she was working on *No One Fears the Woods*, but she cut back on the long hours after her kids were born. You should have heard Bryan bitch about it." Zoe rolled her eyes. "He acts like she had children just to punish him."

"I wouldn't blame her if she did," I said.

I was thinking about Reagan Davis. About how I wished Bryan hadn't been able to get away with completely erasing her from the narrative.

"You'll have a good time talking to her," Zoe said.

We were meeting in Madeline's office, not in a conference room. It was right across from Bryan's office. His door was closed, but still, I kept my gaze down as we passed in front of it. In my memory, the whole room became even more alien and spaceship-like. I even imagined it being ice-cold, a black, starless galaxy.

Madeline's office was the complete opposite. There was an enormous red couch along one wall, covered in fluffy gray pillows.

The rug was bright slashes of color and wherever there wasn't a comfy-looking chair, there were bookcases, crammed full with books. Her desk was tiny compared to Bryan's—a simple wood top balanced on a skinny triangle. There was a Wallace & Gromit clock on the wall.

I loved it so much I wanted to cry.

"Come in, come in." Madeline herself was white and of average height with thick dark hair lined with gray. It was pulled back in a twist, but some of it was escaping against her neck. She wore thin tortoiseshell frames and a blue polka-dot blouse with a pencil skirt.

I realized I recognized her from the intern banquet—she'd been the other woman sitting at Bryan's table.

"Please sit anywhere," she said, pulling out a chair from the other side of her desk.

I didn't get to one of the individual chairs in time and had to sit next to Bear on the sofa. His leg was wedged against mine. I tried to ignore it. To ignore him. It was hard—he still smelled like pencil shavings. It was one of my favorite smells.

"It's a pleasure to meet you all," Madeline said.

She had a nice smile. Her bottom teeth were crooked.

"Is everyone excited about the showcase next week?" She laughed when none of us responded. "I can see that you're all in crunch mode. It's a very distinct expression—and one I see a lot around here." She crossed her eyes and let her mouth hang open a little, a pretty good impression of how some of us looked at that moment.

I gave her the best smile I could manage. It felt rude not to.

"I know this is probably the last thing you want to do right now," she said. "I imagine everyone is distracted—thinking about everything they need to accomplish today. I'll make this easy for you. I'll tell you a little bit about what it means to be a producer and then I'll send you on your way. It will be a short lecture today."

I could see why Zoe liked her, but the PA had also called her tough. The only person capable of standing up to Bryan. And others had all but called her a bitch. Madeline seemed friendly. And nice. Not like the badass warrior producer I'd been warned about.

"I'm sure you've heard that producing is mostly about scheduling and money," Madeline said. "And that's part of it, but it's so much more. Instead of boring you with a laundry list of things that a producer does, I thought I would tell you what qualities I think a good producer needs."

Nick might not have thought this kind of stuff was important, but I did. And maybe that spark of interest I felt meant that I hadn't given up. Not completely.

"A good producer is someone who understands how creative people work," Madeline said. "They recognize when artists need to be left alone and when they need structure. Support. Sometimes when they need limitations."

I saw some of the other interns tuning out. Tentatively, I raised my hand. I didn't know if she was expecting questions, but Madeline turned to me with a smile.

"What do you mean by artists needing limitations?" I asked. "Isn't that bad for creativity?"

"Great question," she said. "What's your name?"

"Hayley."

"Hayley." Madeline gave me a knowing look. "Well, Hayley, sometimes giving an artist unlimited resources, funds, and time can actually have the opposite effect on creativity. There are too many options, too many choices. Having some restraints, whether its budget or schedule or a combination of the two, can sometimes force an artist to think outside the box. To find alternative solutions."

She leaned forward onto her hand. "I always think of *Jaws* as the best example of this. Spielberg couldn't get the shark to work. It kept breaking, looked fake on camera, and just wasn't doing what it needed to do. In the end, it was his editor Verna Fields who figured out how to make it work. She cut the film so you rarely see the shark. Nowadays, Spielberg, with his massive budgets and unlimited access to CG, might not have needed her to problem-solve the way she did, and I don't think the movie would have worked nearly as well."

Madeline looked at me.

"I'm interested in what people do when their options are taken away. It's not just about creativity, it's about tenacity. It's about taking risks. It's about believing in yourself."

left Madeline's office feeling inspired and confused and completely turned upside down. After my question, it had felt like she'd spoken directly to me during the entire lecture. It had been soothing and encouraging, but overwhelming, too.

And I still didn't have any answers. I didn't know what to do. About anything.

We'd run out of time on the short because maybe we'd never really had enough time. It would have never worked. Madeline could talk about restraints, but sometimes they were just roadblocks. Nothing—not even tenacity—could get you around them.

"Hayley." Bear stopped me just before I reached the staircase. It was the first time we'd really spoken since we'd broken up.

"I'm late for a meeting," I said.

"Sally told me that you stopped working on the short," he said.

I couldn't look at him.

"Maybe we could talk?" he asked. "You could come over tonight?"

I could tell that he was glad—that he thought I'd made the right decision. That maybe everything could go back to the way it had been before. But I just felt sick about it.

"I don't think so," I said.

"I don't understand," he said.

"Exactly."

My eyes were burning by the time I got to Sloane's office. I pressed my knuckles against my face—ordering myself to keep it together. Then I knocked on her door.

"Hayley!" She gave me a hug before pulling me into her office and closing the door. "I have something for you."

She grabbed a box from the floor and set it on her desk with a loud *thump*.

"Open it," she said.

I wrestled with the overlapping cardboard sleeves to discover that the box was full of special-edition BB Gun sketchbooks.

"I have another brand that I usually use, but they give them to us for free here, so I wanted you to have them," Sloane said.

I was speechless. In front of me were enough sketchbooks to last years.

Before I'd started this internship, Bryan's seal of approval was all I had needed to guide me. Now, I didn't even know if I liked the sketchbooks because they were good or because Bryan said they were good.

"Thank you." I didn't want to be rude. It was an incredibly thoughtful, kind gift. I just didn't know what to do with it.

"That's not all," Sloane said. "I heard you've been busy."

She had a big, expectant smile on her face. A smile that faded when a tear escaped my dumb, traitorous eye and began rolling down my cheek. Why did I keep crying in front of her? It was so fucking embarrassing.

"Hey, hey, hey," she said. "I'm sorry. It's just—Zoe told me about your short film and, oh, Hayley, it's okay. What's wrong?"

I was fully sobbing now—the stress of the short, of everything that had happened with Bear, and twenty minutes of what felt like Madeline Bailey directly addressing my innermost conflict and *still* not giving me a solution, had obviously gotten to me.

I felt like a complete failure.

Sloane grabbed a box of tissues from somewhere and sat me down in her chair. I took a handful and shoved them into my face. I fell apart, snot coming out of my nose, my shoulders heaving with huge, lung-punching sobs as everything poured out of me. When I was done, the tissues were a soggy mess in my hands and my whole body ached.

"Feel better?" Sloane asked when I lifted my head.

She handed me a fresh pile of tissues. This time I dabbed my face a little more delicately.

"What happened?" she asked.

I shrugged. I didn't even know where to begin.

Sloane crossed her arms. "Come on," she said. "Is this about the short?"

That seemed like a good enough place to start. I nodded.

"Zoe told me you guys were making something really special and that all of sudden you pulled the plug on it."

There was that spark again. A warm, happy feeling at hearing that Zoe liked the short. That it was special. I wanted so badly for my work to be seen as special.

I wanted to be special.

Maybe that had been my problem all along. Maybe Bryan was right about caring too much about credit. Except, he didn't seem to mind getting all the credit for the work BB Gun Films did. I felt so confused and unsure of everything.

Not that any of it mattered. If Zoe had said that to Sloane about our short, she was probably just being nice.

I sniffed. "It was a bad idea," I said.

"It definitely was a daring one." Sloane leaned against her bookcase. "What exactly were you hoping to accomplish?"

"I wanted to prove Bryan wrong," I said.

It was as if I'd just told Sloane I was my own evil twin. She went so still that it felt like the universe had hit pause. Then she straightened. Slowly.

"What do you mean?" she asked.

"Nothing," I said, but it was too late.

"Hayley," Sloane said. "Why did you want to prove Bryan wrong?"

I'd never told her the details of what had happened with Nick. Before or after. Only Bear knew what Bryan had said to me, and even that had been the abridged version. I let out a breath. I'd been carrying all of it—Bryan's words, his assessment of me—around for weeks.

"I got called to Bryan's office," I said.

I could barely look at her, glancing around her office instead. "Again?"

"A few weeks ago. After I—after I yelled at Nick."

"You never told me exactly what had happened with that," she said.

I focused on her bookcase. At the framed drawing that had been placed facedown on the shelf. The one I didn't have to look at to remember.

"Nick stole my idea," I said. "I'd written a new script for his short and he gave it to Bryan and told him it was his."

There was a long pause, and I looked up to find Sloane staring at me with her mouth wide open. "Why didn't you tell me?" she asked.

What could I say? That I'd been too ashamed? That I didn't want to disappoint her? That I didn't say anything because I was afraid she'd tell me that Bryan was right? How much more crying did I want to do in front of Sloane? At what point did it become truly ridiculous?

"What did Bryan say to you in that meeting?" she asked.

I hesitated. Would it do any good to rehash all this now? The internship was almost over.

"Hayley." There was something in Sloane's voice. Almost as if she was bracing for the worst, but also like she was prepared. As if she knew already but was just waiting to hear it out loud. Besides crying even more in front of her, what else did I have to lose? I didn't have the short, I didn't have Bear.

So I told her. I told her *everything*. From Bryan saying that I wasn't talented enough to direct a short, to informing me that all I was good for was inspiring other people. When I was done, Sloane was silent. For a long time. A long, long time. I waited.

Sloane put her hand on her lips, then lowered it. She opened her mouth, and then closed it. Her nostrils flared.

"Excuse me," she said.

Then she turned away from me, hands clenched into fists.

"That self-centered piece of shit," she shouted at the ceiling. "Fuck you, BB Gun Films, and fuck you, Bryan. FUCK! YOU!"

I stared at her, shocked. When she was done, she let out a breath, her entire body deflating a little as she turned back to me.

"Hayley," she said. "I'm so, so sorry."

I was still too stunned to say anything, and a little surprised that no one came bursting through her door wondering what all the shouting and profanity had been about.

Sloane sat down. She inhaled and then exhaled, tucking her hair behind her ears.

"Bryan Beckett is the worst," she said. "Don't believe anything he said to you."

"But—"

Sloane held up a hand. I shut my mouth.

"My first year here," she said, "there was only one other woman in the story department, and I was one of the few people of color in the whole building. It was me, Isaac, Ron, and some other artists who no longer work here. Everyone else was white. Most of them were male."

Maybe things had changed, but they hadn't changed *that* much.

"I had a meeting with Bryan after my probationary period was up," she said. "I wanted to renegotiate my salary, which I'd found out was a fraction of what Josh was getting." Sloane gave me a knowing look. "Oh yeah, Josh and I were hired at the same time."

"But he's the executive head of story," I said.

Sloane's chair squeaked as she scooted forward. "I like Josh—I do—but he's good at two things: drawing, and kissing Bryan Beckett's ass. And he's only *really* good at one of them."

That might have been funny if it didn't suck so very much. I thought about Josh's mural—the one on prominent display in the lobby of the theater with a large plaque. It was entirely forgettable. Not like Sloane's mural. How beautiful and vibrant it was. And how it was hidden in a hallway deep inside the building with nothing to indicate who had drawn it.

"I came into the meeting prepared," Sloane said. "I had a whole argument laid out for why I deserved to be getting the same salary as someone with the same amount of experience. Of course, I didn't realize that Josh had been hired right out of CalAn, while I had three years at other studios under my belt. I should have been getting paid more to begin with."

She shook her head. "Anyway. Bryan not only told me that he would not be giving me a raise, but that I should be grateful for the job I already had. You see, I was a 'diversity hire.'" She used aggressive air quotes. "He hadn't really wanted to hire me. He would have preferred someone with a more *universal* perspective, but Madeline was forcing his hand."

I liked Madeline more and more. It was also, almost verbatim, what Bryan had said to me. I'd seen Sloane's work. Calling her nothing more than a diversity hire was beyond insulting.

"I went to my mentor," Sloane said. "Monica. The only other woman in our department. I thought she'd understand—give me advice, or at least commiserate with me about how shitty the process was."

She'd mentioned Monica before.

"She told me that she'd had to deal with the same thing when she started out, and that I needed to suck it up." Sloane gestured toward her bookcase. "You know that drawing of me—the caricature?"

I nodded.

"*She* drew it," Sloane said. "After we had that conversation. She passed it around in a story meeting—basically as a way to tell everyone that I was being ungrateful. Difficult. Bryan thought it was hilarious. Monica was 'one of them,' he said. And I wasn't. Years later, that's how still some people see me. As a bitch."

I got chills. Bad ones.

"Why did you keep the drawing?" I thought of the caricature Nick had done of me. How glad I was that it was at the bottom of some trash bag somewhere.

"At first I kept it up so that people would think I was in on the joke," Sloane said. "Acted like it didn't bother me. And when Monica retired, I thought about throwing it out, but I felt I needed the reminder. That I couldn't let *that* define who I was. Because this place can mess with your head. They'll try to tell you who you are. And you'll start believing it, if you're not careful."

I could see that. A part of me still wanted to believe in Bryan—in what he said—despite everything that had happened.

"Why didn't you warn me?" I asked.

"I should have," she said. "But I saw how excited you were about the program—about Bryan's work—and I didn't want to ruin it for you. It's clear you love animation and I didn't want to be the person that made you question that. And I thought—I *hoped*—that things would be different for you."

"But they weren't," I said. "They aren't."

When Sloane said that I loved animation, I realized I didn't know if that was true anymore. It had been magical to me once. I didn't know if it still was.

Rolling her chair backward, Sloane pulled a book from the shelf. She handed it to me.

"Have you ever heard of Lotte Reiniger?" she asked.

The book was a collection of her art. Shadow puppets, like the kind of animation that Sally did. I'd never heard the name before, nor had I ever seen her work.

"Most people think that Walt Disney directed the first full-length animated feature in 1937," Sloane said. "But Lotte Reiniger made *The Adventures of Prince Achmed* in Germany in 1926. That's eleven years before *Snow White and the Seven Dwarfs.*"

I flipped the pages of the book Sloane had given me. Lotte Reiniger's work was beautiful. Simple, yet elegant. Dynamic.

"She also pioneered the use of the multiplane camera, but barely anyone's heard of her. There were plenty of female animators—even in the early days—we just don't know about them. Artists like Reiko Okuyama and Brenda Banks and Retta Scott and Faith Hubley and Evelyn Lambart and Lillian Friedman Astor and Helena Smith Dayton and Makiko Futaki and Joy Batchelor and Laverne Harding and Edith Vernick and Christine Jollow and so many more. All of our heroines have been erased from the story. No wonder we've never felt like we belonged."

I was overwhelmed.

"What Bryan said is not about you," Sloane said. "It's about him. It's what comes from growing up in an industry that ignores its own history. Women have been shut out of animation, making us believe it's because *we're* not good enough. That our stories aren't worth telling."

She stood. "But they're wrong. Bryan was wrong about me, and he's wrong about you."

I sat there, letting her words sink in.

"You should finish your short," Sloane said.

"It's too late," I said. "There's not enough time."

"If we restart work right now, there's a chance."

"We?"

"Hell yeah," she said. "Look, maybe this industry hasn't changed as fast as I would like, but things *are* different. I might not have had the mentor *I* wanted—the mentor I needed—when I was starting out, but there's no way I'm going to let history repeat itself."

She put her hand on my shoulder.

"We're in this together," she said. "We might not change Bryan's mind and we probably won't change the animation industry—but at least we'll have control over *this* story."

She straightened.

"Come on," she said. "Let's make a movie."

CHAPTER TWENTY-NINE

With Sloane's encouragement, I gathered the rest of the girls, Avengers-style, and we hit the ground running. Again.

It didn't take much to get everyone back on board, and the time off actually ended up being more beneficial than anything. After a break from the project, I could see certain things more clearly now—the problems, yes, but also the solutions.

Together, we ate, slept, and breathed animation. It was exactly what I had hoped for when I'd first imagined this internship—working as a team, building something together. With Sloane and Zoe coaching us from the sidelines, we worked until I was sure none of us ever wanted to see a golem again.

But we were triumphant.

"I knew you wouldn't quit," Sally said.

Our room was a chaotic mess. All the work that we'd done away from the studio was here. As the final week of the internship came to a close, I had completely given up on trying to keep my desk clear.

It didn't bother me anymore. I'd done some of the best work of my life surrounded by drawings, pens scattered everywhere, my own pencil flying over the page as I did my part to bring Miriam and the golem to life.

"I hope it's worth it," I said.

We had one last day at the studio. The day after that—Saturday— we'd be packing up our things and hosting our parents at the end-of-the-summer banquet in the CalAn dining hall. Then on Sunday, we'd be going back to the studio for the last time—screening the short films in the theater for our parents, the studio, and the press.

We'd finished the final shot an hour ago.

Gathering around Emily's computer, with the lights off, we watched the short. It was the first time we'd seen it all the way through.

It was five minutes long—only a fraction of the story I'd intended to tell. There was no dialogue. The only noise was some eerie guitar strings, courtesy of Caitlin, and some minimal sound design—footsteps and wind—that Jeannette had managed to make on her phone. Parts of the animation felt jerky at times, and Miriam's design wasn't as consistent as I would have liked, but it was finished. And it was good.

It wasn't how I had pictured it in my head—not even close— but I could see the fingerprints of every single person who'd worked on it. Sally's golem was ingenious, and she'd made him stoic, yet tender. Rachel's backgrounds were stark and devastating, while Emily had woven Miriam within it like needlepoint. Caitlin had been in charge of the few close-ups of Miriam's face, and she'd discovered sadness in the stern lines, while Jeannette had found ways to bring the dusty environments to life.

I could even see Sloane and Zoe's work. How Sloane had urged us to linger on moments that we had been leaving too soon. The way that Zoe had encouraged us to simplify our settings in order to get more done.

I saw Bear's influence, too. The way Miriam rubbed the back of her neck when she looked up at the golem. I'd animated it, but I'd been thinking of him.

"We did it," Emily said when it was over.

Caitlin turned the lights back on. We blinked at one another.

"We did it," Sally said.

I felt a spark inside of me. Something that felt a little like magic. We were all bleary-eyed and half dead from exhaustion, but we celebrated.

Cranking Sally's "Hero's Journey" mix, we FaceTimed Sloane and Zoe so they could join in, all of us belting out the words to "Into the Unknown" and "How Far I'll Go." It was a good thing that we were the only people on the hall—no doubt if the guys had heard us, they would have complained.

My throat was sore; my back ached from spending hours bent over my desk, but I felt better than I had in weeks. It barely hurt to think about Bear at all.

"What did Sloane say about John?" Sally asked as we cleared off our beds. We'd opened a few bottles of sparkling apple cider, and a box or two of doughnuts. Now there was trash strewn everywhere. I had no idea how six of us ended up using as many napkins as we did.

I shook my head. "She said she'd ask him in the morning."

We still didn't have a way to get it into the final presentation. I'd counted on Bear for that—hoping that his relationship with John would have been enough to convince the editor to do something that could possibly get him fired.

Zoe wasn't comfortable asking, and I didn't blame her. Sloane was our next, best chance.

"It could go either way," she'd said.

I was still amazed that we had completed a five-minute short—a *good* five-minute short—in the free time we'd had between our other projects. I wanted to see it on the big screen. I wanted everyone to see it. Wanted my parents and Zach to see it. Wanted Bryan to see it.

Maybe Bear was right—maybe it wouldn't be enough. Maybe it wouldn't drown out that little voice in the back of my head—a voice that sounded a lot like Bryan Beckett—telling me that I wasn't as talented as I thought I was.

Maybe that voice would never go away. But I wouldn't know unless I tried.

When Sloane took me out for lunch on my last day, she still hadn't spoken to John.

"Do you have the final cut?" she asked.

I handed her the flash drive. It was warm—I'd been carrying it around since we finaled it, my hand in my pocket, the drive pressed hard against my palm. As we sat down to eat, I kept tracing the indent it had left.

It was a nearby Mexican place that Sloane had told me was her go-to post-production celebration spot. It was huge—the inside designed to look like it was outside, with a fake veranda and a real tree in the middle of the room. Each table was decked out with colorful flags, plastic tablecloths, and big bowls of fresh chips.

"If he says yes, I'll just give it right to him," Sloane said.

Neither of us brought up what would happen if he said no.

"It's good," Sloane said. "I'm really proud of you."

I nodded, my lips clamped together. I'd already cried enough in front of Sloane—I didn't want to make a habit of it.

"Have you thought about what you want to do next?" she asked.

"I don't even know where to start," I said.

She laughed. "You said that to me your first day here, remember?"

It felt like it had been years. I'd been so sure of myself—of everything—back then.

"I remember that you also asked me what I loved about animation," I said.

"Ah yes." Sloane took a sip of the margarita she'd ordered. "The *big* question."

"I said something about the details," I said. "Repeated something that Bryan had said."

Sloane nodded.

I hadn't trusted myself back then—hadn't trusted what I believed.

"It's more than that," I said. "It's always been more than that." I still couldn't really put it into words. "Animation is—"

It was magic and it was power, and it was something I could do really well. It was a part of me and outside of me. It was feeling nostalgic for something that hadn't even happened. It was gravity. It just *was*.

Sloane looked down and I realized I'd put my hand over my heart.

"I know exactly what you mean," she said.

There was a reception in the cafeteria at the end of the day. It seemed like all we would be doing for the next few days would be going to parties or little gatherings like this.

I saw Ron setting out tiny cupcakes. "Last day," he said.

I nodded. "Will you be at the screening on Sunday?"

"'Fraid not," he said. "Above my pay grade."

That was disappointing. I wanted Ron to see my film almost as much as I wanted Bryan to see it. Maybe even more. After all, if one counted the tea and the doughnuts, he'd provided a vital type of support to all of us.

"I'll find a way to see the final projects," Ron said. "All of them."

I hadn't told him that we were making a fifth, secret film, but I was pretty sure he knew. I was pretty sure that Ron knew everything that happened in the studio.

"I'm going to miss you guys," Ron said. "You all brought fresh neuroses to the studio."

I laughed. "I'm going to miss you, too."

He waved a hand. "You're just going to miss the doughnuts."

I wanted to hug him, but before I could decide if it was appropriate or not, Ron was looking over my shoulder and waving. I glanced back to find Bear coming toward us.

"I should go," I said.

Ron gave me a surprised look. "Oh?"

Apparently, he *didn't* know everything.

"Yeah," I said. "Bye, Ron."

"Bye, Hayley."

My shirtsleeve brushed against Bear's shoulder as I passed him. I didn't look up. Didn't look back. I just kept walking.

CHAPTER THIRTY

Mom had been thrilled to get my call. "I brought you a few options," she said, practically hidden behind dresses as she elbowed her way into my dorm room.

She dumped them all on the bed and turned to sweep me up into a hug. I leaned into it. I'd forgotten how much I missed her hugs. She smelled like flour.

"It's been a long couple of weeks," she said. "I love your father, and I love your brother, but Hayley, it's not the same without you."

It was almost too much to hear. Almost.

"Thanks for bringing these over," I said.

We still had a few hours until the reception on campus, but I'd decided I wanted to wear something different from what I'd been wearing all summer.

It was funny. During the chaotic rush to finish our short, I'd never been more grateful for my uniform. I'd barely remembered to brush my teeth, let alone had time to decide what to wear every morning. Bryan was right. Dressing the same every single day made it easier to focus all your attention on the work.

It was just that I realized, when we were done, that I didn't want to focus all my attention on the work. I was beyond proud of what we'd done, but I was pretty sure when I thought about this internship, I wasn't going to remember the golem shot we had to half-ass, or the wonky animation on Miriam, or even the story problems we couldn't quite fix.

I was going to remember lunches with Sloane. Shuttle rides with Sally. Sheet masks and popcorn with the other girls.

I was going to remember Bear.

The work was the work, but in the end, it wasn't everything.

There was more. *I* was more.

As of tonight, I was ready to step out from Bryan Beckett's shadow. And a new dress felt like just the right start.

"I went shopping on my way here," Mom said. "They all still have the tags on, so I'll take back whatever you don't like."

She had brought armfuls. "I also have the one from Stella's wedding," Mom held up a green dress with a big, swishy skirt. "And the one from your cousin's bar mitzvah."

It was a black-and-white sheath that I'd thought made me look at least twenty. Maybe even twenty-one. I took my time with the bounty of dresses she'd brought me. I'd missed this. Missed how clothes could make you feel like a new person when you most needed to.

One of the new dresses was white with black polka dots all over, and puffy sleeves. I held it up against me as I looked in the mirror. Unlike the one from the bar mitzvah, it made me look my own age. It made me look like me.

"This one," I said.

Mom beamed. "I hoped you would like it."

I hung it up in the closet alongside the green dress and the bar mitzvah dress. Mom was sitting on my bed and patted the spot next to her.

"Tell me about the internship," she said. "We missed hearing from you."

I sat. "I was busy," I said.

"I know." She took my face in her hands, her thumbs against my cheeks. She hadn't done something like that since I was a kid—I hadn't let her. It was a little embarrassing, but also a little nice and no one was around so I just let her be my mom. "You're always busy."

"I like being busy," I said.

It was true, but I had also started to think about other things I could do to keep myself busy. Things that didn't necessarily have to do with animation. I didn't think I'd start running or join the soccer team like Sally and Jeannette. I was pretty sure I didn't have the talent for music like Caitlin or the patience for plants like Emily, but it had become clear to me, the more we all worked together, how much the things they did outside of animation informed the work they did for it.

Animation would probably always be first in my heart, but maybe it wasn't such a bad idea to make room for other stuff as well. I'd even promised Samantha and Julie I'd go on a hike with them when we were all home, something I'd never really felt I had time for.

I was going to make time now. For them. For my family. For new things.

"Was the program everything you hoped it would be?" Mom asked.

I wanted to tell her about the short film. Wanted to tell her everything that had happened this summer, but I didn't know how to tell her or what she would say.

Mom patted my knee. "You know I love your father, right?"

I nodded.

She looked up at the ceiling. "Sometimes, though, he can be such a schmuck."

I was so surprised that I laughed. Mom laughed too.

"He told me what he said to you the night you called. The night you found out about the director position." She sighed. "I could have throttled him."

"It's okay," I said.

"No, honey, no it's not," Mom said. "But it's my fault too. We haven't been doing a very good job supporting you, have we?"

I lifted my shoulder in a half-shrug.

"When you told us about the internship, you were so sure you'd get in, but I was worried," she said. "I know you think that I don't understand animation, and maybe I don't understand everything about it, but I can tell how important it is to you. I also know how hard it is to be an artist. Not from personal experience, but I know what it's like to love an artist. I saw how devastated your father was when he didn't get into grad school. I don't think he ever fully recovered from that rejection, and I didn't want to see that happen to you."

"But I did get in," I said.

"I know," Mom said. "It scared me a little, I guess. I worried that the further you went, the harder it would be when you did face rejection. Because rejection is part of the deal, isn't it? I didn't want you to find yourself in a position where you didn't have options. I wanted to protect you, I guess."

I understood. Because right now, part of me still wanted to give up. It was hard—so hard—and the thought of having to fight *all the time* just to be seen made me feel worn-out. Like I wanted to curl into a little ball and go to sleep. Turn off. Shut down.

"But I can't protect you from something that's a part of life—something you're going to face whether you're an artist or not," Mom said. "And that's when I realized something. I always thought that you took after your father—your ambition, your artistry—and you do. But what I realized is that you take after me, too. Your stubbornness?" Mom pointed to her chest. "That comes from me."

I'd never really thought about it that way.

"Your father let one rejection stop him," she said. "You won't. Because I didn't. You think it's easy going back to school at my age? No. It's hard. But I do it because it's worth it. Because I *know* I'm good at it. And that confidence, that strength to keep trying, that's what you have. No matter what, I know you'll find your way."

It was like I was seeing Mom for the first time. And seeing myself in her. It was nice.

"*This* is where you belong," she said. "And I'm so, so proud of you."

I wore the polka-dot dress to the reception on campus. Sally did my makeup—gold eyeliner and a bright, bold lip. I half hoped that Nick would come over to stare at my mouth and make some comment about how fake I was. The internship was basically over; there wasn't much they could do to me if I kneed him in the balls.

The dining hall still looked like the dining hall—it wasn't decked out the way they'd done at the studio cafeteria that first week—but there were high, round tables covered in tablecloths and trays of tiny hors d'oeuvres.

My parents and Zach hadn't arrived yet, but Sloane was there, talking to a tall white woman with wavy brown hair and one gray streak at her temple.

"Hayley." Sloane gave me a hug. "You look great."

"Thanks. You too."

Sloane was wearing a beautiful silk dress that looked like it had been purposefully stained with streaks of color. She looked stunning as always.

"So, this is Hayley," the woman with the gray streak said. "I've heard a lot about you."

"Thanks?" I hoped it was a compliment.

"Sloane has been telling me how talented you are. I think she described you having 'a singular vision.' High praise, indeed."

I looked at Sloane, who beamed at me.

"It's true," she said. "If this is the kind of stuff you're doing at seventeen, I can't even imagine what you'll be doing when you're my age."

It was the nicest thing anyone had ever said to me.

Still, it didn't completely drown out Bryan's voice.

"Sloane tells me you've had an interesting summer," the woman said. "Was it everything you hoped it would be?"

We hadn't been officially introduced, but I didn't know how to address that, so I just didn't.

"Not exactly," I said. "It was challenging. But good. Sloane was a great mentor. The best."

"I paid her to say that," Sloane said, but I could tell that she was pleased.

"I'm not surprised at all," the woman said. "Sloane is one of a kind. She *also* has a singular vision." She looked at Sloane expectantly.

"I'm still thinking about it," Sloane said cryptically. "It's a big change."

The woman held up her hands in a gesture that was surprisingly familiar to me. "I know, I know," she said. "I'm being impatient."

"Understandably," Sloane said. "I'm excited for you to get back in the game."

"Me too," the woman said. "There's no point in regretting things that have already happened, but I wish I hadn't given up so easily back then."

I listened, the two of them so focused on what they were talking about that I was pretty sure they'd forgotten about me. Just for a moment, though. Sloane looked at me and smiled.

"This new generation, however," she said. "They're not going to put up with that crap."

The woman with the gray streak nodded. "That's what I've heard." She looked at me. "I've been told you took on the king. And won."

It was clear they were talking about Bryan.

"I don't think I won," I said. "I mean, I still didn't get to direct a short."

I hadn't heard if Sloane had managed to convince John to put our film in the lineup, and even if he had, I didn't think it was a good idea to tell a stranger about our plan. Despite Sloane's obvious respect for her.

"It's more than that," the woman said. "It's holding on to your confidence—your sense of self-worth—in the face of all of this." She waved her hand at the people gathered for the reception. "It's believing that you have talent, even when the loudest voices in the room are telling you that you don't."

She put her hand on my shoulder. "Don't ever let them tell you that you're not good enough."

Looking past me, she let out a sigh and leaned toward Sloane. "You know, I wish I'd never suggested he start wearing the same thing every day," she said.

I looked back and saw that Bryan was standing across the room with Bear.

"I was just tired of picking out his outfits every morning," she said. "Good to see you, Sloane. And nice to meet you, Hayley."

"Great seeing you, Reagan," Sloane said.

I stared as Reagan Davis, formerly Reagan Beckett, crossed the room toward her son and ex-husband.

"That's Bear's mom?" I asked, even though I already knew the answer.

"Did I not introduce you?" Sloane asked. "Sorry about that."

"It's okay," I said, unable to take my eyes off of Reagan.

She gave Bear a hug before turning to her ex-husband, her stiff body language indicating her discomfort. Still, they leaned toward each other, exchanging cheek kisses.

"She deserved credit on *A Boy Named Bear*, didn't she?" I asked.

"Yep," Sloane said. "That was before my time, but if you ask anyone in the studio who worked on that movie, they'll tell you that Reagan is the only reason it got made. She was the person who kept Bryan from getting distracted—gave him necessary limitations on what they could do."

Limitations. Madeline Bailey had talked about limitations. How they could force an artist to do something they might have never considered. How certain artists could take those limitations and make something extraordinary.

"She gave up her whole career to work on that movie," Sloane said. "She's an incredible editor in her own right, but after everything that happened with the divorce and the settlement, she just stopped working. Focused on raising Bear."

Bear had said that giving up that fight had been the best thing his mother had done. That it had saved her. Him.

I didn't think that was true.

"That's too bad," I said.

"Yeah," Sloane said, but she was smiling. "It was."

There was something she wasn't telling me, but I could sense that now wasn't the time or the place to get details.

"Did you give the flash drive to John?" I asked.

Her smile faded. "Hayley," she said. "I don't know if he's going to do it."

I'd been bracing for that response, but it didn't make it hurt any less. I had to start accepting that just because you worked really hard at something, just because you thought you were good enough, that you had something special to offer, it didn't mean that other people would agree. Or even give you a chance to prove it.

"Okay," I said.

"I gave him the film," Sloane said. "Told him how important it was, but this is the first BB Gun film that he's the lead editor on. There's a lot riding on how well he tows the family line."

"I understand," I said.

"Don't give up," Sloane said. "He didn't say no. He just said he'd have to think about it."

I didn't have much time to be disappointed before my parents and Zach arrived at the reception. I hadn't seen Dad and Zach in weeks. I'd missed them, but it was still a little awkward. I introduced them to Sloane.

"Hayley is an incredibly focused young woman," she said.

Zach started humming the Oompa Loompa song under his breath. I pinched his arm.

"I think she has so much potential," Sloane said.

"Is this the kind of potential that would be better suited after four years at college?" Mom asked. "At an arts college, perhaps?"

"Mom," I said, even though I didn't really mind this time.

"I'd be happy to discuss the pros and cons of a college degree when it comes to getting a job in animation." Sloane winked at me. "A lot of my peers attended CalAn."

The two of them walked away, leaving me, Dad, and Zach.

"Hey, mini cupcakes," Zach said, and headed over to the dessert table where Sally was putting some macarons on her plate.

Dad had his hands in his pockets, swaying back and forth. It was clear that Mom had had words with him, and he was now expected to fix the mess he'd made. I wasn't going to make it hard for him, but I wasn't going to make it easy, either. I was kind of tired of making things easier for guys in my life.

"Want to get some food?" he asked.

"Sure."

We each got a tiny round plate, Dad piling on as much shrimp, little crab cakes, and slices of bruschetta as he could manage. I took some mini egg rolls.

"Look at all this stuff," Dad said. "Quite the spread."

I nodded.

"Your mom says you really enjoyed the internship," Dad said, as we took our food to a table. "Learned a lot."

"Yeah," I said.

We sat there, eating in silence.

"I messed up, huh, kiddo?"

I didn't say anything.

"I'm proud of you, Hayley, it's just . . ." Dad sighed. "I might also be a little jealous, too."

My eyebrows shot up.

"Jealous of me?"

"It's your tenacity," he said. "How driven you are."

I thought about what Mom had said—how Dad had given up after getting rejected from grad school.

"I know you don't think animation is serious, Dad, but it's important to me," I said.

He lowered his crab cake. "I know," he said. "I guess I just couldn't figure out how to be supportive." Dad ran a hand through his hair. His glasses were smudgy. "But that's not your problem," he said. "That's my problem. And it's something I'll be better about. At least, I can try."

I nodded, rocking back on my heels.

"Do you really think I'm a spoiled brat?" I asked.

He didn't say anything, and when I glanced up, I saw the shock on his face.

"Did I say that?" he asked.

"Sort of," I said.

He closed his eyes for a moment. "You're not a brat," he said. "You're amazing."

"Really?"

He put his hand over mine. "Of course. You're my favorite daughter, after all."

"I'm your only daughter."

He squeezed my hand. This was about as honest and open as we'd ever been and I was glad for it, but we were also in the middle of the CalAn dining hall and it wasn't exactly the best place to be emotional.

I cleared my throat.

"If you really want to make it up to me, they're coming out with a new Wacom tablet this year," I said.

Dad laughed. "We'll see," he said, and stole one of my egg rolls.

After the reception, Sally went to bed, but I couldn't sleep. I didn't know what was going to happen tomorrow, but I couldn't help hoping that everything would work out—that John would say to hell with his career and add our short film to the lineup. That Bryan would be forced to watch something that I made. That he, and Nick, and everyone else who had made me feel like I didn't belong there would see exactly what I was capable of.

Still in my polka-dot dress, I went for a drive.

It was the perfect California night. For the first time ever, I wanted to do the thing I saw people do in movies. I rolled down my windows and went down the 101. I didn't have anywhere to go, I just wanted to drive—just wanted to go fast. My hair blew up and around my face as the car flew down the freeway.

In a few weeks, I'd be back at school. Senior year.

After talking to Sloane, Mom hadn't given up hope that I'd apply to college. But at least she'd accepted that this was what I wanted to do.

"Why not CalAn?" she'd asked as I had walked my parents and Zach to their car.

"I'll think about it," I'd told her.

"That's all I ask."

This was the year where I was supposed to figure out what I wanted. I'd started the internship thinking that I knew. Thinking that I had a plan.

Even if John didn't put our short into the final screening, even if Bryan never saw what I was truly capable of doing—was BB Gun Films still where I wanted to end up? I'd been so sure that there was a place for me at the studio—that once I was here, I'd finally feel like I belonged.

I didn't know what I wanted anymore. Or, I did, but my plan wasn't as clear-cut as it had been a few weeks ago.

I was blasting my favorite piece of animation score—"Test Drive" from *How to Train Your Dragon*. As the music swelled, I could feel my heart turn over.

I thought about everything that had happened over the past few weeks. I thought about everyone I had met—Zoe, Isaac, Ron, and Sloane. Madeline Bailey. Even Reagan Davis. I thought about what they had taught me—about art, about myself. About facing obstacles. About having fun.

I thought about my friends. About Sally, Caitlin, Emily, Jeannette, and Rachel. How together we had made something out of nothing. How we'd taken an idea, and with paper and pencil, we'd made it come alive.

Bryan believed that the only thing that mattered was the final product. I didn't think I believed him anymore. I was proud of what we had accomplished, but I knew—with L.A. speeding past, with the summer nearly behind me—that the thing that mattered the most to me wasn't the film I had made.

It was everything else.

Maybe I didn't need Bryan to see the short. Maybe I didn't

need to prove to him that I was talented. I knew who I was. What I was capable of.

Maybe that was enough.

Bear was outside the dorms when I got back. Like he had been waiting for me.

"I saw you talking to my mom," he said.

"She's nice." I jingled my car keys in my hand. All that exhilaration I'd felt wilted like my wild hair. I didn't want to talk to him. I didn't want to look at him. My heart began to hurt again.

"She liked you," he said.

I nodded.

"I heard you finished the short," he said.

"It doesn't matter," I said. "John probably won't screen it."

Bear frowned. "Hayley, I—" he said, but I held up my hand.

"Can we not?" I asked. "I'm tired, and tomorrow's a big day. For you, at least."

At first it seemed like he was going to argue with me, but he just nodded and stepped aside to let me pass.

CHAPTER THIRTY-ONE

The theater was crowded. Bryan was sitting up toward the front with Bear, Reagan, and most of the press. Sloane had saved me, Zach, and my parents some seats toward the back, and I saw Sally and her parents sitting right in the middle.

I'd told her—told all the girls—that our short probably wasn't going to be shown. And when I said that it was okay, that we should be proud of what we had done, this time I meant it. Still, I couldn't help that jittery, double-time heartbeat I felt when I allowed myself to hope that I might be wrong.

I'd worn my green dress, with my hair down. As the doors of the theater closed, I started fidgeting with a lock of it—smoothing it and twisting it between my fingers. The lights dimmed and the crowd grew silent.

Bryan rose from the audience and stepped onto the stage.

"Welcome," he said, arms spread wide.

Zach leaned over Mom. "Is that Willy Wonka?" he asked. I shushed him.

Onstage, Bryan continued. "I am so pleased to welcome you all to the first BB Gun summer film festival. We have four incredible short films to share with you today."

I watched the back of Bear's head. He turned to say something to his mom, who put her hand on his shoulder.

"I am so proud of the work our interns have done," Bryan said. "The caliber of talent here is truly incredible, and I'm certain you'll see—as I do—the future of animation here in these projects." He smiled at the crowd. "But you didn't come here to listen to me talk," he said.

There was a ripple of laughter. That was exactly what the press had come here to do.

"I'll step aside and let these talented directors introduce their projects."

Before everything had ended between me and Bear, he'd told me that his father was making each of the directors speak about their movie.

"I know my dad wants me to say something about how I was inspired by him—how he's always pushed me to do better—but I'm not going to do it," Bear had said. "I should just stand up there—in front of everyone—and tell the press how he was a shitty father who forced me to do an internship I didn't want to do."

I had no idea what he was going to say.

The first two films were introduced and screened. Eddie and Jeff didn't stumble too much over their words as they talked about their films, but I think they knew—as well as the rest of us—that everyone was just waiting for Bear's movie.

Nick's film was second to last. Sloane and I exchanged a look as he got up onstage, looking like a sweatier, shorter version of Bryan.

"Hi, uh, I'm Nick," he said. His voice was shaking. His hands, too.

If he hadn't been such an asshole to me and everyone, I might have felt bad for him.

"My film is a modern retelling of *Jack and the Beanstalk*," he read robotically from the piece of paper he was holding. "I was inspired by filmmakers like Tarantino, and Bryan Beckett, of course."

He gestured awkwardly toward Bryan, who waved at the crowd.

"I please hope you enjoy it," Nick said.

I rolled my eyes as the lights went down.

It was immediately apparent that Nick had ended up using the script I'd written. He was lucky I didn't stand up in the middle of the screening and yell at him for being a thief and a liar. It wasn't worth it. Despite stealing my script, Nick had still managed to fuck up his film, adding back unnecessary—and bad—jokes and overstuffing the plot to the point of nonsense. Whatever he had been trying to accomplish with his film fell flat. I didn't want to claim any part of it.

The applause was polite but quieted quickly as Bear got on the stage. He didn't have anything in his hands—apparently, he hadn't written anything down.

"Hey," he said.

There was some laughter. He had a completely different energy from the other guys—all of whom had seemed deeply uncomfortable to be onstage. Bear appeared fine, relaxed, even. He wasn't trying to impress anyone. He was just Bear.

"My film doesn't have a title," he said. "I thought about calling it *Bear's Fantasia*, but that was shot down."

He looked out into the chuckling audience. I knew he was looking for me.

"It's not really a story," he said. "It's more of a bunch of feelings. So. Yeah."

With that, he got off the stage. Applause was scattered and confused.

Bryan stood up again. "We'll have a Q-and-A after this," he said. "Where the directors can speak about their work in more detail."

That hadn't been in the program. Had he just added it at the last minute because of Bear's lackluster introduction?

The short was good. Unlike Nick's film, it was something I was proud to have my name on. It wasn't really a traditional story, but it was beautiful and evocative. The animation was gorgeous—Sally's especially.

I hadn't seen the credits, but there was a quiet little gasp that went through the crowd when the cards came up and Bear had listed me as the codirector. All around me, I saw people whispering to one another. Up at the front of the theater, Bryan turned sharply toward Bear.

"I didn't know you were so involved," Dad said.

"It was really beautiful," Mom said.

"It didn't suck," Zach said. A high compliment, especially in front of our parents.

"Thanks," I said.

I waited for the lights to come up, for Bryan to drag the directors back up onstage to answer questions, but the theater stayed dark. My heart began to beat faster.

Bryan shifted in his seat, turning around to face the projection booth, just as the opening image of my short film flashed across the screen. I grabbed Sloane's hand.

"He did it," I said.

"Shh," she said.

The confused murmurs died out as Sally's golem appeared. Our film was half the length, and rougher in places than some of the other shorts, but it was good. It was really good.

Part of me wished that it wasn't dark, that I could watch the faces of everyone around me. I caught a glimpse of Mom—her face barely illuminated—and her eyes were wide, her mouth hanging open. Even Zach seemed focused on the screen.

Sloane squeezed my hand as the last frame came up.

Directed by Hayley Saffitz.

"You did this?" Dad asked.

"That . . . wasn't bad." Zach sounded a little stunned.

"It was incredible," Mom said.

There were tears in her eyes. I looked away fast, so I wouldn't get weepy as well.

People were applauding. Really applauding. Sloane was on her feet, and a few other people followed suit. I saw Isaac standing—and Bear as well. He had turned, facing the back of the theater. The lights came up and his eyes found mine. His mom was standing next to him, and he bent his head toward her, pointing in my direction.

Reagan's eyes widened with recognition when she saw me, and she smiled and waved. I didn't know what to do, so I waved back. Suddenly half of the theater was turning around to stare at me.

"Hayley." Bryan was onstage. He was smiling, but I could tell he was furious.

"Why don't you come down here?" he said.

Now *everyone* was looking at me.

I got up from my seat, awkwardly maneuvering in front of my parents' knees and out into the aisle. My palms were damp, but I didn't wipe them on my dress, afraid they'd leave big, wet hand-prints on the skirt. My ankles felt wobbly as I walked toward the front of the theater, and I wasn't certain I would get there without falling flat on my face.

"I need a moment with our directors," Bryan said to the press. He was still smiling, his teeth clenched together. "Come with me," he said.

Nick shot me a look as he got up from his seat and followed Bryan through a door at the side of the stage. Jeff and Eddie trailed after him.

"That was great," Bear said.

I looked up at him.

"Really great," he said.

"Thanks," I said.

He put his hand on my back. Gently. I leaned into it.

"Let's do this," I said.

CHAPTER THIRTY-TWO

Bryan was facing away from us, his shoulders hunched. Eddie and Jeff suctioned themselves to a wall, trying to look as unobtrusive as possible, while Nick was hovering dangerously close to Bryan.

"Which of you knew about this?" Bryan turned to face us.

Bear cheerfully raised a hand. "I helped," he said.

Bryan looked at Eddie and Jeff, the two of them pale and nervous.

"Go back to your seats," he said.

They fled eagerly. Nick was standing next to Bryan, his hands on his hips. While Bryan had been speaking, Nick's head had bounced up and down like a bobblehead.

"I knew they were up to something," Nick said. "I just knew it."

Bryan turned toward him. "Who are you?"

Nick shrank back. "I'm Nick," he said. "I directed *Jack and the Beanstalk*."

Bryan closed his eyes, pinching his nose between his fingers. "Go away," he said.

"I—"

"Go. Away," Bryan said.

"But my film—"

"Was serviceable," Bryan said, like the word tasted bad in his mouth.

It was almost worse than saying it was terrible.

All of the color drained from Nick's face and he pushed past us, scrambling for the door. It slammed closed and Bryan fixed me with a stare so intense that I was pretty sure my heart fully stopped.

"Who the hell do you think you are?" Bryan asked.

I knew he wasn't really asking so I said nothing.

"I did not put this whole internship together so some little brat could show up my son at the last minute." He waved his hand toward the door. "That's all they're going to be talking about, you realize that, don't you? Not Bear's film—not my legacy—but your half-finished, half-assed fucking short."

His words hurt, but I also knew he wouldn't have been this upset if my film had actually been bad. That was what was really making him angry—that my project was the best of the bunch.

"It's good, and you know it," Bear said.

Bryan's eyes shifted toward his son.

"Bear," he said. "I'd hate to know how you were involved in all of this."

"I just drew some stuff for them," he said. "Oh, and I made sure that it got added to the lineup."

I looked at him. He smiled.

"After all I've done for you. This whole thing—" Bryan made a sweeping gesture. "This whole thing was for you, and this is how you repay me?"

Bear crossed his arms. "I didn't ask for it," he said.

"No, of course you didn't. You never would." There was a strain in Bryan's voice, real frustration, real disappointment. "That's your problem, Bear. You have so much potential, and you're wasting it."

It was immediately clear that Bryan loved Bear. Wanted what

was best for him. But it was also clear that he wasn't listening. That he didn't *see* Bear at all.

"You and your mother were perfectly content to hide your talents," Bryan said. "Keeping them buried in sketchbooks and those little cartoons you did for the school paper. But *this* is what you were meant to do."

"This is what *you* want me to do," Bear said. "You never even gave me a chance to consider it on my own."

Bryan ignored him. It was like he had blinders on. All he could see—all he could think about—was what *he* thought was best for Bear. He was completely missing out on who Bear actually was. It made me sad for him.

Not that sad, of course. He was still the brains behind a multibillion-dollar company, with four Oscars under his belt. But he couldn't see what he already had.

"What am I going to do now?" Bryan ran a hand over his face. "What am I going to tell the press? They were here for you, Bear. Not her."

Bear's expression was defiant. "I don't know, Dad. You could tell them the truth. That you rigged this whole internship to make me look good and Hayley beat you at your own game."

Bryan faced me. "When I told you to inspire him, this isn't what I meant."

Any sympathy I'd felt for Bryan disappeared quickly.

"Excuse me?" Bear asked. "You told Hayley to do *what?*"

I hadn't told Bear about *that* part of my conversation with his father.

"You're gross," Bear said to his dad.

"And you're so infatuated that you can't see straight."

Bear reached out and linked our fingers together. "Her short was better than mine and you know it," he said.

"I want a moment alone with Hayley," Bryan said.

"Fuck no," Bear said.

"Watch your language," Bryan said.

"It's okay," I said.

"Hayley—" Bear said, but I put my hand on his arm.

"I'll be okay." I had no idea if that was true, but I wanted to hear what Bryan would say.

"I'm going to be right outside," Bear said.

The door closed and Bryan stood there with his hands on his hips. Not looking at me.

He took a deep breath, thinking. "Here's what we're going to do," he said. "You're going to go out there and you're going to tell the press that this was a surprise that we planned for them. That we weren't sure you were going to finish the project in time. That we didn't want to get their hopes up if it didn't come together."

"I'm not going to do that," I said.

He blinked, like he had forgotten I was there.

"Listen to me," he said. "You made that movie because of me. Because you needed me to tell you no. *I* did this. And you're going to go out there and you're going to tell the press exactly that."

I shook my head.

His face turned an unpleasant shade of red. "Then your career in animation will be over before it even begins," he said.

I didn't respond.

Suddenly, he laughed. A loud bark of a laugh. A mean laugh. I took a step back, startled.

"It doesn't matter," he said. "It doesn't even matter." He looked at me. "Because I *own* your short. Every frame of that thing belongs to me."

My heart sank into my toes. "What?"

"When you joined this internship, you signed that all away," he said. "Everything you worked on in *my* studio during the internship *I* sponsored, belongs to BB Gun Films."

Little black spots began appearing in front of my eyes and the whole ground seemed to shift beneath me. I felt unsteady. Like I might fall.

Because he was right.

"It doesn't matter what you tell them," Bryan said. "Because I can do whatever I want with your little film. No one will ever know that you made it. You can't use it in your portfolio, you can't put it on a résumé. I can bury it—lock it away in our archives so no one else can ever see it."

"But you won't."

I hadn't even heard the door open. I *definitely* hadn't heard Reagan come in.

Bryan and I both turned to stare at her.

"Stay out of this, Reagan," Bryan said.

She smiled. "You're going to give Hayley the rights to *her* film, Bryan."

He crossed his arms. "Or what?"

"Or I'll go to the press and tell them that the great Bryan Beckett isn't above stealing from a teenage girl."

"You can't tell them anything," Bryan said. "Everyone who walks through these doors signs an NDA. No one speaks to the press. No one."

"I didn't sign a goddamn thing when I came here today," she said.

Bryan went white.

"After what you pulled with me on *A Boy Named Bear* you must be the stupidest man alive to think I'd sign a single thing you put in front of me."

"You're not allowed in the studio unless—"

"I still have plenty of friends here, Bryan," Reagan said. "People actually like me."

Bryan's jaw was moving, but no sound was coming out.

"Hayley, Bear's waiting for you," Reagan said. "Bryan and I have a few things we need to discuss. It'll only be a few moments."

CHAPTER THIRTY-THREE

s everything okay?" Bear asked.

"I think your mom might be tearing your dad a new one," I said.

I kept my voice low—I could see reporters straining to hear what we were talking about.

"Good," Bear said. "I'm pretty sure it's long overdue."

I looked at him. His expression was cautious, and I noticed his hands at his sides, flexing. Unflexing. He was nervous.

He really was very cute.

"You got the film into the lineup?" I asked.

His grin was a little sheepish. "Yeah," he said.

"Why?" I asked. "What made you change your mind?"

"I might have overheard you talking to my mom last night," he said. He moved us farther from the row of press who were starting to get restless during Bryan's absence. "I thought my mom was glad that she'd stopped fighting my dad for credit," Bear said. "I didn't realize that she regretted giving it up."

He shifted on his feet. "And I thought about what you said— that it wasn't really about credit, it was about recognition, and I realized I was wrong. I knew how important the short was to you, but I didn't really understand why. I'm sorry."

I put my hand out, resting my palm against Bear's chest. He put his hand on top of mine.

"Thank you," I said. "And you were right."

He lifted an eyebrow.

"About chasing approval. About going outside once in a while. About a lot of things that I want to do differently."

"Are you saying I inspired you, Hayley Saffitz?" Bear asked.

I smiled.

"I do love you, you know," he said.

Magic. Gravity.

"Yeah," I said. "I love you too."

He smiled at me, putting his hands around my waist. But before he could kiss me, the door next to the stage flew open and Bryan stalked back out into the theater. I didn't know what Reagan had said to him, but he wore the expression of a little kid who had just gotten his favorite toy taken away. The sour look on his face quickly vanished as he remembered that he had an audience, and by the time he stepped on the stage, he was wearing a smile.

"Okay, folks," he said. "Who wants to ask our directors some questions?"

Sally was waiting for me outside the theater.

"That. Was. Epic," she said. "I can't believe it worked. It was incredible. My parents were totally shocked—Maurene, too. She said it's the best animation I've ever done. She said I should totally use it on my reel if I want to apply to CalAn, which I definitely do."

Thanks to Reagan, Sally would be able to do exactly that.

"It looked good on the big screen, didn't it?" I asked.

She grinned. "It looked *so* good."

There was a loud squeal and pretty soon we were caught up in a group hug with Caitlin, Jeannette, Rachel, and Emily.

"You did it!" Caitlin said. "You fucking did it!"

"*We* did it," I said.

"What did Bryan say to you?" Emily asked.

"What did *you* say to him?" Rachel asked.

I shook my head. "It doesn't matter."

They stared at me.

"Are you kidding? It totally matters," Jeannette said.

I'd kept my mouth shut during the Q&A where most of the questions had been a less-direct version of what the girls were asking me now. Everyone wanted to know where the short had come from and why Bryan hadn't announced it at the beginning of the festival.

But even though Reagan hadn't signed an NDA, I had. I knew I had to be careful about what I said. Especially with the media still milling around.

"Let's just say that he was impressed with our tenacity," I said.

It was miles away from the truth, but I had a feeling deep down inside that if Bryan Beckett ever allowed himself to look at this situation from another perspective, he might actually feel that way. After all, he'd made an entire career out of skirting the rules.

"This was a pretty good summer," Sally said as we all moved farther away from the theater. From the crowds. "I can't believe everything we got done. It's kind of amazing, isn't it? We're a little like superheroes."

"The summer wasn't as restful as I would have hoped," Caitlin said. "But pretty good nonetheless."

"I don't think an animation life is a restful one," I said.

"Probably not." Caitlin grinned. "But it's still the only life I'm interested in."

I saw my parents standing off to the side, talking to each other. Zach was hovering there, hands in his pockets, looking awkward. When he caught me looking, he lifted his eyebrows and started making kissy faces in Bear's direction. I rolled my eyes, but I knew that I owed everyone in my family some answers. Not just about Bear, but about the whole short film that I hadn't told them about.

"I should go," I said.

"Yeah," Emily said.

"Me too," Jeannette said.

"My parents are waiting," Rachel said.

None of us moved.

"I'm going to miss you guys," Sally said. Her eyes were a little shiny.

I shuffled my feet. I'd done way more than enough crying this summer.

"I'm going to miss you too," I said.

We fell into a big octopus-style tangle, where we were hugging and patting one another on the back and leaning hard into one another. I thought I saw Caitlin wiping her eyes, but I couldn't be sure. I definitely wasn't doing the same thing.

"Don't forget to take the plants with you," Emily said.

She'd given me her enormous collection because she couldn't take them on the plane. I'd told her that I couldn't promise I'd keep them alive. She'd said she would expect daily updates. Caitlin had made us all a Spotify playlist to listen to when we missed one another. Jeannette said she'd have her parents record her soccer games so we could watch.

It was weird that I wouldn't be seeing them every day anymore.

"I'll text you guys when I get home," Sally said.

"I'm definitely going to be applying to CalAn," Caitlin said. "You guys should too."

"All of us back together in the dorms again?" Emily asked.

We exchanged grins. I could just imagine the kind of mischief we'd get up to.

"Okay." Slowly, one by one, we all started shuffling away.

"Bye," Rachel said.

"Bye," Caitlin said.

"Miss you," Jeannette said.

"Ta-ta," Emily said.

Soon it was just me and Sally.

"Bye." She gave me a hug.

"See you soon," I said.

EPILOGUE

From ANIMATION_STEW.COM

EX-WIFE OF BRYAN BECKETT ANNOUNCES FOUNDING OF NEW STUDIO, SQUARE PEG PRODUCTIONS; POACHES PRODUCER, ARTISTS FROM BB GUN FILMS

Reagan Davis, formerly Reagan Beckett, has announced the founding of a new animation studio, Square Peg Productions. The animation editor is best known for her work on the first three seasons of the cult classic stop-motion show *Dancing Through History*, as well as her previous marriage to renowned director and producer Bryan Beckett.

The announcement came a few days after the culmination of BB Gun Films's first internship, where students were invited to work alongside artists for the summer and produce a series of short films. Bear Beckett, the namesake and inspiration behind BB Gun's inaugural film, *A Boy Named*

Bear, was one of the student directors who presented a short at the press screening. In addition to the announced projects, the audience was surprised by the addition of a fifth film.

During the Q&A following the screening, Bryan Beckett evaded questions about the unexpected inclusion of the fifth short. When asked, the director, Hayley Saffitz, would only say that she was grateful to the students who helped make her project possible.

There has been no statement indicating whether the internship will continue in the future, though Reagan Davis has announced that her new studio will hold yearly internships for high school and college students.

Davis has not worked publicly in animation since her divorce, but she will be joined by several BB Gun Films alumni, including producer Madeline Bailey and story artists Isaac Flores and Sloane Li.

It is expected that there will be additional staffing announcements in the coming weeks.

Bryan Beckett and BB Gun Films had no comment.

• • •

One week after the internship ended, and two weeks before my senior year began, I was back at BB Gun Films. Bryan had summoned me.

Greg, the studio security guard, waved when I drove up to the gate.

"Good to see you again, Hayley," he said when I pulled up to his booth. "Heard about your film. Impressive stuff."

"Thanks, Greg," I said.

He didn't have to tell me where to park. I knew where to go.

"He's going to offer you a job," Bear told me. He was in the passenger seat. He'd asked to come along.

"You don't know that," I said.

"Yeah, I do," he said. "Because I know my dad."

Secretly, I thought the same thing, but I didn't know how I felt about it, so it seemed easier to just to pretend that I'd been called back to the studio for some other reason.

I parked the car—on the Bear level, of course—and we walked over to the studio entrance. Even though I'd just spent the entire summer walking in and out of the enormous metal doors, I still got a little thrill when I approached. I wondered if that feeling would ever really go away.

"Have you talked to him lately?" I asked. "Your dad?"

"He's on his apology tour," Bear said. "That's where he sends me lots of stuff and no apologies."

"What did he send you?" I asked.

He shot me a sideways look. "I might have gotten the new Wacom tablet," he said.

I narrowed my eyes at him.

"You can come over and use it whenever you want," Bear said.

"We'll see how busy I am with school," I said.

He poked me in the side.

My parents liked Bear. They hadn't liked that I'd kept him a secret from them, but after he and his mom came over for Shabbat the other night, it seemed like almost all the adults were on board with us spending time together. Even Zach liked him, and kept threatening to spend time with him one-on-one. I was planning on introducing him to Samantha and Julie next weekend.

"Maybe *you* can talk her into applying to college," Mom had said once she found out that's what Bear planned to do. To my annoyance, he had been doing exactly that.

"You just spent a whole summer at a studio," he said. "You know the hours they keep. Wouldn't college be a nice break from that?"

I wondered if Mom would be so happy to have Bear on her side if she heard that he considered college to be a "nice break." But they weren't the only ones who wanted me to consider it. Sally kept forwarding me the e-mails she was getting from CalAn.

Think of how cool we could make our room if we were staying the whole year, she would write. Or, *Maurene is going to be teaching there—we'd automatically be her favorites.*

I was tempted. Very tempted. But I was keeping that to myself for now. I hadn't decided what I wanted to do and was kind of enjoying not having a plan.

"Are you sure you don't want to go rock climbing after this?" Bear asked as we checked in at the front desk.

I looked down at my outfit—my nicest jeans, low-heeled boots, and a linen shirt—all of which were definitely not rock-climbing appropriate. "I thought we were going to the aquarium."

"I guess we can do that today," he said. "But next time . . ." He mimed climbing a wall.

I rolled my eyes. "What are you going to do while I'm talking to your dad?" I asked.

"Probably wander around and cause trouble," he said.

"You're going to the cafeteria to see if Ron has any doughnuts."

"That sounds about right," he said. "I'm also going to try to poach him for my mom."

"You are not."

But Bear just shrugged, arms out, as he walked away.

I stuck my visitors' badge to the cardigan I'd pulled out of my bag. Even though it was sweltering outside, I hadn't forgotten how cold they kept it in the studio. Heading upstairs, I almost automatically turned the corner toward Sloane's office, forgetting that she wasn't there anymore. She'd be starting at Reagan's company next week.

"We're all in cubicles in some old factory building downtown," she'd told me. "None of the amenities of BB Gun Films, but they'll have me shadowing the director of their first film. Bryan never let me do anything like that."

She'd made me promise I'd come visit soon. She also told me that she'd thrown away the drawing her former mentor had done of her.

"I don't need it anymore," she'd said.

Bryan's assistant got me a bottle of water. I was too nervous to drink, so I just twisted the cap off and on and off a few times while I waited.

"Hayley." Bryan was standing in his doorway, smiling at me. "Come on in."

His office was just as vast and white as I remembered. Just

as cold, too. I pulled my sweater tighter around me, but still felt goose bumps rising up on my arms.

We both sat—me in the weird half-egg chair, him behind his desk. He steepled his fingers and looked at me. I looked back, unsure if it would be rude not to.

"I'm very impressed with you, Hayley," he said.

I braced myself.

"I know that the press has been reaching out to you," he said. "Asking for interviews, wanting to know what happened during the internship."

It was true. I was pretty sure that everyone who'd worked at BB Gun Films over the summer had gotten a call or an e-mail from someone wanting to do a story about the secretive internship, but it seemed like I was getting the bulk of the attention. Especially after I'd been named in the *Animation Stew* article. I'd had to set all my social media stuff to private because people kept sending me messages. I wondered if that's how it was for Bear all the time.

"You handled yourself very well at the Q-and-A," Bryan said. "Very professionally. And I've been paying attention."

His office smelled a little like chalk.

"We need a game plan." He placed his hands flat on the table. "Saying nothing will just increase speculation about what happened during the internship. It will take on a life of its own— unless we set the record straight."

My chair squeaked as I shifted my hips.

"We both know that you wouldn't have even made that film if it wasn't for me," Bryan said. "I saw something in you, Hayley. I knew that you wouldn't do your best work if opportunity was just handed to you. I knew you needed a challenge. Needed to be pushed."

I sat there, listening to him rewrite history. Knowing that he truly believed everything he was saying. That he thought he was the hero of this story. Of *my* story.

"You and I are alike," he said. "We think outside the box. We're special."

I'd always wanted Bryan Beckett to tell me I was special.

"This is what we're going to do," he said, as if I had brought him a problem and he had just come up with the solution. "I had my PR team write up a statement."

He reached into a drawer and pulled out a piece of paper, sliding it across the desk.

"It clarifies the situation," Bryan said. "It says that I knew exactly what I was doing when I denied you the director position. That I knew someone like you would thrive in the face of rejection. That this was all part of the plan. That it was a test. One that you passed with flying colors."

I reached forward and took the piece of paper. His desk was cold, but still, I dragged a finger along the top of it just to say I had. He'd summed up the statement neatly. He just hadn't mentioned the last line.

"You want me to work here?" I asked.

He beamed at me. "After you graduate high school, of course. Think of the publicity. You'll be the youngest storyboard artist we've ever had."

It was what I had dreamed of when I imagined Bryan Beckett offering me a job at BB Gun Films. But better. Bear had been right.

I thought about the box of sketchbooks that Sloane had given me. The box that was now under my desk at home. Since finishing the internship, I'd tried a few different kinds of sketchbooks and discovered that I actually *did* agree with Bryan about the special-edition BB Gun version being the best. Or, at least, being my favorite.

It wasn't that I hadn't learned things from Bryan. I had. I'd learned a lot. And I knew that if I took the job here, I'd keep learning, but not in the way I was pretty sure I needed to.

If I stayed here, I'd become the kind of artist that *he* wanted me to be. All I had to do was approve a press release that told the world that Bryan had done me a favor by rejecting my pitch. That I had done what I'd done because of him.

I could say yes and go back to becoming Bryan Beckett 2.0.

"No," I said.

Because even though part of his version of the story was true—I *had* been motivated to prove myself—I knew that when it came down to it, I had made the short for me. Because I'd known all along that it was good enough.

That *I* was good enough.

Bryan stared at me. "No?" he repeated.

"No, thank you," I clarified.

There was a long silence.

"And why the hell not?"

I didn't know if he'd understand.

"All I wanted was a chance," I said. "You should have given me that."

"I'm giving you one now," he said.

I shook my head. I knew the chance he was giving me wasn't

really the one I needed. I didn't need more of *his* influence. I needed to discover my own. I needed to figure out who I was now that I'd stopped trying to be him.

"You're making a huge mistake," Bryan said. "Do you think opportunities like this happen every day?"

"No," I said. "I know they don't. But I also know that you could have taken a chance on me—and you didn't. You didn't see my potential. I'm just starting out. If I can accomplish what I did this summer at seventeen, can you imagine what I'll accomplish by the time I'm your age?"

I pushed the statement back at him.

"You're the one who made the mistake," I said. "Because *I'm* the opportunity that *you* missed out on."

Bryan looked at me. I held my breath. I was pretty sure very few people had ever spoken to him the way I just had. I waited for him to start shouting or throwing things.

Instead, something in his face shifted. Something in his eyes.

His gaze sharpened. Focused. On me. It felt like he was looking at me—and actually seeing *me* for the first time since I'd stepped foot in his studio. His jaw—which had been taut with anger—relaxed. He leaned back.

He was seeing me, but I was seeing him, too. The dark circles under his eyes. The ink smudge on one of his fingers. A little red nick under his ear. His eyebrows were bushy. His nails uneven. And suddenly he wasn't Bryan Beckett, animation genius, studio CEO, artistic revolutionary. He was Bryan Beckett. A guy.

"You *are* like me, aren't you?" He asked it with a certain kind of surprise.

I wondered what he was seeing. "I don't know," I said.

He nodded. Just a little bob of his head, but there was some sadness there. Some regret. Like he knew he'd made a mistake, but we both knew that he'd never admit it out loud.

"Bear tells me that you two are seeing a lot of each other," he said.

Bryan Beckett. Dad.

"Yeah," I said.

"He likes you."

"I like him," I said.

Bryan smiled. It was a very dad-like smile—one I'd seen on my own dad's face many times. A mixture of pride and hesitancy. Wanting to ask more, but also knowing I probably wouldn't tell him anything.

"I suppose I'll be seeing you around, then," Bryan said. "Thank you for coming in today, Hayley."

He stood. Held out his hand.

"Thank *you*," I said.

Bear was waiting for me at the bridge.

"How'd it go?" he asked.

"You were right," I said. "He did offer me a job."

"Did you tell him my mom beat him to it?"

I smiled. Reagan's offer had come right after the announcement that she was starting her own studio. She wanted me to be a story apprentice there.

"The position's yours after you graduate high school," she'd said. "Or we can hold it until you graduate college. Your choice."

It was nice to have a choice. To take some time to think about what I wanted to do next.

"How does it feel to have two studios competing for you?" Bear asked.

"Pretty good."

I'd tell him that I turned his dad down another time. Right now, I just wanted to enjoy this moment.

"I have something for you." Bear handed me a folded piece of paper.

Opening it, I found the drawing he'd done of me a while back—a little smudged, a little creased.

"You're pretty amazing, Hayley Saffitz," he said.

"I know." I bumped my hip against his.

He laughed.

"And you know why?" I asked.

"Why?"

I looked down at the water—a pair of ducks were floating toward us. One duck with its beautiful green feathers and another with speckled brown coloring. The water was clear enough that I could see their little feet paddling beneath the surface. They didn't look any different from other ducks I'd seen, but there was undeniably something special about them.

I looked back at Bear's drawing. Traced the look that promised trouble.

"Because I was drawn that way," I said.

ACKNOWLEDGMENTS

The first movie I ever saw was *An American Tail*. Like Hayley, I fell completely in love with animation.

Unlike Hayley, however, I'm a lousy artist. I can manage a decent stick figure once in a while, but when it comes to storytelling, I'm far more effective with words than I could ever be with drawings.

Eventually I discovered that there was a whole career path within animation that didn't require drawing skills. Production management. That's right, I was Zoe and I loved it. Over several years, I had the opportunity to work at four different studios (Nickelodeon, Disney, Dreamworks, and Sony Pictures Imageworks) and on four different films (*The Princess and the Frog*, *Tangled*, *The Croods*, and *Hotel Transylvania*). Animation was— and still is—a form of magic to me.

Drawn That Way is a deeply personal book—I might not have Hayley's drawing skills, but I certainly have her ambition. And I know what it feels like to struggle to be seen.

You're holding this book in your hands because of Elizabeth Bewley. Elizabeth, you saw Hayley and you saw me. It's not hyperbole to say that you've changed my life and I'm so grateful to have you as an agent and friend.

Thank you to the entire team at Simon & Schuster. Amanda Ramirez, you have the enthusiasm of a thousand editors! Thank you for loving this book. Thank you to Sarah Creech for an amazing cover and to Francesca Protopapa for her gorgeous cover art. I'm beyond grateful to Arielle Jovellanos. Your illustrations—how perfectly you captured Hayley and her world—are more than I could have ever hoped for. Thanks to Morgan York, Justin Chanda, Chava Wolin, Annika Voss, Shivani Annirood, and the myriad of talented, dedicated people who touched this book and helped bring it into the world.

I'm beyond lucky to have the support of so many wonderful women. Sally Bergom and Caitlin Gutenberger, who shared their names, their animation expertise, and most importantly their witchy ways. My friends and colleagues, Zan Romanoff, Katie Cotugno, Maurene Goo, Sarah Enni, Robin Benway, Brandy Colbert, Margot Wood, Preeti Chhibber, and Victoria Ying. This is the best job in the world because I get to work alongside all of you.

Thank you, Emily, Rachel, and Jeannette, for being my favorite nieces and character namesakes.

Greg Bonsignore, you're the only person I know who loves *A Goofy Movie* as much I do, and the only other person who would teach themselves the "I2I" dance. Love *is* the reason why.

There's no family quite like mine and thank goodness for it. Thank you for always seeing me and loving what you saw.

Mom and Dad, thank you for putting books in my hands from the very beginning and always, always believing that I could do exactly what I set out to do. Bubbe, you gave me the gift of stubbornness and an unshakeable sense of self. Adam and Abra, thank you for being the willing (and sometimes unwilling) participants in all my early attempts at storytelling, from puppets to plays to short films. You made all this possible. Amy and Tim. Loving Sussmans isn't easy, but it's worth it, I hope. Keith, we miss you.

John. You are always my first reader, my forever champion, my whole heart. Teenage me could not dream of a love like yours, and adult me is beyond grateful for it.

Basil and Mozzarella. You're dogs and you're awesome.

And thank you, dear reader. It's been a journey getting this story onto the page, and I'm so glad you're here to greet it.